THE PENGUIN

THE PENGUIN
ELIZABETHAN VERSE

# THE PENGUIN BOOK OF
# ELIZABETHAN VERSE

INTRODUCED AND EDITED BY
EDWARD LUCIE-SMITH

PENGUIN BOOKS

Penguin Books Ltd, Harmondsworth, Middlesex, England
Penguin Books Inc., 7110 Ambassador Road, Baltimore, Maryland 21207, U.S.A.
Penguin Books Australia Ltd., Ringwood, Victoria, Australia

—

First published 1965
Reprinted 1968, 1971

—

Copyright © Edward Lucie-Smith, 1965

—

Made and printed in Great Britain
by Richard Clay (The Chaucer Press) Ltd,
Bungay, Suffolk
Set in Monotype Bembo

*Cover pattern by Stephen Russ*

FOR
PHILIP HOBSBAUM

# CONTENTS

*My grateful thanks are due to all those
who offered me their suggestions, and especially
to Philip Hobsbaum, Peter Porter,
and Anthony Hartley*

# INTRODUCTION

THE anthologist labours under one heavy burden – the burden of being expected to justify himself, of having to 'explain'. Ideally, a book like this should explain itself – the choice of poems should make all the necessary points. Nevertheless, since Elizabethan poetry is so rich, so complex, and in some important aspects so little known, a few words about first principles might possibly prove helpful to the reader.

To begin with, there is the question of my use of the adjective 'Elizabethan'. I have chosen to interpret it fairly strictly, to mean 'poets whose reputations were made or largely sustained during the reign of Elizabeth'. At one end of the scale, this has meant the omission of earlier Tudor poets such as Wyatt. At the other, it has led to some controversial inclusions. Here are poems not only by Jonson, but also by such characteristically 'Jacobean' figures as Middleton and Donne. While it would be pointless to argue the case for each and every inclusion, I ought perhaps to give reasons for interpreting the word 'Elizabethan' in this way. The answer is a simple one. You cannot, in my opinion, use it simply as a criterion of style. In fact, there is no homogeneous Elizabethan style. Donne's early poetry was written some time before Elizabeth's death, and seems to have circulated widely in manuscript. His poems are as much a part of the climate of the 1590s as the satires of Marston or the erotic mythological poems of Shakespeare. However, Donne is not widely represented here, in view of the excellent selection from his work which is to be found in Helen Gardner's Penguin, *The Metaphysical Poets*. The case of Middleton is rather different. I have chosen to illustrate a side of his work which is little known, though very generally despised – the non-dramatic poetry which he wrote in his youth. Some of it was published under Elizabeth, some at the very beginning of the next reign. In these odd, but often striking, poems, Middleton shows us what young poets were thinking and feeling at the moment of Elizabeth's death.

This rather strictly historical approach has led to two other features of the book – the paradoxical fact that the poets are printed in alphabetical order, and the fact that I have throughout the book drawn very largely on extracts from long poems, at the expense of shorter ones which might have been printed complete The alphabetical order is a tribute to the richness of the period. The time-span involved is so narrow, the connexions between poets so intricate, and the dates themselves so uncertain, that it seemed better to stick to an order which made no sort of comment at all. A 'composed' order would have been forensic rather than historical, and would have been based more upon hypothesis and received opinion than upon ascertainable fact. To justify my use of extracts, and even of extracts from plays, instead of complete poems, I might simply point out, if challenged, that the Eliza-bethans themselves were fond of making books of extracts, as *England's Parnassus* shows. But this would be a flippant reply to a serious question. The real answer is that our view of Elizabethan literature has been cruelly distorted by our cult of the 'complete poem'. It has led, in anthologies, to the over-representation of the lyrical and pastoral sides of Elizabethan poetry, and to the re-printing of much that is vapid, boring, and second-rate. The best Elizabethan poetry is often to be found in the poets' longer and more ambitious efforts. It is only here that we can appreciate the superb variousness of Elizabethan writers, the wide range of modes in which they were prepared to work, and also a certain Augustan solidity and toughness which contrasts with their reputation for extravagance. In any case, it is not the anthologist's task to provide the lazy reader with literature in capsule form – 'swallow this and there's no need to bother with any more'. Instead, it is his job to encourage the reader to go on searching, to follow up what he has liked.

There is also the vexed question of proportion. I am sure there will be some readers – but I hope not very many – whose first act, on picking up this book, will be to count through the pages, checking how many have been allotted to this poet or that. For them, the anthologist is no better than a social secretary. It is his job to know the *placement* at the Banquet of the Immortals, to see that Drayton sits higher at table than Nicholas Breton. I have tried, as I will explain later, to ignore this kind of thing altogether, in favour of a freer, more organic choice. But one apology I must make, and that is for my treatment of Shakespeare. Shakespeare haunts the anthologist. Any selection is bound to be inadequate – Shakespeare deserves better than to be read in extract. However, the choice I have made acknowledges one fact – that we value Shakespeare not as the author of *Venus and Adonis* and *The Rape of Lucrece*, but as the poet of the plays. Indeed, if only in an unsystematic kind of way, I have tried to give due weight to the fact that much of the greatest Elizabethan poetry was written for the stage.

This, then, is the scaffolding on which the book has been built. What of the result? I have already hinted that this is not a 'balanced' anthology in the old sense. True, there has been some attempt to do justice to themes which have not received their proper weight in the past. Elizabethan satire, Elizabethan translations, the Elizabethan use of classical metres, the influence of Ovid and of Ariosto on Elizabethan poets – all of these topics are fairly abundantly illustrated. But an anthology is sure to fail if it is merely a collection of 'themes' of this sort.

The anthologist's real function seems to me to be threefold. First, he must try to discover what seem to him the important characteristics of the period he is illustrating. Secondly, he must ask himself what these characteristics mean to him – how they impinge on his own taste, judgement, and sensibility. Lastly, he must try to stand a little farther off, and see (as far as his own blinkered intelligence will allow) how the past relates to the present. Anthologies are ephemeral things. They sum up an attitude to the past, held at a particular moment by a particular person. That is why there can be no such thing as a 'perfect' anthology of Elizabethan verse. A time will certainly come when this selection will no longer seem relevant. If it said anything that once needed saying, it will already have had its effect. As a writer, I hope that what I have chosen will be useful to other writers, that it will either help the literature of the present to find a new direction, or will confirm a trend which already exists. But my main thought is for those who are not writers. This book will do a useful job if it enables them not only to see Elizabethan poetry afresh but to gain new insights into the literature of their own time. In fact, this book is a tool, and tools are made to be used rather than admired.

The point at which to begin using it is, I think, with a common difficulty – the difficulty we have, so to speak, in 'getting through' to certain Elizabethan poets. With Drayton, for example, we admire the richness of imagery, the smooth rhythm, yet somehow we feel that something is being denied us, even in the poet's most splendid passages. The pulse does not quicken to them, as it quickens to *King Lear*, or to some of the most celebrated poems of Ralegh or of Donne. And this *frisson* is what we have come to accept as the criterion of 'real poetry'. It has been often, but vainly, pointed out that the Elizabethans would not have understood this complaint. What made them admire Spenser, for example, was the fine surface of his work, the poet's ingenuity and power over the word. They were not, of course, unaware that poetry could be made to carry an intensely personal message. At moments, the Elizabethans could write this sort of poem better than it has ever been written. Chidiock Tichborne's single, heart-rending lyric: 'My prime of youth is but a frost of cares' is an example. Though more complex, some of Shakespeare's sonnets are certainly filled with an immense pressure of personal feeling. This is still not to say that the Elizabethans regarded poetry as 'a murderous art' (to borrow an extravagant phrase from a well-known reviewer of contemporary verse). For them, poetry and the extreme situation existed together only by coincidence – though, when the extreme moment came, the Elizabethan poets were not abashed by it. We must remember, when critics seem to demand that modern poets should write like Lear in his agony, that Lear himself is, after all, only an impersonation on the part of a prosperous bourgeois of Stratford. We have no proof that Shakespeare ever felt such emotions *in propria persona*. Surely *King Lear* does him more honour if we assume that he did not.

What we ought to ask ourselves is whether, in looking always for the *frisson*, in demanding a drop of genuine heart's blood in every line, we are making the right demand. A poet once remarked to me that the toughest and fiercest young critics of contemporary verse are always crying out for 'the soft, the moonlit, and the dimpled'. The paradox is there, and it is an amusing one. But the disease of judging a poem entirely by its emotional content has spread even to those with a less pronounced taste for marshmallow. But is it the task of the poet to bring us emotion raw, or even emotion cooked? It seems to me that his main job is to produce a work of art, and that works of art can be of very different kinds. The Elizabethans understood that 'art' and 'artifice' are, after all, not so very far apart. Nourished on the classics as they were, they retained a healthy respect for the devices of rhetoric. As men of the late Renaissance, they also had a taste for ornament – one which we may legitimately feel was often rather naïve. Above all, they believed in the supremacy of the word, the word in all its variousness. For them, poetry was the apotheosis of the word, and it is the splendour of language which the Elizabethan poets bring to us. Their reverence was given, not to the narrowly romantic idea of 'being moved' by a poem, but to the riches of the English tongue, and to the innumerable beautiful and ingenious things which could be made by using it.

We are sometimes amazed at the enthusiasm which the Elizabethans showed for making translations. Translating, because the poet's own feelings are not involved, has sometimes been regarded as an inferior craft. Our amazement is likely to increase when we realize that, in the sixteenth century, a man who was able to read English was quite likely to be able to read Latin, and perhaps Greek, French, and Italian also. But, for the Elizabethans, to give easier access to a masterpiece was only a small part of the business of the translator. They looked at the monuments of other literatures with a sort of covetousness. They wanted to take them over lock, stock, and barrel, to make them for ever part of the tradition of English. That is why Harington's *Ariosto* and Fairfax's *Tasso* continue to hold their place as English poems. To find translations so faithful to the spirit, yet so frequently unfaithful to the sense, of the originals from which they are taken, we must travel forward in time to the work of Pound and of Robert Lowell. It is no coincidence that Pound is an admirer of Golding, the Elizabethan translator of Ovid.

In England, though not in America, there was till recently a foolish suspicion of all literature in a foreign tongue. This tendency implanted itself especially among teachers of English. Perhaps the fashion is by now almost over. The great translations are, nevertheless, only a small part of the broad terrain of Elizabethan poetry and some aspects of its achievement seem to labour under prejudices which are yet more barbarous. Modern critics – many of them – are apt to say that certain things are, or are not, 'legitimate' in poetry. If they are too intelligent to assert this, then they are still apt to imply it. When they turn to Elizabethan literature, they must undoubtedly find much to shock them. There is, for example, the willingness of the Elizabethan poets to write verse which was meant to be used in some purely practical way. William Hunnis's *A Meditation to be Said of Women with Child*, included in this volume, is a simple and touching example. Often these 'useful' poems were commissioned for some special occasion. This was the origin of Peele's famous lyric: 'His golden locks time hath to silver turned', which was written to be sung at a ceremony held in the Queen's presence in 1590, when Sir Henry Lee retired from his office as Queen's Champion on the grounds of old age.

Still more distressing to the purists must be the amount of 'journalism' to be found in Elizabethan verse. As everyone knows, journalism is by now a peculiarly dirty word in the critic's vocabulary. One of its advantages is that it is imprecise, that it condemns rather than characterizes. Yet, however we choose to understand it, a great deal of Elizabethan verse seems to fall under this heading. One might point to the extract from Drayton's *The Barons' Wars* in this book, to Marston's magnificent *In Lectores Prorsus Indignos* (thronged with 'brand-names' as it is), to Breton's *Pasquil's Madcap*, even to Tourneur's *A Funeral Poem Upon the Death of Sir Francis Vere*. These poems are mostly very different in style and tone, but they have a journalistic appetite for facts, and a willingness to work *from* the facts, from the surface inwards. Yet I feel no disappointment in the poetry thus created. It seems to me very fine of its kind, though there are other kinds. Its inclusiveness, its refusal to make finicking distinctions between fact and feeling (for in the last resort how do we gauge emotions without facts to support us?) are part of its strength.

One of the chief fascinations of the Elizabethan poets – always provided that we approach them with reasonable objectivity – is their wide range. I have tried to illustrate this as well as I could in the space allowed me. Elizabethan poetry defies most attempts to divide it into categories. Within it, we find echoes of all previous, and many subsequent styles. It may perhaps be fanciful to find a likeness to Wordsworth in the anonymous lyric: 'In midst of woods or pleasant grove', but there is certainly an anticipation of Rochester in the cynical song: 'If fathers knew but how to leave/Their children wit, as they do wealth.' This is pure Restoration in tone, though published in 1600. Thomas Bastard, an almost forgotten poet who is not represented in the *Oxford Book of Sixteenth-Century Verse*, has a turn of mind and a turn of phrase which remind me of Herrick. Tourneur's couplets in *A Funeral Poem Upon the Death of Sir Francis Vere* startlingly resemble those of Dryden.

In general, when we try to understand the poetry written in the reign of Elizabeth, it is better to assume that it is intellectual, sophisticated, and written by men who exercised a close conscious control over what they were doing. Despite the genius of Sidney, the pastoral lyric and the romantic sonnet do not provide the easiest method of approach. Often these are conventional yet subtly ambiguous in a way which we find it hard to analyse. What we should look at first is some of the great Elizabethan poetry of argument. Sir John Davies has probably been given something like his due for *Orchestra* and *Nosce Teipsum*, but there remain Chapman, and Greville, and even Marston. Chapman's *To the Reader*, the poem which he prefaced to his translation of the *Iliad*, provides a good example of the unique blend of passion and didacticism which the Elizabethan poets were able to achieve. It is interesting to see how the force and vehemence of Chapman's intellectual convictions (rather than feelings) are conjured up by the imagery he uses:

> as a sort of beasts,
> Kept by their guardians, never care to hear

Their manly voices but, when in their fists,
   They breathe wild whistles, and the beasts' rude ear
Hears their curs barking, then by heaps they fly
   Headlong together – so men, beastly given,
The manly soul's voice (sacred poesy,
   Whose hymns the angels ever sing in heaven)
Contemn and hear not; but when brutish noises
   (For gain, lust, honour in litigious prose)
Are bellowed out, and crack the barbarous voices
   Of Turkish stentors, oh! ye lean to those,
Like itching horse to blocks or high may-poles,
   And break nought but the wind of wealth, wealth, all
In all your documents; your asinine souls
   (Proud of their burthens) feel not how they gall.

Gradually, as one reads the Elizabethan poets, one begins to realize how this quality of the trained and obedient intellect underlies even those of their works which seem lightest and most graceful. Many poems rely for their construction on a pattern of syllogistic logic, which was one of the basic tools of Elizabethan education. Daniel's enchanting *Ulysses and the Siren*, for example, takes the pattern of a formal scholastic disputation, where a series of propositions are put forward by one speaker, to be refuted by the other. We find this syllogistic process being used by Gascoigne and his contemporaries, just as we find it in Jonson.

In an introduction of this kind it is not possible to take up more than a few themes; a great deal must go unsaid. The two themes which I should like to end by discussing are not perhaps the most central, but they have the merit of being well illustrated in this book. One important, and often misunderstood, characteristic of Elizabethan poetry is its instinctive classicism. The bold extravagance of both plot and language which we find in the Elizabethan drama have perhaps led people to minimize the importance of this. Yet it remains surprising how close are the links between much that was written in the sixteenth century, and the work of Pope and Dryden. Often it begins to seem as if the whole Metaphysical movement was only an irrelevant episode in the history of English poetry. Already in Gascoigne we find that hard, definite way of using words which is one of the marks of genuine classicism. Indeed, it is the 'apparent' quality we find in Gascoigne, the fact that in his work nothing is slurred, nothing veiled, which has led Professor Yvor Winters to rate him so highly, perhaps above his true worth. It is true that this early group of writers – Gascoigne, Turberville, and Googe – is separated from the rest of Elizabethan verse by the revolution which Spenser brought about. Yet the classical strain persists – in Daniel, in Drayton, in Jonson. We find it in Marlowe's *Hero and Leander*, and even in Dekker's elegant Prologue to *The Whore of Babylon*. Jonson is the poet in whom Elizabethan classicism culminates. He has learnt from Latin the power of packing meaning and yet more and richer meaning into a particular pattern of simple words. The *Elegy* which begins with the line: 'If beauty be the mark of praise' is probably the supreme example. If classicism implies density and weight of language, then Jonson is arguably more classical than Dryden himself.

Side by side with Elizabethan classicism, there exists a neglected vein of experiment. True enough, we pay lip-service to the idea that all Elizabethan poetry was experimental, and in a sense this is precisely what it was. Spenser, though it takes some effort to think of him as an experimentalist and a revolutionary, was both of these things, and on a truly formidable scale. But this is not quite the kind of experiment which I am talking about, the kind of experiment which has been successfully absorbed into the main-stream of English literature. What concerns me here are those experiments which remain a little apart, stranded by the tide of history. One such experiment was the Elizabethan vogue for classical metres in English, of which the strangest surviving monu-ment is Richard Stanyhurst's *First Four Books of Virgil*.

The *First Four Books of Virgil* seems to me a remarkable poem which has been made the target of a great deal of undeserved abuse. At its best, it has an excitement of rhythm and of language which should atone for some extravagances, and even for the chaotic state of the text. Stanyhurst was a classicist of a kind – but Elizabethan experiments in classical metres are often unexpected. In Stanyhurst's vigorously alliterative lines we catch an echo, not so much of Virgil, as of *Piers Plowman*. Among the effects which classical metres could produce in other hands, we find the charming mischief of Campion's *The Eleventh Epigram*, the dreaminess of Sidney's 'Oh Sweet Woods', the passionate simplicity of the poem in phaleuciacs which is signed with the initials A.W.

As well as the poets who interested themselves in classical metres, there existed another and more radical school of experiment among the Elizabethan writers. This school was more concerned with the subject-matter of poetry than with questions of technique. It was linked with the feeling of dissatisfaction with society which grew up at the end of Elizabeth's reign. Many poets seem to have felt this emotion – we find evidence of it in Shakespeare. Only a few raised dissatisfaction almost to the status of a principle. For the first time we find a sort of aggression among poets, a desire to affront the reader's susceptibilities and shatter his expectations. We are probably not wrong if we suppose that these writers thought of themselves as being 'modern', almost in the sense that we would use the word now. Tourneur's early poem, *The Transformed Metamorphosis*, was described by Churton Collins, who edited it, as 'Alexandrian' – he compared it to the work of Lycophron. The contemporary reader will probably be far more struck by its deliberately *avant-garde* qualities. *The Transformed Metamorphosis*, though it contains only a very little good poetry, has something about it which reminds us of the early experiments of Eliot and Pound.

The most powerful of all these 'radical' writers at the end of the reign is John Marston, and it is perhaps damning to the whole school that so powerful a writer should have failed to establish himself in the front rank. Or perhaps this is simply the fault of our own squeamishness. Marston is certainly very fascinating, with his tone of sexual disgust, his marriage of deliberate ugliness and poetic power, his mixture of reasoned social criticism and instinctive rage against himself and his surroundings:

> Our adverse body, being earthly, cold,
> Heavy, dull, mortal, would not long enfold
> A stranger inmate, that was backward still
> To all his dungy, brutish, sensual will. ...

But we must beware of reading Marston as if he were a contemporary poet – even if we can only read him with contemporary eyes. The Elizabethans had a great, but by now somewhat deceptive, gift for immediacy. By this I mean two things. One is that they had the habit of building poems out of whatever came to hand. We see this habit at work most blatantly in the plays, which were written under pressure, and written with money in mind. If we do not understand the circumstances in which it was written, the play or the poem can deceive or confuse us. The other kind of immediacy is the nobler sort. The Elizabethans had a marvellous command of imagery, and they made images from everything about them. Though, as I have said, Elizabethan writers are often classical, if we treat them as 'classics' in the old schoolroom sense, and insist that they go on stilts and behave with a proper dignity, we can end by missing some of the greatest pleasures which they have to offer. But this is perhaps the same thing as saying that there is no such thing as a 'legitimate' or an 'illegitimate' subject in Elizabethan poetry. There is another thing which I should like to say again – and that is that anthologies are ephemeral things, tools but not monuments. I hope the reader will put this book to work for his own purposes. If he fails to agree with some, or indeed all, of the ideas which I have put forward here, that does not matter. The important thing is that he should read and judge the poems by his own lights, and use them to form his own conclusions, not only about the Elizabethans, but about the art of poetry.

*

## NOTE ON THE TEXT

For the sake of clarity and consistency, the text here presented is a modernized one. This decision was forced by the fact that certain poets – notably Barnabe Barnes and Stanyhurst – left their work in a state which I thought would present grave difficulties to most readers. Barnes's *Sestina* and the extract from Stanyhurst's *First Four Books of Virgil* are probably the most heavily edited texts in the volume. Stanyhurst did, I know, set store by his curious spellings, as part of his system of metre. But either he did not carry his intentions out, or the result was muddled by his Dutch printer. In modernizing the text, I was also influenced by the general consideration that the orthography and punctuation are often not the poet's own, but those of the printer or of some third party. This is especially true of the extracts from plays.

A point which may possibly offend some readers is that I have reverted to the now old-fashioned practice of always printing 'ed' in full where it falls at the end of a word; but of marking the 'e' with an accent where the syllable is meant to be sounded (except where it is always sounded). The reason is that I find this the most helpful system when reading aloud, and I hope this book will be used often for such a purpose.

The dates placed at the ends of most of the poems are not intended to indicate the date of the text used, but the date of first publication. In some cases, the poet issued a revised text. When the poem concerned remained unpublished till after the seventeenth century, I have not given a date. Instead, I have tried to indicate the accepted authority both for its 'Elizabethanism' and for giving it to the poet under whose name it appears. This authority is usually a contemporary or near contemporary manuscript. In the case of plays, I have sometimes given dates of performance, especially if the play was printed only long after its first production.

# ELIZABETHAN
# VERSE

# ANONYMOUS LYRICS FROM
# SONG-BOOKS

## *When I Was Otherwise Than Now I Am*

WHEN I was otherwise than now I am,
   I lovèd more, but skillèd not so much;
Fair words and smiles could have contented then,
   My simple age and ignorance was such.
But at the length experience made me wonder
That hearts and tongues did lodge so far asunder.

As watermen which on the Thames do row
   Look to the east, but west keeps on their way,
My sovereign sweet her countenance settled so
   To feed my hope, while she her snares might lay.
And when she saw that I was in her danger,
Good God, how soon she provèd then a ranger.

I could not choose but laugh, although too late,
   To see great craft deciphered in a toy.
I love her still, but such conditions hate
   Which so profanes my paradise of joy.
Love whets the wits, whose pain is but a pleasure,
A toy by fits to play withal at leisure.

[William Byrd, *Songs of Sundry Natures*, 1589]

## *Arise, Get Up, My Dear*

ARISE, get up, my dear, make haste, begone thee!
Lo where the bride, fair Daphne, tarries on thee!
   Hark! yon merry wanton maidens squealing:
   Spice-cake, sops in wine, are now a dealing!
      Then run apace,
      Get a bride-lace,

And a gilt rosemary branch while yet there is catching,
    And then hold fast for fear of old snatching.
        Alas, my love, why weep she?
    Oh fear not that the next day keep we.
Hark yon minstrels! List, how fine they firk[1] it!
        And see how the maids jerk it!
            With Kate and Will,
            Tom and Jill.
            Now a trip,
            Then a skip,
            Finely set aloft,
            There again as oft.
        Hey ho, fine brave holiday!
        All for fair Daphne's wedding day!

[Thomas Morley, *Canzonets or Little Short Songs to Three Voices*, 1593]

## In Midst of Woods or Pleasant Grove

IN midst of woods or pleasant grove
    Where all sweet birds do sing,
Methought I heard so rare a sound,
    Which made the heavens to ring.
The charm was good, the noise full sweet,
    Each bird did play his part;
And I admired to hear the same;
    Joy sprung into my heart.

The blackbird made the sweetest sound,
    Whose tunes did far excel,
Full pleasantly and most profound
    Was all things placèd well.
Thy pretty tunes, mine own sweet bird,
    Done with so good a grace,
Extols thy name, prefers the same,
    Abroad in every place.

Thy music grave, bedeckèd well
  With sundry points of skill,
Bewrays thy knowledge excellent,
  Engraftèd in thy will.
My tongue shall speak, my pen shall write,
  In praise of thee to tell.
The sweetest bird that ever was,
  In friendly sort, farewell.

         [John Mundy, *Songs and Psalms*, 1594]


## Now is the Month of Maying

Now is the month of maying,
When merry lads are playing
Each with his bonny lass
Upon the greeny grass.

The Spring, clad all in gladness,
Doth laugh at Winter's sadness,
And to the bagpipe's sound
The nymphs tread out their ground.

Fie then! why sit we musing,
Youth's sweet delight refusing?
Say, dainty nymphs, and speak,
Shall we play barley-break?[1]

        [Thomas Morley, *First Book of Ballets to Five Voices*, 1595]

## *Thule, the Period of Cosmography*

THULE, the period of cosmography,
   Doth vaunt of Hecla, whose sulphureous fire
Doth melt the frozen clime and thaw the sky;
   Trinacrian Etna's flames ascend not higher;
These things seem wondrous, yet more wondrous I,
Whose heart with fear doth freeze, with love doth fry.

The Andalusian merchant, that returns
   Laden with cochineal and china dishes,
Reports in Spain how strangely Fogo[1] burns
   Amidst an ocean full of flying fishes:
These things seem wondrous, yet more wondrous I,
Whose heart with fear doth freeze, with love doth fry.

[T. Weelkes, *Madrigals of 6 parts*, 1600]

## *Fine Knacks for Ladies*

FINE knacks for ladies, cheap, choice, brave and new!
   Good pennyworths – but money cannot move:
I keep a fair but for the Fair to view –
   A beggar may be liberal of love.
Though all my wares be trash, the heart is true,
              The heart is true.

Great gifts are guiles and look for gifts again;
   My trifles come as treasures from my mind:
It is a precious jewel to be plain;
   Sometimes in shell the orient'st pearls we find.
Of others take a sheaf, of me a grain!
              Of me a grain!

Within this pack pins, points, laces, and gloves,
   And divers toys fitting a country fair;
But in my heart, where duty serves and loves,
   Turtles and twins, court's brood, a heavenly pair –
Happy the heart that thinks of no removes!
                 Of no removes!

            [John Dowland, *Second Book of Airs*, 1600]


## If Fathers Knew But How To Leave

IF fathers knew but how to leave
   Their children wit, as they do wealth;
And could constrain them to receive
   That physic which brings perfect health,
The world would not admiring stand
A woman's face and woman's hand.

Women confess they must obey;
   We men will needs be servants still.
We kiss their hands, and what they say
   We must commend, be't ne'er so ill.
Thus we like fools admiring stand
Her pretty foot and pretty hand.

We blame their pride, which we increase
   By making mountains of a mouse.
We praise because we know we please.
   Poor women are too credulous
To think that we admiring stand
Or foot, or face, or foolish hand.

        [Robert Jones, *First Book of Songs and Airs*, 1600]

## Weep You No More, Sad Fountains

WEEP you no more, sad fountains:
   What need you flow so fast?
Look how the snowy mountains
   Heaven's sun doth gently waste.
     But my sun's heavenly eyes
      View not your weeping,
      That now lies sleeping
     Softly, now softly lies
       Sleeping.

Sleep is a reconciling,
   A rest that peace begets.
Doth not the sun rise smiling
   When fair at ev'n he sets?
     Rest you then, rest, sad eyes,
      Melt not in weeping
      While she lies sleeping
     Softly, now softly lies
       Sleeping.

[John Dowland, *Third Book of Airs*, 1603]

# From *The Wisdom of Doctor Dodypol*

## Act Three, Scene Five

ENCHANTER: Hast thou forgot me then? I am thy Love,
Whom sweetly thou wert wont to entertain
With looks, with vows of love, with amorous kisses.
Look'st thou so strange? Dost thou not know me yet?

LUCILIA: Sure I should know you.

ENCHANTER: Why, Love, doubt you that?
'Twas I that led you through the painted meads,
Where the light fairies danced upon the flowers,
Hanging on every leaf an orient pearl,
Which, struck together with the silken wind
Of their loose mantles, made a silver chime.
'Twas I that, winding my shrill bugle horn,
Made a gilt palace break out of the hill,
Filled suddenly with troops of knights and dames,
Who danced and revelled; whilst we sweetly slept
Upon a bed of roses, wrapt all in gold.
Dost thou not know me now?

LUCILIA: Yes, now I know thee.

ENCHANTER: Come then, confirm this knowledge with a kiss.

LUCILIA: Nay, stay; you are not he: how strange is this!

ENCHANTER: Thou art grown passing strange, my Love,
To him that made thee so long since his bride.

LUCILIA: Oh was it you? Come then. Oh stay awhile.
I know not where I am, nor what I am;
Nor you, nor these I know, nor anything.

[1600]

# A.W.

Many attempts have been made to discover the personality concealed by these initials in Davison's anthology, *A Poetical Rhapsody*. One suggestion is that they cover not one personality but several, and stand for 'Anonymous Writer'. For a guess at the author of at least one of the A. W. poems, see my note to Stanyhurst's *Prayer to the Trinity*.

## Eternal Time, That Wastest Without Waste

ETERNAL Time, that wastest without waste,
That art, and art not, diest, and livest still;
Most slow of all, and yet of greatest haste;
Both ill and good, and neither good nor ill:
How can I justly praise thee, or dispraise?
Dark are thy nights, but bright and clear thy days.

Both free and scarce, thou giv'st and tak'st again;
Thy womb that all doth breed, is tomb to all;
What so by thee hath life, by thee is slain;
From thee do all things rise, by thee they fall:
Constant, inconstant, moving, standing still;
*Was, Is, Shall be*, do thee both breed and kill.

I lose thee, while I seek to find thee out;
The farther off, the more I follow thee;
The faster hold, the greater cause of doubt;
*Was, Is*, I know; but *Shall* I cannot see.
All things by thee are measured; thou, by none:
All are in thee; thou, in thyself alone.

[*A Poetical Rhapsody*, 1602]

A.W.

## *Upon Visiting His Lady By Moonlight*

THE night, say all, was made for rest;
    And so say I, but not for all:
To them the darkest nights are best
    Which give them leave asleep to fall;
        But I that seek my rest by light
        Hate sleep, and praise the clearest night.

Bright was the moon, as bright as day,
    And Venus glistered in the west,
Whose light did lead the ready way,
    That brought me to my wishèd rest:
        Then each of them increased their light
        While I enjoyed her heavenly sight.

Say, gentle dames, what moved your mind
    To shine so fair above your wont?
Would Phoebe fair Endymion find?
    Would Venus see Adonis hunt?
        No, no, you fearèd by her sight
        To lose the praise of beauty bright.

At last for shame you shrunk away,
    And thought to reave the world of light;
Then shone my dame with brighter ray,
    Than that which comes from Phoebus' sight:
        None other light but hers I praise,
        Whose nights are clearer than the days.

[*A Poetical Rhapsody*, 1602]

## Smooth are Thy Looks

SMOOTH are thy looks, so is the deepest stream;
Soft are thy lips, so is the swallowing sand;
Fair is thy sight, but like unto a dream;
Sweet is thy promise, but it will not stand.
   Smooth, soft, fair, sweet, to them that lightly touch;
   Rough, hard, foul, sour to them that take too much.

Thy looks so smooth have driven away my sight,
Who would have thought that hooks could be so hid?
Thy lips so soft have fretted my delight,
Before I once suspected that they did.
   Thy face so fair hath burnt me with desire,
   Thy words so sweet were bellows for the fire.

And yet I love the looks that made me blind,
And like to kiss the lips that fret my life,
In heat of fire an ease of heat I find,
And greatest peace of mind in greatest strife.
   That if my choice were now to make again,
   I would not have this joy without this pain.

[*A Poetical Rhapsody*, 1602]


## Phaleuciacs

TIME nor place did I want, what held me tongue-tied?
What charms, what magical abusèd altars?
Wherefore wished I so oft that hour unhappy
When with freedom I might recount my torments,
And plead for remedy by true lamenting?
Dumb, nay dead in a trance I stood amazèd,
When those looks I beheld that late I longed for;
No speech, no memory, no life remainèd,

Now speech prateth, apace my grief bewraying,
Now bootless memory my plaints remembereth,
Now life moveth again, but all avails not.
Speech, life and memory die altogether;
With speech, life, memory, love only dies not.

[*A Poetical Rhapsody*, 1602]

# SIR FRANCIS BACON

## (1561–1626)

Sir Francis Bacon, the famous essayist and philosopher, wrote few poems, and the one printed in this book is by far the best known. Bacon's glittering public career in the reigns of Elizabeth and James I was helped by his friendship with, and subsequent abandonment of, the Earl of Essex. After achieving the Lord Chancellorship and a viscountcy, Bacon was accused of taking bribes and disgraced.

## The World's a Bubble

THE world's a bubble, and the life of man
    Less than a span,
In his conception wretched, from the womb,
    So to the tomb;
Curst from the cradle, and brought up to years,
    With cares and fears.
Who then to frail mortality shall trust,
But limns on water, or but writes in dust.

Yet since with sorrow here we live oppressed,
    What life is best?
Courts are but only superficial schools
    To dandle fools.
The rural parts are turned into a den
    Of savage men.
And where's a city from all vice so free,
But may be termed the worst of all the three?

Domestic cares afflict the husband's bed,
    Or pains his head.
Those that live single take it for a curse,
    Or do things worse.

Some would have children; those that have them none,
   Or wish them gone.
What is it then to have or have no wife,
But single thraldom, or a double strife?

Our own affections still at home to please
   Is a disease;
To cross the sea to any foreign soil,
   Perils and toil.
Wars with their noise affright us; when they cease,
   W'are worse in peace.
What then remains, but that we still should cry,
Not to be born, or being born to die?

     [T. Farnaby, *Florilegium Epigrammatum graecorum*, 1629]

# BARNABE BARNES

## (1570–1609)

Barnes was the younger son of Richard Barnes, Bishop of Durham. He studied at Brasenose College, Oxford. His poems show a liking for complicated verbal patterns, which he often fails to control. But he can manage strange, obsessional effects as in the triple sestina printed here. The extravagance of his style laid him open to attack, and he was ridiculed by both Nashe and Campion.

## Sestina

THEN first with locks dishevellèd and bare,
Strait girded, in a cheerful calmy night;
Having a fire made of green cypress wood,
And with male frankincense on altar kindled,
I call on threefold Hecate with tears,
And here, with loud voice invocate the furies

For their assistance: to me with their furies,
Whilst snowy steeds in coach bright Phoebe bear.
Ay me, Parthenophe smiles at my tears!
I neither take my rest by day, or night,
Her cruel loves in me such heat have kindled.
Hence, goat, and bring her to me raging wood![1]

Hecate, tell which way she comes through the wood.
This wine about this altar, to the furies
I sprinkle, whiles the cypress boughs be kindled,
This brimstone earth within her bowels bare,
And this blue incense sacred to the night.
This hand, perforce, from this bay this branch tears.

So be she brought which pitied not my tears,
And as it burneth with the cypress wood
So burn she with desire by day and night.

38

You gods of vengeance, and revengeful furies,
Revenge, to whom I bend on my knees bare!
Hence, goat, and bring her with love's outrage kindled!

Hecate, make signs, if she with love come kindled;
Think on my passions, Hecate, and my tears.
This rosemary (whose branch she chiefly bare,
And lovèd best), I cut both bark and wood,
Broke with this brazen axe, and in love's furies,
I tread on it, rejoicing in this night,

And saying, 'Let her feel such wounds this night!'
About this altar, and rich incense kindled,
This lace and vervain to love's bitter furies
I bind, and strow, and with sad sighs and tears
About I bear her image, raging wood.
Hence, goat, and bring her from her bedding bare!

Hecate, reveal if she like passions bear.
I knit three true-lover's knots (this is love's night)
Of three discoloured silks, to make her wood,
But she scorns Venus till her loves be kindled,
And till she find the grief of sighs and tears:
Sweet Queen of Loves, for mine unpitied furies,

Alike torment her with such scalding furies!
And this turtle, when the loss she bare
Of her dear make, in her kind did shed tears,
And mourning did seek him all day and night:
Let such lament in her for me be kindled,
And mourn she still, till she run raging wood.

Hence, goat, and bring her to me raging wood!
These letters, and these verses to the furies,
Which she did write, all in this flame be kindled:
Me, with these papers, in vain hope she bare,

That she to day would turn mine hopeless night.
These as I rent and burn, so fury tears

Her hardened heart, which pitied not my tears.
The wind-shaked trees make murmur in the wood,
The waters roar at this thrice-sacred night,
The winds come whisking still to note her furies:
Trees, woods, and winds, a part in my plaints bare,
And knew my woes, now joy to see her kindled –

See where she comes, with loves enraged and kindled!
The pitchy clouds in drops send down their tears,
Owls scritch, dogs bark, to see her carried bare;
Wolves yowl and cry, bulls bellow through the wood,
Ravens croak. Now, now, I feel love's fiercest furies!
See'st thou that black goat, brought this silent night

Through empty clouds by th' daughters of the night?
See how on him she sits, with love-rage kindled,
Hither perforce brought with avengeful furies?
Now I wax drowsy, now cease all my tears,
Whilst I take rest and slumber near this wood:
Ah me! Parthenophe naked and bare!

Come, blessed goat, that my sweet lady bare!
Where hast thou been, Parthenophe, this night?
What – cold? Sleep by this fire of cypress wood
Which I much longing for thy sake have kindled.
Weep not! Come, loves, and wipe away her tears.
At length yet, wilt thou take away my furies?

Ay me, embrace me! See those ugly furies!
Come to my bed, lest they behold thee bare,
And bear thee hence – they will not pity tears,
And these still dwell in everlasting night.
Ah, love's sweet love sweet fires for us hath kindled,
But not inflamed with frankincense or wood.

The furies, they shall hence into the wood,
Whiles Cupid shall make calmer his hot furies,
And stand appeasèd at our fires kindled.
Join, join, Parthenophe! Thyself unbare,
None can perceive us in the silent night.
Now will I cease from sighs, laments, and tears;

And cease Parthenophe, sweet, cease thy tears.
Bear golden apples thorns in every wood,
Joy heavens, for we conjoin this heavenly night;
Let alder trees bear apricocks (die furies!),
And thistles pears, which prickles lately bare.
Now both in one with equal flame be kindled.

Die, magic boughs, now die, which late were kindled!
Here is mine heaven; loves drop instead of tears.
It joins! it joins! ah, both embracing bare!
Let nettles bring forth roses in each wood;
Last ever-verdant, woods! Hence, former furies!
Oh die, live, joy! What? Last continual, night!

Sleep Phoebus still with Thetis! Rule still, night!
I melt in love, love's marrow flame is kindled:
Here will I be confirmed in love's sweet furies.
I melt! I melt! Watch, Cupid, my love-tears:
If these be furies, oh let me be wood!
If all the fiery element I bare,

'Tis now acquitted. Cease your former tears,
For as she once with rage my body kindled,
So in hers am I burièd this night.

[*Parthenophil and Parthenophe*, 1593]

## *A Blast of Wind, a Momentary Breath*

A BLAST of wind, a momentary breath,
A watery bubble symbolised with air,
A sun-blown rose, but for a season fair,
A ghostly glance, a skeleton of death;
A morning dew, pearling the grass beneath,
Whose moisture sun's appearance doth impair;
A lightning glimpse, a muse of thought and care,
A planet's shot, a shade which followeth,
A voice which vanisheth so soon as heard,
The thriftless heir of time, a rolling wave,
A show, no more in action than regard,
A mass of dust, world's momentary slave,
  Is man, in state of our old Adam made,
  Soon born to die, soon flourishing to fade.

[*Spiritual Sonnets*, 1595]

# RICHARD BARNFIELD
## (1574–1627)

Like Barnes, Barnfield was a student at Brasenose. He proceeded
B.A. in 1592. His three books of verse: *The Affectionate Shepherd*
(1594), *Cynthia* (1595), and *The Encomion of Lady Pecunia* (1598)
were all published before he was twenty-five. Sidney was Barnfield's
great admiration, and *Cynthia* was dedicated to Sidney's Stella,
Penelope Rich. He was a friend of Thomas Watson.

## My Flocks Feed Not

MY flocks feed not,
My ewes breed not,
My rams speed not,
     All is amiss.
Love is dying,
Faith's defying,
Heart's denying,
     Causer of this.

All our merry jigs are quite forgot;
All my lady's love is lost, God wot;
Where our faith was firmly fixed in love,
There annoy is placed without remove.

     One seely[1] cross
     Wrought all my loss,
Oh frowning Fortune, cursèd fickle dame!
     For now I see
     Inconstancy
More in women than in many men to be.

     In black mourn I,
     All fear scorn I,
     Love hath forlorn me,
          Living in thrall.

43

Heart is bleeding,
All help needing,
Oh cruel speeding
   Fraught with gall!

My shepherd's pipe will sound no dea ;
My wether's bell rings doleful knell;
My curtall[1] dog that wont to have played,
Plays not at all, but seems afraid.

My sighs so deep
Procures to weep
With howling noise to see my doleful plight.
How sighs resound
Through harkless ground,
Like thousand vanquished men in bloody fight.

Clear wells spring not,
Sweet birds sing not,
Loud bells ring not
   Cheerfully,
Herds stand weeping,
Flocks all sleeping,
Nymphs back creeping
   Fearfully.

All our pleasures known to us poor swains,
All our merry meetings on the plains,
All our evening sports from us are fled,
All our loves are lost, for Love is dead.

Farewell, sweet lass,
The like ne'er was
For sweet content, the cause of all my woe.
Poor Corydon
Must live alone,
Other help for him I know there's none.

          [Thomas Weelkes, *Madrigals*, 1597]

## To His Friend Master R.L., in Praise of Music and Poetry [1]

IF music and sweet poetry agree,
As they must needs (the sister and the brother),
Then must the love be great 'twixt thee and me,
Because thou lov'st the one, and I the other.
Dowland to thee is dear, whose heavenly touch
Upon the lute doth ravish human sense;
Spenser to me, whose deep conceit is such
As passing all conceit, needs no defence.
Thou lov'st to hear the sweet melodious sound
That Phoebus' lute (the queen of music) makes;
And I in deep delight am chiefly drowned
Whenas himself to singing he betakes.
    One god is god of both (as poets feign),
    One knight loves both, and both in thee remain.

[Poems in Divers Humours, 1598]


## A Comparison of the Life of Man

MAN'S life is well comparèd to a feast,
Furnished with choice of all variety:
To it comes Time; and as a bidden guest
He sits him down, in pomp and majesty:
The threefold age of Man the waiters be.
    Then with an earthen voider,[2] made of clay,
    Comes Death, and takes the table clean away.

[Poems in Divers Humours, 1598]

# THOMAS BASTARD

## (1566–1618)

A country clergyman who made pitiably small headway in life, Bastard published his book, *Chrestoleros*, in 1598. It was much ridiculed, but Harington defended it. Bastard died, touched in his wits, in a debtors' prison in Dorchester.

## De Puero Balbutiente

METHINKS 'tis pretty sport to hear a child,
Rocking a word in mouth yet undefiled;
The tender racquet rudely plays the sound,
Which, weakly bandied, cannot back rebound;
And the soft air the softer roof doth kiss,
With a sweet dying and a pretty miss,
Which hears no answer yet from the white rank
Of teeth, not risen from their coral bank.
The alphabet is searched for letters soft,
To try a word before it can be wrought,
And when it slideth forth, it goes as nice
As when a man does walk upon the ice.

[*Chrestoleros*, 1598]

## De Sua Clepsydra

SETTING mine hour-glass for a witness by
To measure study as the time did fly:
A lingering muse possessed my thinking brain:
My mind was reaching, but in such a vein,
As if my thoughts, by thinking brought asleep
Wingless and footless, now like snails did creep.
I eyed my glass, but he so fast did run,
That e'er I had begun, the hour was done.

46

The creeping sands with speedy pace were flit,
Before one reason crept out of my wit.
When I stood still, I saw how time did fly:
When my wits ran, time ran more fast than I.
Stay here: I'll change the course, let study pass,
And let time study while I am the glass.
What touch ye, sands? are little mites so fleet?
Can bodies run so swift that have no feet?
And can ye tumble time so fast away?
Then farewell hours, I'll study by the day.

[*Chrestoleros*, 1598]

## Ad Lectorem de Subiecto Operis Sui

THE little world the subject of my muse,
Is an huge task and labour infinite;
Like to a wilderness or mass confuse,
Or to an endless gulf, or to the night:
How many strange meanders do I find?
How many paths do turn my straying pen?
How many doubtful twilights make me blind,
Which seek to limn out this strange All of men?
Easy it were the earth to portray out,
Or to draw forth the heavens' purest frame,
Whose restless course by order whirls about
Of change and place, and still remains the same.
But how shall men's, or manners' form appear,
Which while I write, do change from what they were?

[*Chrestoleros*, 1598]

# FRANCIS BEAUMONT
## (1584–1616)

A prolific dramatist in the Jacobean period, in collaboration with John Fletcher, Beaumont was a somewhat uneven writer of non-dramatic verse. *Salmacis and Hermaphroditus* is an early effort in the elegant and witty tradition of Marlowe's *Hero and Leander*.

## *Mercury Aids Bacchus' Revenge Upon Phoebus*
### From *Salmacis and Hermaphroditus*

AND now the Sun was in the middle way,
And had o'ercome the one half of the day,
Scorching so hot upon the reeking sand,
That lies upon the near Egyptian land,
That the hot people burnt e'en from their birth,
Do creep again into their mother earth,
When Mercury did take his powerful wand,
His charming caduceus in his hand,
And a thick bever which he used to wear,
When aught from Jove he to the Sun did bear,
Which did proceed from Phoebus' glittering sight.
Clad in these powerful ornaments he flies,
With outstretched wings up to the azure skies:
Where seeing Phoebus in his orient shrine,
He did so well revenge the god of wine,
That whilst the Sun wonders his chariot reels,
The crafty god had stole away his wheels.

[1602]

# NICHOLAS BRETON

(1545?–1626?)

Breton was the son of a rich London merchant, and stepson to the poet George Gascoigne. A prolific and popular author in prose and verse, Breton is usually valued more for his somewhat insipid pastoral poems than for his religious and satirical ones. I prefer these latter, and have represented them here. Breton's authenticated writings suggest that he leant towards Puritanism.

## From *The Pilgrimage to Paradise*

WHEN, passing on, they fell into a wood,
A thicket full of brambles, thorns and briars;
A graceless grove, that never did man good,
But wretched endings of the world's desires;
Where snakes and adders, and such venomed things,
Had slain a number with their cruel stings.

Some metamorphosed like Actaeon were,
Diana smiling at their lewd desires;
Some semitawres,[1] and some more half a bear,
Other half swine, deep wallowing in the mires:
All beastly minds, that could not be reformed,
Were to the shapes of their own shame transformed.

There might he see a monkey with an ape,
Climbing a tree and cracking of a nut;
One sparrow teach another how to gape,
But not a tame one, taught to keep the cut;[2]
And many a jackdaw, in his foolish chat,
While parrots prated of they knew not what.

There might he see bears baited all with dogs,
Till they were forced to fly into their dens;
And wild boars beating of the lesser hogs,
While cocks of game were fighting for their hens;

49

A little ferret, hunting of a coney;
And how the old bees sucked the young bees' honey.

There might he hear the lions in their roaring,
While lesser beasts did tremble at the sound;
There might he see bulls one another goring,
And many a hart sore hunted with a hound;
While Philomene, amid the queachy[1] spring,
Would cease her note to hear the cuckoo sing.

There might he see a falcon beaten down
By carrion crows, that crossed her in her flight;
A russet jerkin face a velvet gown,
While base companions braved a noble knight;
And crafty foxes creep into their holes,
While little hops were climbing lofty poles.

There might he see the satyrs in their dances,
Half men, half beasts, or devils in their kinds;
There might he see the Muses, in their trances,
Lie down as dead, as if they had no minds;
There might he see, in all, so little good,
As made him wish he had been through the wood.

Yet in the path wherein he sweetly passed,
No evil thing had power to take a place,
No venomed serpent might his poison cast,
No filthy monster, nor ill-favoured face;
No lion, bear, dog, monkey, fox, or crow,
Could stop the way where virtue was to go.

[1592]

## From *Pasquil's Madcap*

LET but a fellow in a fox-furred gown,
A greasy night-cap and a drivelled beard,
Grow but a bailiff of a fisher-town,
And have a matter 'fore him to be heard;
Will not his frown make half a street afeared?
   Yea, and the greatest codshead gape for fear
   He shall be swallowed by this ugly bear.

Look but on beggars going to the stocks,
How master constable can march before them,
And while the beadle maketh fast the locks,
How bravely he can knave them and be-whore them,
And not afford one word of pity for them,
   When it may be poor honest seely[1] people
   Must make the church make curtsy to the steeple.[2]

Note but the beadle of a beggar's spittle,
How (in his place) he can himself advance,
And will not of his title lose a tittle,
If any matter come in variance,
To try the credit of his countenance:
   For whatsoever the poor beggars say,
   His is the word must carry it away.

Why, let a beggar but on cock-horse sit,
Will he not ride like an ill-favoured king?
And will it not amaze a poor man's wit
That cuckoos teach the nightingale to sing?
Oh this same wealth is such a wicked thing
   'Twill teach an owl in time to speak true latin,
   And make a friar forswear Our Lady's matin.

Take but a peasant newly from the cart,
That only lives by puddings, beans, and pease,
Who never learnèd any other art,

But how to drive his cattle to the leas,
And after work, to sit and take his ease:
   Yet put this ass into a golden hide,
    He shall be groom unto a handsome bride.

Take but a rascal with a roguish pate,
Who can but only keep a counting book,
Yet if his reck'ning grow to such a rate
That he can angle for the golden hook,
However so the matter be mistook,
   If he can cle'erly cover his deceit,
    He may be held a man of deep conceit.

Find out a villain, born and bred a knave,
That never knew where honesty became,
A drunken rascal and a dogged slave,
That all his wits to wickedness doth frame,
And only lives in infamy and shame;
   Yet let him tink upon the golden pan,
    His word may pass yet for an honest man.

Why, take a fiddler with but half an eye,
Who never knew if *Ela*[1] were a note,
And can but play a round or hey-de-gey,
And that perhaps he only hath by rote,
Which now and then may hap to get a groat;
   Yet if his crowd be set with silver studs,
    The other ministers may go and chew their cuds.

[1600]

NICHOLAS BRETON

## A Doleful Fancy

SORROW rip up all thy senses,
　　Nearest unto horror's nature;
Taste of all thy quintessences
　　That may kill a wretched creature.

Then, behold my woeful spirit,
　　All in passions overthrown,
And, full closely, like a ferret,
　　Seize upon it for thine own.

But if thou do grow dismayed,
　　When thou dost but look on me,
When my passions, well displayed,
　　Will but make a blast of thee,

Then in grief of thy disgraces,
　　Where my fortunes do deface thee,
Tell thy muses to their faces,
　　They may learn of me to grace thee.

For thy sighs, thy sobs and tears
　　But thy common badges been,
While the pain the spirit bears
　　Eats away the heart unseen.

Where, in silence swallowed up,
　　Are the sighs and tears of love,
Which are drawn to fill the cup
　　Must be drunk to death's behove.

Then, beholding my heart's swoon,
　　In my torments more and more,
Say, when thou dost sit thee down,
　　Thou wert never graced before.

[*Melancholic Humours*, 1600]

NICHOLAS BRETON

## Hymn

WHEN the angels all are singing,
All of glory ever springing,
In the ground of high heaven's graces
Where all virtues have their places:
   Oh that my poor soul were near them,
   With an humble heart to hear them!

Then should Faith in Love's submission,
Joying but in Mercy's blessing,
Where that sins are in remission,
Sing the joyful soul's confessing,
   Of her comfort high commending,
   All in glory, never ending.

But, ah wretched sinful creature,
How should the corrupted nature
Of this wicked heart of mine
Think upon that love divine
   That doth tune the angels' voices
   While the host of heaven rejoices?

No, the song of deadly sorrow,
In the night that hath no morrow,
And their pains are never ended
That have heavenly powers offended,
   Is more fitting to the merit
   Of my foul infected spirit.

Yet while Mercy is removing
All the sorrows of the loving,
How can Faith be full of blindness
To despair of Mercy's kindness;
   While the hand of heaven is giving
   Comfort from the ever-living?

No, my soul, be no more sorry;
Look unto that life of glory
Which the grace of Faith regardeth,
And the tears of Love rewardeth:
　　Where the soul the comfort getteth
　　That the angels' music setteth.

There when thou art well conducted,
And by heavenly grace instructed,
How the faithful thoughts to fashion
Of a ravished lover's passion,
　　Sing with saints to angels nighest,
　　Halleluiah in the highest!

[*Breton's Longing*, 1602]


## The Worldly Prince Doth In His Sceptre Hold

THE worldly prince doth in his sceptre hold
A kind of heaven in his authorities;
The wealthy miser, in his mass of gold,
Makes to his soul a kind of Paradise;
The epicure that eats and drinks all day,
Accounts no heaven, but in his hellish routs;
And she, whose beauty seems a sunny day,
Makes up her heaven but in her baby's clouts.
But, my sweet God, I seek no prince's power,
No miser's wealth, nor beauty's fading gloss,
Which pamper sin, whose sweets are inward sour,
And sorry gains that breed the spirit's loss:
　　No, my dear Lord, let my Heaven only be
　　In my love's service, but to live to thee.

[*The Soul's Harmony*, 1602]

# NICHOLAS BRETON

## *Oh That My Heart Could Hit Upon a Strain*

OH that my heart could hit upon a strain
Would strike the music of my soul's desire;
Or that my soul could find that sacred vein
That sets the consort of the angels' choir.
Or that that spirit of especial grace
That cannot stoop beneath the state of heaven
Within my soul would take his settled place
With angels' *Ens*,[1] to make his glory even.
Then should the name of my most gracious King,
And glorious God, in higher tunes be sounded
Of heavenly praise, than earth hath power to sing,
Where heaven, and earth, and angels, are confounded.
   And souls may sing while all heart strings are broken;
   His praise is more than can in praise be spoken.

[*The Soul's Harmony*, 1602]

# THOMAS CAMPION
## (1559?–1634)

Campion entered Peterhouse College, Cambridge, but did not proceed to a degree, probably because of his Catholicism. Later, he took a degree in medicine abroad. The most dramatic event in his life was his implication in the Overbury murder. Campion was both musician and poet, and composed the music to his own songs. His *Observations in the Art of English Poesy* (1602) was an extreme, and rather belated, plea for the cause of classical metres in English. Samuel Daniel wrote a reply.

## Follow Your Saint

FOLLOW your saint, follow with accents sweet;
Haste you, sad notes, fall at her flying feet.
There, wrapped in cloud of sorrow, pity move,
And tell the ravisher of my soul I perish for her love.
But if she scorns my never-ceasing pain,
Then burst with sighing in her sight, and ne'er return again.

All that I sung still to her praise did tend.
Still she was first, still she my songs did end.
Yet she my love and music both doth fly,
The music that her echo is, and beauty's sympathy.
Then let my notes pursue her scornful flight;
It shall suffice that they were breathed, and died for her delight.

[*A Book of Airs*, 1601]

## When Thou Must Home

WHEN thou must home to shades of underground,
    And there arrived, a new admirèd guest,
The beauteous spirits do engirt thee round,
    White Iope, blithe Helen and the rest,
To hear the stories of thy finished love
From that smooth tongue, whose music hell can move:

Then wilt thou speak of banqueting delights,
    Of masks and revels which sweet youth did make,
Of tourneys and great challenges of knights,
    And all these triumphs for thy beauty's sake.
When thou hast told these honours done to thee,
Then tell, oh! tell, how thou didst murder me.

[*A Book of Airs*, 1601]

## Hark, All You Ladies

HARK, all you ladies that do sleep;
    The fairy queen Proserpina
Bids you awake and pity them that weep.
    You may do in the dark
What the day doth forbid;
    Fear not the dogs that bark,
        Night will have all hid.

But if you let your lovers moan,
    The fairy queen Proserpina
Will send abroad her fairies ev'ry one,
    That shall pinch black and blue
Your white hands and fair arms
    That did not kindly rue
        Your paramours' harms.

In myrtle arbours on the downs
    The fairy queen Proserpina,
This night by moonshine leading merry rounds
    Holds a watch with sweet love,
Down the dale, up the hill;
    No plaints or groans may move
      Their holy vigil.

All you that will hold watch with love,
    The fairy queen Proserpina
Will make you fairer than Dione's dove;
    Roses red, lilies white,
And the clear damask hue,
    Shall on your cheeks alight:
      Love will adorn you.

All you that love, or loved before,
    The fairy queen Proserpina
Bids you increase that loving humour more:
    They that yet have not fed
On delight amorous,
    She vows that they shall lead
      Apes in Avernus.[1]

*[Astrophel and Stella, 1591]*

## Follow Thy Fair Sun, Unhappy Shadow

FOLLOW thy fair sun, unhappy shadow.
    Though thou be black as night,
    And she made all of light,
Yet follow thy fair sun, unhappy shadow.

Follow her whose light thy light depriveth.
    Though here thou livest disgraced,
    While she in heaven is placed,
Yet follow her whose light the world reviveth.

Follow those pure beams whose beauty burneth,
 That so have scorchèd thee,
 As thou still black must be,
Till her kind beams thy black to brightness turneth.

Follow her, while yet her glory shineth.
 There comes a luckless night,
 That will dim all her light;
And this the black unhappy shade divineth.

Follow still, since so thy fates ordained.
 The sun must have his shade,
 Till both at once do fade,
The sun still proved, the shadow still disdained.

        [*A Book of Airs*, 1601]


## Now Winter Nights Enlarge

Now winter nights enlarge
 The number of their hours,
And clouds their storms discharge
 Upon the airy towers.
Let now the chimneys blaze,
 And cups o'erflow with wine;
Let well-tuned words amaze
 With harmony divine.
Now yellow waxen lights
 Shall wait on honey Love,
While youthful revels, masks, and courtly sights
 Sleep's leaden spells remove.

This time doth well dispense
 With lovers' long discourse.
Much speech hath some defence
 Though beauty no remorse.

All do not all things well:
   Some measures comely tread,
Some knotted riddles tell,
   Some poems smoothly read.
The Summer hath his joys,
   And Winter his delights.
Though Love and all his pleasures are but toys,
   They shorten tedious nights.

[*Two Books of Airs*, 1613(?)]


## Thrice Toss These Oaken Ashes in the Air

THRICE toss these oaken ashes in the air;
Thrice sit thou mute in this enchanted chair;
Then thrice three times tie up this true love's knot,
And murmur soft: 'She will, or she will not.'

Go burn these poisonous weeds in yon blue fire,
These screech-owl's feathers and this prickling briar,
This cypress gathered at a dead man's grave,
That all thy fears and cares an end may have.

Then come, you fairies, dance with me a round;
Melt her hard heart with your melodious sound.
In vain are all the charms I can devise;
She hath an art to break them with her eyes.

[*Two Books of Airs*, 1613(?)]

## Sleep, Angry Beauty

SLEEP, angry beauty, sleep, and fear not me.
For who a sleeping lion dares provoke?
It shall suffice me here to sit and see
Those lips shut up that never kindly spoke.
    What sight can more content a lover's mind
    Than beauty seeming harmless, if not kind?

My words have charmed her, for secure she sleeps;
Though guilty of much wrong done to my love;
And in her slumber, see, she close-eyed weeps:
Dreams often more than waking passions move.
    Plead, sleep, my cause; and make her soft like thee,
    That she in peace may wake and pity me.

[*Two Books of Airs*, 1613(?)]


## Anacreontic Verses[1]

FOLLOW, follow,
Though with mischief
Armed, like whirlwind
Now she flies thee;
Time can conquer
Love's unkindness;
Love can alter
Time's disgraces;
Till death faint not
Then but follow.
Could I catch that
Nimble traitor,
Scornful Laura,
Swiftfoot Laura,
Soon then would I
Seek avengement.

What's th'avengement?
Even submissely
Prostrate then to
Beg for mercy.

[*Observations in the Art of English Poesy*, 1602]


## The Eleventh Epigram[1]

HIS late loss the wifeless Higgs in order
Ev'rywhere bewails to friends, to strangers;
Tells them how, by night, a youngster armèd
Sought his wife (as hand in hand he held her)
With drawn sword to force; she cried; he mainly
Roaring ran for aid, but (ah) returning
Fled was with the prize the beauty-forcer,
Whom in vain he seeks, he threats, he follows.
Changed is Helen, Helen hugs the stranger,
Safe as Paris in the Greek triumphing.
Therewith his reports to tears he turneth,
Pierced through with the lovely dame's remembrance;
Straight he sighs, he raves, his hair he teareth,
Forcing pity still by fresh lamenting.
Cease unworthy, worthy of thy fortunes,
Thou that couldst so fair a prize deliver,
For fear unregarded, undefended,
Hadst no heart, I think; I know no liver.

[*Observations in the Art of English Poesy*, 1602]

# GEORGE CHAPMAN

## (1559?–1634)

Chapman was, on the evidence of his works, one of the most scholarly of Elizabethan poets, and may have studied at both Oxford and Cambridge. He may also have served in the Netherlands under Sir Francis Vere. He seems to have begun his literary career around 1594, when he published *The Shadow of Night* and he commenced dramatist at about the same time, as Henslowe mentions him in his *Diary* for 1595–6. By 1598 he was established in the theatre, and is mentioned by Meres. 1598 also saw the publication of two important works – Chapman's completion of Marlowe's *Hero and Leander*, and the first instalment of his translation of Homer. This latter brought him his most lasting fame. As well as being a scholar, Chapman seems consciously to have wished to raise the status of the poet. At any rate he succeeded in winning a not undeserved respect among his contemporaries and rivals. Jonson, who collaborated with Chapman and Marston in writing *Eastward Ho!*, described Chapman as 'a learned and honest man'. Webster, in the address to the reader prefixed to *Vittoria Corombona*, refers to the 'full and heightened style of Master Chapman'. Prestige was not, however, accompanied by a commensurate financial success.

## To the Reader[1]

Poem Prefixed to Chapman's Translation of the *Iliads*

> WHOM shall we choose the glory of all wits,
>     Held through so many sorts of discipline,
> And such variety of works and spirits;
>     But Grecian Homer? like whom none did shine
> For form of work and matter. And because
>     Our proud doom of him may stand justified
> By noblest judgements, and receive applause
>     In spite of envy, and illiterate pride;
> Great Macedon, amongst his matchless spoil
>     Took from rich Persia (on his fortunes cast)
> A casket finding (full of precious oils)
>     Formed all of gold, with wealthy stones enchased:

He took the oils out; and his nearest friends
   Asked in what better guard it might be used?
All giving their conceipts, to several ends.
   He answered: his affections rather chused
An use quite opposite to all their kinds;
   And Homer's books should with that guard be served,
That the most precious work of all men's minds
   In the most precious place might be preserved.
The fount of wit was Homer, learning's sire,
   And gave Antiquity her living fire.


Volumes of like praise I could heap on this,
   Of men more ancient, and more learn'd than these;
But since true virtue enough lonely is
   With her own beauties, all the suffrages
Of others I omit; and would more fain
   That Homer for himself should be beloved
Who every sort of love-worth did contain.
   Which now I have in my conversion proved;
I must confess, I hardly dare refer
   To reading judgements, since, so generally,
Custom hath made even th'ablest agents err
   In these translations; all so much apply
Their pains and cunnings, word for word to render
   Their patient authors, when they may as well
Mate fish with fowl, camels with whales engender,
   Or their tongue's speech in other mouths compel.
For, even as different a production
   As Greek and English; since as they in sounds
And letters shun our form and unison,
   So have their sense and elegancy bounds
In their distinguished natures, and require
   Only a judgement to make both consent
In sense and elocution, and aspire
   As well to reach the spirit that was spent
In his example, as with art to pierce
   His grammar and etymology of words.

But, as great clerks can write no English verse,
   Because (alas! great clerks) English affords
(Say they) no height, nor copy; a rude tongue
   (Since 'tis their native) – but in Greek or Latin
Their wits are rare, for thence true poesy sprung,
   Though them (truth knows) they have but skill to chat in,
Compared with that they might say in their own;
   Since thither th'others full soul cannot make
The sample transmigration to be shown
   In nature-loving poesy. So the brake
That those translators stick in, that affect
   Their word-for-word traductions (where they lose
The free grace of their natural dialect,
   And shame their authors with a forcèd glose)
I laugh to see; and yet as much abhor
   More licence for the words than may express
Their full compression, and make clear the author.
   From whose truth, if you think my feet digress,
Because I use needful periphrases;
   Read Valla,[1] Hessus,[2] that in Latin prose
And verse convert him; read the Messines[3]
   That unto Tuscan turns him, and the glose
Grave Salel[4] makes in French, as he translates:
   Which (for th'aforesaid reasons) all must do;
And see that my conversion much abates
   The licence they take, and more shows him too,
Whose right not all those great men learn'd have done
   (In some main parts) that were his commentars:
But (as the illustration of the sun
   Should be attempted by the erring stars)
They failed to search his deep and treasurous heart.
   The cause was, since they wanted the fit key
Of nature, in their downright strength of art;
   With poesy, to open poesy.
Which in my poem of the mysteries
   Revealed in Homer, I will clearly prove:
Till whose near birth suspend your calumnies,

And far-wide imputations of self-love.
'Tis further from me than the worst that reads,
   Professing me the worst of all that write;
Yet what, in following one that bravely leads,
   The worst may show, let this proof hold the light.
But grant it clear – yet hath detraction got
   My blind side in the form my verse puts on;
Much like a dunghill mastiff, that dares not
   Assault the man he barks at, but the stone
He throws at him, takes in his eager jaws,
   And spoils his teeth because they cannot spoil.
The long verse[1] hath by proof received applause
   Beyond each number, and the foil
That squint-eyed Envy takes is censured plain,
   For this long poem asks this length of verse,
Which I myself ingenuously maintain
   Too long our shorter authors to rehearse.
And, for our tongue, that still is so impaired
   By travailling linguists, I can prove it clear
That no tongue hath the Muses' utterance heired
   For verse and that sweet music for the ear
Struck out of rhyme, so naturally as this;
   Our monosyllables so kindly fall
And meet, opposed in rhyme, as they did kiss;
   French and Italian, most immetrical;
Their many syllables, in harsh collision,
   Fall as they brake their necks; their bastard rhymes
Saluting as they justled in transition,
   And set our teeth on edge; nor tunes, nor times
Kept in their falls. And methinks, their long words
   Show in short verse, as in a narrow space
Two opposites should meet, with two-hand swords
   Unwieldy, without or use or grace.
Thus having rid the rubs, and strowed these flowers
   In our thrice-sacred Homer's English way,
What rests to make him yet more worthy yours?
   To cite more praise of him were mere delay

To your glad searches, for what those men found
    That gave his praise, past all, so high a place,
Whose virtues were so many, and so crowned,
    By all consents, divine; that not to grace
Or add increase to them the world doth need
    Another Homer; but even to rehearse
And number them, they did so much exceed;
    Men thought him not a man, but that his verse
Some mere celestial nature did adorn.
    And that all may well conclude, it could not be
That for the place where any man was born
    So long and mortally could disagree
So many nations, as for Homer strived,
    Unless his spur in them had been divine.
Then end their strife, and love him (thus revived)
    As born in England; see him overshine
All other-country poets, and trust this –
    That whosoever Muse dare use her wing
When his Muse flies, she will be trussed[1] by his,
    And show as if a barnacle[2] should spring
Beneath an eagle. In none since was seen
    A soul so full of heaven as earth's in him.
Oh! if our modern poesy had been
    As lovely as the ladies he did limn,
What barbarous worlding, grovelling after gain,
    Could use her lovely parts with such rude hate
As now she suffers under every swain?
    Since then 'tis nought but her abuse and fate
That thus impairs her, what is this to her
    As she is real, or in natural right?
But since in true religion men should err
    As much as poesy, should th'abuse excite
The like contempt of her divinity?
    And that her truth, and right saint sacred merits,
In most lives breed but reverence formally,
    What wonder is't if poesy inherits
Much less observance, being but agent for her,

And singer of her laws, that others say?
Forth then, ye moles, sons of the earth abhor her!
   Keep still on in the dirty, vulgar way,
Till dirt receive your souls, to which ye vow;
   And with your poisoned spirits bewitch our thrifts.
Ye cannot so despise us as we you.
   Not one of you above his molehill lifts
His earthy mind; but, as a sort of beasts,
   Kept by their guardians, never care to hear
Their manly voices but, when in their fists,
   They breathe wild whistles, and the beasts' rude ear
Hears their curs barking, then by heaps they fly
   Headlong together – so men, beastly given,
The manly soul's voice (sacred poesy,
   Whose hymns the angels ever sing in heaven)
Contemn and hear not; but when brutish noises
   (For gain, lust, honour in litigious prose)
Are bellowed out, and crack the barbarous voices
   Of Turkish stentors, oh! ye lean to those,
Like itching horse to blocks or high may-poles,
   And break nought but the wind of wealth, wealth, all
In all your documents; your asinine souls
   (Proud of their burthens) feel not how they gall.
But as an ass, that in a field of weeds
   Affects a thistle, and fall fiercely to it;
That pricks, and galls him; yet he feeds, and bleeds;
   Forbears a while, and licks; but cannot woo it
To leave the sharpness; when (to wreak his smart)
   He beats it with his foot; then backward kicks,
Because the thistle galled his forward part;
   Nor leaves till all be ate, for all the pricks;
Then falls to others with as hot a strife;
   And in that honourable war doth waste
The tall heat of his stomach, and his life:
   So, in this world of weeds, you worldlings taste
Your most-loved dainties; with such war, buy peace;
   Hunger for torments; virtue kick for vice;

Cares, for your states, do with your states increase:
   And though ye dream ye feast in Paradise,
Yet Reason's daylight shows ye at your meat,
   Asses at thistles, bleeding as ye eat.

[c. 1609]

## Ulysses Describes His Visit to
## the Underworld[1]

### Translated from the *Odyssey*, Book XI

WHEN to the powers beneath,
The sacred nation that survive with Death,
My prayers and vows had done devotions fit,
I took the offerings, and upon the pit
Bereft their lives. Out gushed the sable blood,
And round about me fled out of the flood
The souls of the deceased. There clustered then
Youths, and their wives, much suffering agèd men,
Soft tender virgins that but new came there
By timeless death, and green their sorrows were.
There men at arms, with armours all imbrued,
Wounded with lances and with falchions hewed,
In numbers up and down the ditch did stalk,
And threw unmeasured cries about their walk,
So horrid that a bloodless fear surprised
My daunted spirits. Straight then I advised
My friends to flay the slaughtered sacrifice,
Put them in fire, and to the Deities,
Stern Pluto and Persephone apply
Exciteful prayers. Then drew I from my thigh
My well-edged sword, stepped in, and firmly stood
Betwixt the press of shadows and the blood,
And would not suffer any one to dip
Within our offering his unsolid lip
Before Tiresias, that did all control.
The first that pressed in was Elpenor's soul,

His body in the broad-wayed earth as yet
Unmourned, unburied by us, since we sweat
With other urgent labours. Yet his smart
I wept to see, and rued it from my heart,
Enquiring how he could before me be
That came by ship? He, mourning, answered me:
'In Circe's house, the spite some spirit did bear
And the unspeakable good liquor there
Hath been my bane. For being to descend
A ladder much in height, I did not tend
My way well down, but forwards made a proof
To tread the rounds, and from the very roof
Fell on my neck and brake it. And this made
My soul thus visit this infernal shade.
And here, by them that next thyself are dear,
Thy wife and father, that a little one
Gave food to thee, and by thy only son
At home behind thee left, Telemachus,
Do not depart by stealth and leave me thus,
Unmourned, unburied, lest neglected I
Bring on thyself th'incensèd Deity.
I know that, sailed from hence, thy ship must touch
On th'Isle Aeaea, where vouchsafe thus much,
Good king, that, landed, thou wilt instantly
Bestow on me thy royal memory,
To this grace, that my body, arms and all,
May rest consumed in fiery funeral.
And on the foamy shore a sepulchre
Erect to me, that after times may hear
Of one so hapless. Let me these implore,
And fix upon my sepulchre the oar
With which alive I shook the agèd seas,
And had of friends the dear societies.'
   I told the wretched soul I would fulfil
And execute to th'utmost point his will;
And all the time we sadly talked, I still
My sword above the blood held, when aside

The idol of my friend still amplified
His plaint, as up and down the shades he erred.
Then my deceasèd mother's soul appeared,
Fair daughter of Autolycus the Great,
Grave Anticlea, whom, when forth I set
For sacred Ilion, I had left alive.
Her sight much moved me, and to tears did drive
My note of her decease; and yet not she
(Though in my ruth she held the highest degree)
Would I admit to touch the sacred blood
Till from Tiresias I had understood
What Circe told me. At the length did land
Theban Tiresias' soul, and in his hand
Sustained a golden sceptre, knew me well,
And said: 'Oh man unhappy, why to hell
Admit'st thou dark arrival and the light
The sun gives leav'st, to have the horrid sight
Of this black region and the shadows here?
Now sheath thy sharp sword and the pit forbear,
That I the blood may taste, and then relate
The truth of those acts that affect thy Fate.'

[*c.* 1614]

## Bussy Wounded by a Pistol Shot [1]

From *Bussy D'Ambois*, Act Five, Scene Four

BUSSY:                'Tis enough for me
    That Guise and Monsieur, Death and Destiny,
    Come behind D'Ambois. Is my body, then,
    But penetrable flesh? And must my mind
    Follow my blood? Can my divine part add
    No aid to th'earthly in extremity?
    Then these divines are but for form, not fact:
    Man is of two sweet courtly friends compact,

A mistress and a servant: let my death
Define life nothing but a courtier's breath.
Nothing is made of nought, of all things made,
Their abstract being a dream but of a shade.
I'll not complain to earth yet, but to heaven,
And, like a man, look upwards even in death.
And if Vespasian thought in majesty
An emperor might die standing, why not I?
Nay, without help, in which I will exceed him;
For he died splinted with his chamber grooms.
Prop me, true sword, as thou hast ever done!
The equal thought I bear of life and death
Shall make me faint on no side; I am up;
Here like a Roman statue I will stand
Till death hath made me marble. Oh, my fame,
Live in despite of murder! Take thy wings
And haste thee where the grey-eyed Morn perfumes
Her rosy chariot with Sabaean spices!
Fly, where the Evening from th'Iberian vales
Takes on her swarthy shoulders Hecate,
Crowned with a grove of oaks: fly where men feel
The burning axletree, and those that suffer
Beneath the chariot of the snowy Bear:
And tell them all that D'Ambois now is hasting
To the eternal dwellers; that a thunder
Of all their sighs together (for their frailties
Beheld in me) may quit my worthless fall
With a fit volley for my funeral. . . .[1]

BUSSY:                    Oh, my heart is broken!
Fate nor these murderers, Monsieur nor the Guise,
Have any glory in my death, but this,
This killing spectacle, this prodigy:
My sun is turned to blood, in whose red beams
Pindus and Ossa (hid in drifts of snow,
Laid on my heart and liver) from their veins
Melt like two hungry torrents, eating rocks,

Into the ocean of all human life,
And make it bitter, only with my blood.
Oh frail condition of strength, valour, virtue,
In me (like warning fire upon the top
Of some steep beacon, on a steeper hill)
Made to express it: like a falling star
Silently glanced, that like a thunderbolt
Looked to have stuck and shook the firmament.

*(Dies.)*

UMBRA: Farewell, brave relics of a complete man,
Look up and see thy spirit made a star;
Join flames with Hercules, and when thou sett'st
Thy radiant forehead in the firmament,
Make the vast crystal crack with thy receipt;
Spread to a world of fire, and the aged sky
Cheer with new sparks of old humanity.

[1607]

# HENRY CONSTABLE

## (1562–1613)

Constable was born in Warwickshire and educated at Cambridge, after which he became a convert to Catholicism and lived mostly abroad. His sonnet-sequence, *Diana* (1592), won him a certain reputation among his contemporaries. A second sequence of *Spiritual Sonnets* was left in manuscript, and remained unpublished till the early nineteenth century. Constable is a rather cloying writer, and has probably been overrated owing to the modern interest in recusant poets.

### To God the Father[1]

GREAT God, within whose simple essence we
Nothing but that which is thyself can find;
When on thyself thou didst reflect thy mind,
Thy thought was God, and took the form of thee:
And when this God, thus born, thou lov'st, and he
Loved thee again, with passion of like kind
(As lovers' sighs which meet become one wind),
Both breathed one sprite of equal deity.
Eternal Father, whence these two do come
And wilt the title of my father have,
And heavenly knowledge in my mind engrave,
That it thy son's true Image may become:
    And cense my heart with sighs of holy love,
    That it the temple of the Sprite may prove.

[*Spiritual Sonnets*, Harleian MSS, 7553]

# SAMUEL DANIEL

## (1562?–1619)

Daniel studied at Magdalen Hall, Oxford, but did not take a degree.
He travelled on the Continent before 1592. Later, he belonged to
the circle of the Countess of Pembroke, and afterwards held various
offices in the household of Anne of Denmark. He was recognized in
his own day as a leading exponent of the plain style. He was a
meticulous workman, and frequently revised his poems.

## From *Musophilus*

YOU mighty Lords, that with respected grace
   Do at the stern of fair example stand,
And all the body of this populace
   Guide with the only turning of your hand,
Keep a right course, bear up from all disgrace,
   Observe the point of glory to our land:

Hold up disgracèd knowledge from the ground,
   Keep virtue in request, give worth her due,
Let not neglect with barbarous means confound
   So fair a good to bring in night anew.
Be not, oh be not, accessory found
   Unto her death that must give life to you.

Where will you have your virtuous names safe laid:
   In gorgeous tombs, in sacred cells secure?
Do you not see those prostrate heaps betrayed
   Your fathers' bones, and could not keep them sure?
And will you trust deceitful stones fair laid,
   And think they will be to your honour truer?

No, no, unsparing time will proudly send
   A warrant unto wrath that with one frown

Will all these mock'ries of vainglory rend,
   And make them as before, ungraced, unknown,
Poor idle honours that can ill defend
   Your memories, that cannot keep their own.

And whereto serve that wondrous *trophei*[1] now,
   That on the goodly plain near Wilton stands?
That huge dumb heap, that cannot tell us how,
   Nor what, nor whence it is, nor with whose hands,
Nor for whose glory, it was set to show
   How much our pride mocks that of other lands?

Whereon, when as the gazing passenger
   Hath looked with greedy admiration,
And fain would know his birth, and what he were,
   How there erected, and how long agone,
Enquires, and asks his fellow traveller
   What he hath heard, and his opinion:

And he knows nothing. Then he turns again,
   And looks, and sighs, and then admires afresh,
And in himself with sorrow doth complain
   The misery of dark forgetfulness;
Angry with time that nothing should remain
   Our greatest wonders–wonder to express.

[1599]

## These Plaintive Verse

THESE plaintive verse, the posts of my desire,
Which haste for succour to her slow regard,
Bear not report on any slender fire,
Forging a grief to win a fame's reward.
Nor are my passions limned for outward hue,
For that no colours can depaint my sorrows;
Delia herself, and all the world, may view
Best in my face where cares have tilled deep furrows.

77

No bays I seek to deck my mourning brow,
Oh clear-eyed Rector of the holy hill!
My humble accents bear the olive bough
Of intercession, but to move her will.
  These lines I use to unburden mine own heart;
  My love affects not fame, nor 'steems of art.

[*Delia*, 1592]


## Care-Charmer Sleep

CARE-CHARMER sleep, son of the sable night,
Brother to death, in silent darkness born,
Relieve my languish, and restore the light,
With dark forgetting of my care's return.
And let the day be time enough to mourn
The shipwreck of my ill-adventured youth;
Let waking eyes suffice to wail their scorn,
Without the torment of the night's untruth.
Cease, dreams, the images of day-desires,
To model forth the passions of the morrow;
Never let rising sun approve you liars,
To add more grief to aggravate my sorrow.
  Still let me sleep, embracing clouds in vain;
  And never wake to feel the day's disdain.

[*Delia*, 1592]

SAMUEL DANIEL

## Let Others Sing of Knights and Paladins[1]

LET others sing of knights and paladins
In agèd accents and untimely words;
Paint shadows in imaginary lines,
Which well the reach of their high wits records:
But I must sing of thee, and those fair eyes.
Authentic shall my verse in time to come;
When yet th'unborn shall say, 'Lo where she lies,
Whose beauty made him speak that else was dumb.'
These are the arks, the trophies I erect,
That fortify thy name against old age;
And these thy sacred virtues must protect
Against the dark, and time's consuming rage.
    Though th'error of my youth in them appear,
    Suffice they show I lived and loved thee dear.

[*Delia*, 1592]


## Chorus of Egyptians
From *Cleopatra*[2]

OH fearful frowning Nemesis,
    Daughter of Justice most severe,
    That art the world's great arbitress,
    And queen of causes reigning here:
Whose swift-sure hand is ever near
    Eternal Justice, righting wrong:
    Who never yet deferrest long
    The proud's decay, the weak's redress,
But through thy power everywhere,
    Doth raze the great, and raise the less;
    The less made great doth ruin too,
    To show the earth what heaven can do.

Thou from dark-closed Eternity,
　　From thy black cloudy hidden seat,
　　The world's disorders dost descry:
　　Which when they swell so proudly great,
Reversing th'order Nature set,
　　Thou giv'st thy all-confounding doom,
　　Which none can know before it come.
　　Th'inevitable destiny,
Which neither wit nor strength can let,
　　Fast chained unto necessity,
　　In mortal things doth order so,
　　Th'alternate course of weal or woe.

Oh how the powers of heaven do play
　　With travailèd mortality,
　　And doth their weakness still betray,
　　In their best prosperity!
When being lifted up so high,
　　They look beyond themselves so far,
　　That to themselves they take no care;
　　Whilst swift confusion down doth lay
Their late proud mounting vanity,
　　Bringing their glory to decay,
　　And with the ruin of their fall,
　　Extinguish people, state and all.

But is it justice that all we,
　　The innocent poor multitude,
　　For great men's faults should punished be,
　　And to destruction thus pursued?
Oh why should th'heavens us include
　　Within the compass of their fall,
　　Who of themselves procurèd all?
　　Or do the gods (in close) decree,
Occasion take how to extrude
　　Man from the earth with cruelty?
　　Ah no, the gods are ever just;
　　Our faults excuse their rigour must.

This is the period Fate set down
   To Egypt's fat prosperity,
    Which now unto her greatest grown
    Must perish thus, by course must die,
And some must be the causers why
   This revolution must be wrought;
    As born to bring their state to nought,
    To change the people and the crown,
And purge the world's iniquity,
   Which vice so far hath overgrown:
    As we, so they that treat us thus,
    Must one day perish like to us.

[1594]

## Ulysses and the Siren

### Siren

Come, worthy Greek! Ulysses, come;
   Possess these shores with me!
The winds and seas are troublesome
   And here we may be free.
Here may we sit and view their toil
   That travail in the deep,
And joy the day in mirth the while
   And spend the night in sleep.

### Ulysses

Fair nymph, if fame or honour were
   To be attained with ease,
Then would I come and rest me there,
   And leave such toils as these.
But here it dwells, and here must I
   With danger seek it forth:
To spend the time luxuriously
   Becomes not men of worth.

### Siren

Ulysses, Oh! be not deceived
   With that unreal name;
This honour is a thing conceived
   And rests on others' fame;
Begotten only to molest
   Our peace, and to beguile
The best thing of our life, our rest,
   And give us up to toil.

### Ulysses

Delicious nymph, suppose there were
   Nor honour nor report,
Yet manliness would scorn to wear
   The time in idle sport;
For toil doth give a better touch
   To make us feel our joy,
And ease finds tediousness as much
   As labour yields annoy.

### Siren

Then pleasure likewise seems the shore,
   Whereto tends all your toil
Which you forgo to make it more,
   And perish oft the while.
Who may disport them diversely
   Find never tedious day,
And ease may have variety,
   As well as action may.

### Ulysses

But natures of the noblest frame
   These toils and dangers please;
And they take comfort in the same
   As much as you in ease;

And with the thought of actions past
   Are recreated still;
When pleasure leaves a touch at last,
   To shew that it was ill.

### Siren

That doth opinion only cause,
   That's out of custom bred,
Which makes us many other laws,
   Than ever nature did.
No widows wail for our delights,
   Our sports are without blood;
The world we see by warlike wights
   Receives more hurt than good.

### Ulysses

But yet the state of things require
   These motions of unrest;
And these great spirits of high desire
   Seem born to turn them best;
To purge the mischiefs that increase
   And all good order mar,
For oft we see a wicked peace
   To be well changed for war.

### Siren

Well, well, Ulysses, then I see
   I shall not have thee here;
And therefore I will come to thee
   And take my fortunes there.
I must be won that cannot win,
   Yet lost were I not won,
For beauty hath created been
   T'undo, or be undone.

[*Certain Small Poems*, 1605]

## Song
### From *Tethys' Festival*

ARE they shadows that we see,
And can shadows pleasure give?
Pleasures only shadows be,
Cast by bodies we conceive;
   And are made the things we deem
   In those figures which they seem.

But these pleasures vanish fast,
Which by shadows are expressed:
Pleasures are not, if they last;
In their passing is the best.
   Glory is most bright and gay
   In a flash, and so away.

Feed apace then, greedy eyes,
On the wonder you behold;
Take it sudden as it flies,
Though you take it not to hold:
   When your eyes have done their part,
   Thought must lengthen it in the heart.

[1610]

# SIR JOHN DAVIES
## (1569–1626)

Davies studied at Queen's College, Oxford, and later at the Middle
Temple. He was disbarred from 1598 to 1601 for an assault on
Richard Martin, a one-time friend, and seems to have spent this
period of enforced retirement writing poetry. He had a distinguished
public career under James I, and became Speaker of the Irish Parlia-
ment. At the end of his life, he was appointed Lord Chief Justice of
England, but died before he could take up office. His poetry is
distinguished by its superb intellectual energy.

## The General Consent of All
### From *Nosce Teipsum*

FOR, how can that be false, which every tongue
  Of every mortal man affirms for true?
  Which truth hath in all ages been so strong,
  As lodestone-like, all hearts it ever drew.


For, not the Christian, or the Jew alone,
  The Persian, or the Turk, acknowledge this:
  This mystery to the wild Indian known,
  And to the Cannibal and Tartar is.


This rich Assyrian drug grows everywhere;
  As common in the North, as in the East:
  This doctrine does not enter by the ear,
  But of itself is native in the breast.


None that acknowledge God, or providence,
  Their soul's eternity did ever doubt;
  For all Religion takes her root from hence,
  Which no poor naked nation lives without.

For sith the world for Man created was,
   (For only Man the use thereof doth know)
   If man do perish like a withered grass,
   How doth God's Wisdom order things below?

And if that Wisdom still wise ends propound,
   Why made he man, of other creature King;
   When (if he perish here) there is not found
   In all the world so poor and vile a thing?

If death do quench us quite, we have great wrong,
   Sith for our service all things else were wrought,
   That daws, and trees, and rocks, should last so long,
   When we must in an instant pass to nought.

But blest be that Great Power, that hath us blest
   With longer life than Heaven or Earth can have;
   Which hath infused into our mortal breast
   Immortal powers, not subject to the grave.

For though the Soul do seem her grave to bear,
   And in this world is almost buried quick,
   We have no cause the body's death to fear,
   For when the shell is broke, out comes a chick.

[1599]

## From *Orchestra*[1]

BEHOLD the world, how it is whirlèd round!
   And for it is so whirled, is namèd so;
In whose large volume many rules are found
   Of this new art, which it doth fairly show.
   For your quick eyes in wandering to and fro,
     From east to west, on no one thing can glance,
     But, if you mark it well, it seems to dance.

First you see fixed in this huge mirror blue
    Of trembling lights a number numberless;
Fixed, they are named, but with a name untrue;
    For they all move and in a dance express
    The great long year that doth contain no less
        Than threescore hundreds of those years in all,
        Which the sun makes with his course natural.

What if to you these sparks disordered seem,
    As if by chance they had been scattered there?
The gods a solemn measure do it deem
    And see a just proportion everywhere,
    And know the points whence first their movings were,
        To which first points when all return again,
        The axletree of heaven shall break in twain.

Under that spangled sky five wandering flames,
    Besides the king of day and queen of night,
Are wheeled around, in all their sundry frames,
    And all in sundry measures do delight;
    Yet altogether keep no measure right;
        For by itself each doth itself advance,
        And by itself each doth a galliard dance.

Venus, the mother of that bastard Love,
    Which doth usurp the world's great marshal's name,
Just with the sun her dainty feet doth move,
    And unto him doth all her gestures frame;
    Now after, now afore, the flattering dame
        With divers cunning passages doth err,
        With him respecting that respects not her.

For that brave sun, the father of the day,
    Doth love this earth, the mother of the night;
And, like a reveller in rich array,
    Doth dance his galliard in his leman's sight,

Both back and forth and sideways passing light.
His gallant grace doth so the gods amaze,
That all stand still and at his beauty gaze.


But see the earth when she approacheth near,
How she for joy doth spring and sweetly smile;
But see again her sad and heavy cheer,
When changing places he retires a while;
But those black clouds he shortly will exile,
And make them all before his presence fly,
As mists consumed before his cheerful eye.


Who doth not see the measure of the moon?
Which thirteen times she danceth every year,
And ends her pavan thirteen times as soon
As doth her brother, of whose golden hair
She borroweth part, and proudly doth it wear.
Then doth she coyly turn her face aside,
That half her cheek is scarce sometimes descried.


Next her, the pure, subtle, and cleansing fire
Is swiftly carried in a circle even,
Though Vulcan be pronounced by many a liar
The only halting god that dwells in heaven;
But that foul name may be more fitly given
To your false fire, that far from heaven is fall,
And doth consume, waste, spoil, disorder all.


And now behold your tender nurse, the air,
And common neighbour that aye runs around;
How many pictures and impressions fair
Within her empty regions are there found,
Which to your senses dancing do propound?
For what are breath, speech, echoes, music, winds,
But dancings of the air, in sundry kinds?

For, when you breathe, the air in order moves,
  Now in, now out, in time and measure true,
And when you speak, so well she dancing loves,
  That doubling oft and often redoubling new
  With thousand forms she doth herself endue;
    For all the words that from your lips repair
    Are nought but tricks and turnings of the air.

Hence is her prattling daughter, Echo, born,
  That dances to all voices she can hear.
There is no sound so harsh that she doth scorn,
  Nor any time wherein she will forbear
  The airy pavement with her feet to wear;
    And yet her hearing sense is nothing quick,
    For after time she endeth every trick.

And thou, sweet music, dancing's only life,
  The ear's sole happiness, the air's best speech,
Lodestone of fellowship, charming rod of strife,
  The soft mind's paradise, the sick mind's leech,
  With thine own tongue thou trees and stones canst teach,
    That when the air doth dance her finest measure,
    Then art thou born, the gods' and men's sweet pleasure.

Lastly, where keep the winds their revelry,
  Their violent turnings and wild whirling hays,
But in the air's tralucent gallery?
  Where she herself is turned a hundred ways,
  While with those maskers wantonly she plays.
    Yet in this misrule they such rule embrace
    As two, at once, encumber not the place.

If then fire, air, wandering and fixed lights,
  In every province of th' imperial sky,
Yield perfect forms of dancing to your sights,
  In vain I teach the ear that which the eye,

With certain view, already doth descry;
 But for your eyes perceive not all they see,
 In this I will your senses' master be.

For lo! the sea that fleets about the land,
 And like a girdle clips her solid waist,
Music and measure both doth understand;
 For his great crystal eye is always cast
 Up to the moon, and on her fixèd fast;
  And as she danceth in her pallid sphere,
  So danceth he about the centre here.

Sometimes his proud green waves in order set,
 One after other, flow unto the shore;
Which when they have with many kisses wet,
 They ebb away in order, as before;
 And to make known his courtly love the more,
  He oft doth lay aside his three-forked mace,
  And with his arms the timorous earth embrace.

Only the earth doth stand forever still:
 Her rocks remove not, nor her mountains meet,
Although some wits enriched with learning's skill
 Say heaven stands firm and that the earth doth fleet,
 And swiftly turneth underneath their feet;
  Yet, though the earth is ever steadfast seen,
  On her broad breast hath dancing ever been.

For those blue veins that through her body spread,
 Those sapphire streams from which great hills do spring,
The earth's great dugs, for every wight is fed
 With sweet fresh moisture from them issuing,
 Observe a dance in their wild wandering;
  And still their dance begets a murmur sweet,
  And still the murmur with the dance doth meet.

[*Orchestra, or A Poem of Dancing*, 1596]

SIR JOHN DAVIES

## Of a Gull

OFT in my laughing rhymes I name a gull,
But this new term will many questions breed;
Therefore at first I will express at full
Who is a true and perfect gull indeed:
A gull is he who fears a velvet gown,
And when a wench is brave dares not speak to her;
A gull is he which traverseth the town,
And is for marriage known a common wooer;
A gull is he which while he proudly wears
A silver-hilted rapier by his side
Endures the lies and knocks about the ears,
Whilst in his sheath his sleeping sword doth bide;
A gull is he which wears good handsome clothes,
And stands in presence stroking up his hair,
And fills up his unperfect speech with oaths,
But speaks not one wise word throughout the year.
   But to define a gull in terms precise,
   A gull is he which seems, and is not, wise.

[*Epigrams and Elegies*, c.1595]

## A Gulling Sonnet[1]

THE sacred muse that first made love divine
Hath made him naked and without attire;
But I will clothe him with this pen of mine,
That all the world his fashion shall admire:
His hat of hope, his band of beauty fine,
His cloak of craft, his doublet of desire,
Grief, for a girdle, shall about him twine,
His points[2] of pride, his eyelet-holes of ire,
His hose of hate, his codpiece of conceit,
His stockings of stern strife, his shirt of shame,
His garters of vain-glory gay and slight,
His pantofles[3] of passion will I frame;
    Pumps of presumption shall adorn his feet,
    And socks of sullenness exceeding sweet.

[Chetham MS. 8012]

# JOHN DAY

## (fl. 1606)

Little seems to be known about Day. He may have been writing for
the stage as early as 1593, and is mentioned in Henslowe's *Diary* for
1598 as a collaborator of Henry Chettle. He also collaborated with
Dekker and worked on his own. Henslowe often lent him small
sums, which suggests that he had some difficulty in making a living.

### *Character Three – Thraso or Polypragmus, the Plush Bee*

#### From *The Parliament of Bees*

POLYPRAGMUS: The room smells: foh, stand off. –
    Yet stay; d'ye hear
    O' the saucy sun which, mounted in our sphere,
    Strives to outshine us?
SERVANT: So the poor bees hum.
POLYPRAGMUS: Poor bees! potguns,[1] illegitimate scum,
    And bastard flies, taking adulterate shape
    From reeking dunghills. If that meddling ape,
    Zanying my greatness, dares but once presume
    To vie expense with me, I will consume
    His whole hive in a month. Say, you that saw
    His new-raised frame, how is it built?
SERVANT: Of straw
    Dyed in quaint colours; here and there a row
    Of Indian bents, which make a handsome show.
POLYPRAGMUS: How! Straw and bents, say'st? I will have one
    built
    Like Pompey's theatre; the ceiling gilt
    And interseamed with pearl, to make it shine
    Like high Jove's palace: my descent's divine.
    My great hall I'll have paved with clouds; which done,
    By wondrous skill, an artificial sun

Shall roll about, reflecting golden beams,
Like Phoebus dancing on the wanton streams.
And when 'tis night, just as that sun goes down,
I'll have the stars draw up a silver moon
In her full height of glory. Overhead
A roof of woods and forests I'll have spread,
Trees growing downwards, full of fallow-deer;
When of the sudden, listening, you shall hear
A noise of horns and hunting, which shall bring
Actaeon to Diana in the spring,
Where all shall see her naked skin; and there
Actaeon's hounds shall their own master tear,
As emblem of his folly that will keep
Hounds to devour and eat him up asleep.
All this I'll do, that men with praise may crown
My fame for turning the world upside-down.

[Earliest known edition 1641, but a lost edition of 1607(?)]

# THOMAS DEKKER

## (c. 1570–c. 1632)

Dekker was a prolific dramatist and author of numerous pamphlets. His plays were often written in collaboration. He evidently lived a hand-to-mouth existence and was once imprisoned for debt for as long as three years. He attacked Jonson in *Satiromastix* (1602), in return for Jonson's attack on him in *The Poetaster.*

## Song

### From *The Shoemaker's Holiday*

OH! the month of May, the merry month of May,
   So frolic, so gay, and so green, so green, so green!
Oh! and then did I unto my true Love say,
   Sweet Peg, thou shalt be my Summer's Queen.

Now the nightingale, the pretty nightingale,
   The sweetest singer in all the forest's choir,
Entreats thee, sweet Peggy, to hear thy true Love's tale:
   Lo! yonder she sitteth, her breast against a briar.

But oh! I spy the cuckoo, the cuckoo, the cuckoo;
   See where she sitteth; come away, my joy:
Come away, I prithee, I do not like the cuckoo
   Should sing where my Peggy and I kiss and toy.

Oh! the month of May, the merry month of May,
   So frolic, so gay, and so green, so green, so green!
And then did I unto my true Love say,
   Sweet Peg, thou shalt be my Summer's Queen.

[1600]

## *Song*

### From *Patient Grissill*

ART thou poor, yet hast thou golden slumbers?
    Oh sweet content!
Art thou rich, yet is thy mind perplexed?
    Oh punishment!
Dost thou laugh to see how fools are vexed
To add to golden numbers, golden numbers?
Oh sweet content! Oh sweet content!
    Work apace, apace, apace, apace;
    Honest labour bears a lovely face;
   Then hey nonny nonny, hey nonny nonny!

Canst drink the waters of the crispèd spring?
    Oh sweet content!
Swim'st thou in wealth, yet sink'st in thine own tears?
    Oh punishment!
Then he that patiently want's burden bears
No burden bears, but is a king, a king!
Oh sweet content! Oh sweet content!
    Work apace, apace, apace, apace;
    Honest labour bears a lovely face;
   Then hey nonny nonny, hey nonny nonny!

[1603]

## THOMAS DEKKER

### *Prologue*
#### From *The Whore of Babylon*

THE charms of silence through this square be thrown,
That an un-used attention (like a jewel)
May hang at every ear, for we present
Matter above the vulgar argument:
Yet drawn so lively, that the weakest eye,
(Through those thin veils we hang between your sight
And this our piece) may reach the mystery:
What in it is most grave, will most delight.
But as in landskip, towns and woods appear
Small afar off, yet to the optic sense,
The mind shows them as great as those more near;
So, wingèd Time that long ago flew hence
You must fetch back, with all those golden years
He stole, and here imagine still he stands,
Thrusting his silver lock into your hands.
There hold it but two hours – it shall from graves
Raise up the dead; upon this narrow floor
Swell up an ocean (with an armèd fleet),
And lay the dragon at a dove's soft feet.
These wonders sit and see, sending as guides
Your judgement, not your passions: passion slides,
While judgement goes upright: for though the Muse
(That's thus inspired) a novel path does tread,
She's free from foolish boldness, or base dread.
Lo, scorn she scorns, and Envy's rankling tooth,
For this is all she does – she wakens Truth.

[1607]

# JOHN DONNE
## (1572–1631)

Donne was brought up as a Catholic, and studied at both Oxford and Cambridge. In 1592 he entered Lincoln's Inn. He was a volunteer with the Earl of Essex on the expedition to Cadiz of 1596, and the 'Islands Voyage' of 1597. On his return he entered the service of Sir Thomas Egerton, Keeper of the Great Seal, and in 1601 he eloped with Egerton's niece and was dismissed. The same year seems to have seen his final abandonment of Catholicism. After much heart-searching, he was ordained an Anglican priest in 1615. In 1621 he became Dean of St Paul's. His work seems to have circulated widely in manuscript, but as a gentleman he disdained to publish. Only work written during Elizabeth's reign is represented here.

## The Perfume

ONCE, and but once, found in thy company,
All thy supposed escapes are laid on me;
And as a thief at bar, is questioned there
By all the men, that have been robbed that year,
So am I (by this traitorous means surprised)
By thy hydroptic father catechised.
Though he had wont to search with glazèd eyes,
As though he came to kill a cockatrice,
Though he hath oft sworn, that he would remove
Thy beauty's beauty, and food of our love,
Hope of his goods, if I with thee were seen,
Yet close and secret, as our souls, we'have been.
Though thy immortal mother which doth lie
Still buried in her bed, yet will not die,
Takes this advantage to outsleep daylight,
And watch thy entries, and returns all night,
And, when she takes thy hand, and would seem kind,
Doth search what rings, and armlets she can find,
And kissing notes the colour of thy face,
And fearing lest thou'art swoll'n, doth thee embrace;

To try if thou long, doth name strange meats,
And notes thy paleness, blushing, sighs, and sweats;
And politicly will to thee confess
The sins of her own youth's rank lustiness;
Yet love these sorceries did remove, and move
Thee to gull thine own mother for my love.
Thy little brethren, which like fairy sprights
Oft skipped into our chamber, those sweet nights,
And kissed, and ingled on thy father's knee,
Were bribed next day, to tell what they did see:
The grim eight-foot-high iron bound serving-man,
That oft names God in oaths, and only then,
He that to bar the first gate, doth as wide
As the great Rhodian Colossus stride,
Which, if in hell no other pains there were,
Makes me fear hell, because he must be there:
Though by thy father he were hired to this,
Could never witness any touch or kiss.
But Oh, too common ill, I brought with me
That, which betrayed me to mine enemy:
A loud perfume, which at my entrance cried
Even at thy father's nose, so were we spied.
When, like a tyran king, that in his bed
Smelt gunpowder, the pale wretch shiverèd.
Had it been some bad smell, he would have thought
That his own feet, or breath, that smell had wrought.
But as we in our Isle emprisonèd,
Where cattle only, 'and diverse dogs are bred,
The pretious unicorns, strange monsters call,
So thought he good, strange, that had none at all.
I taught my silks, their whistling to forbear,[1]
Even my oppressed shoes, dumb and speechless were,
Only, thou bitter sweet, whom I had laid
Next me, me traitorously hast betrayed,
And unsuspected hast invisibly
At once fled unto him, and stayed with me.
Base excrement of earth, which dost confound

Sense, from distinguishing the sick from sound;
By thee the seely[1] amorous sucks his death
By drawing in a leprous harlot's breath;
By thee, the greatest stain to man's estate
Falls on us, to be called effeminate;
Though you be much loved in the Prince's hall,
There, things that seem, exceed substantial.
Gods, when ye fumed on altars, were pleased well,
Because you'were burnt, not that they liked your smell;
You'are loathsome all, being taken simply alone,
Shall we love ill things joined, and hate each one?
If you were good, your good doth soon decay;
And you are rare, that takes the good away.
All my perfumes I give most willingly
To'embalm thy father's corse; what? will he die?

[*Poems*, 1633]


## The Storm [1]

THOU which art I ('tis nothing to be so),
Thou which art still thyself, by these shalt know
Part of our passage; and, a hand, or eyes
By Hilliard[2] drawn is worth an history,
By a worse painter made; and (without pride)
When by thy judgement they are dignified,
My lines are such: 'tis the pre-eminence
Of friendship only to'impute excellence.
England to whom we'owe, what we be, and have,
Sad that her sons did seek a foreign grave
(For, Fate's or Fortune's drifts none can soothsay,
Honour and misery have one face and way.)
From out her pregnant entrails sighed a wind
Which at th'air's middle marble room[3] did find
Such strong resistance, that itself it threw
Downward again; and so when it did view

How in the port, our fleet dear time did lease,
Withering like prisoners, which lie but for fees,[1]
Mildly it kissed our sails, and, fresh and sweet,
As to a stomach starved, whose insides meet,
Meat comes, it came; and swole our sails, when we
So joyed, as Sara'her swelling joyed to see.
But 'twas but so kind, as our countrymen,
Which bring friends one day's way, and leave them then.
Then like two mighty kings, which dwelling far
Asunder, meet against a third to war,
The South and West winds joined, and, as they blew,
Waves like a rolling trench before them threw.
Sooner than you read this line, did the gale,
Like shot, not feared till felt, our sides assail;
And what at first was called a gust, the same
Hath now a storm's, anon a tempest's name.
Jonas, I pity thee, and curse those men,
Who when the storm raged most, did wake thee then;
Sleep is pain's easiest salve, and doth fulfil
All offices of death, except to kill.
But when I waked, I saw, that I saw not;
Ay, and the sun, which should teach me'had forgot
East, West, Day, Night, and I could only say,
If'the world had lasted, now it had been day.
Thousands our noises were, yet we'mongst all
Could none by his right name, but thunder call:
Lightning was all our light, and it rained more
Than if the sun had drunk the sea before.
Some coffined in their cabins lie,'equally
Grieved that they are not dead, and yet must die;
And as sin-burdened souls from graves will creep,
At the last day, some forth their cabins peep:
And tremblingly'ask what news, and do hear so,
Like jealous husbands, what they would not know.
Some sitting on the hatches, would seem there,
With hideous gazing to fear away fear.
Then note they the ship's sicknesses, the mast

Shaked with this ague, and the hold and waist
With a salt dropsy clogged, and all our tacklings
Snapping, like too-high-stretched treble strings.
And from our tottered sails, rags drop down so,
As from one hanged in chains, a year ago.
Even our ordinance, placed for our defence,
Strive to break loose, and scape away from thence.
Pumping hath tired our men, and what's the gain?
Seas into seas thrown, we suck in again;
Hearing hath deafed our sailors; and if they
Knew how to hear, there's none knows what to say.
Compared to these storms, death is but a qualm,
Hell somewhat lightsome, and the'Bermuda calm.[1]
Darkness, light's elder brother, his birthright
Claims o'er this world, and to heaven hath chased light.
All things are one, and that one none can be,
Since all forms, uniform deformity
Doth cover, so that we, except God say
Another *Fiat*,[2] shall have no more day.
So violent, yet long these furies be,
That though thine absence starve me,'I wish not thee.

[*Poems*, 1633]

# MICHAEL DRAYTON

## (1563–1631)

Drayton is *par excellence* the professional poet of his time, though he
did not enter either university, and his education was confined to his
period of service as a page in the household of Sir Henry Goodere.
In spite of the fact that he was forced to work as a hack playwright
for Henslowe in the late 1590s, he seems to have had a reasonably
successful as well as a prolific career. In the course of it he attempted
most of the stock Elizabethan genres, and usually met with applause.
Some of his historical narrative poems were often reprinted. Time,
however, eventually overtook him, and he was disappointed when
his long-meditated *Poly-Olbion* (published in two parts, 1612 and
1622) was overshadowed by more recent fashions.

## *Mortimer and Queen Isabella at Nottingham Castle*

### From *The Barons' Wars*, Canto Six[1]

THE night waxed old (not dreaming of these things),
And to her chamber is the Queen withdrawn,
To whom a choice musician plays and sings
While she sat under an estate[2] of lawn,
In night-attire, more god-like glittering
Than any eye had seen the cheerful dawn,
 Leaning upon her most-loved Mortimer,
 Whose voice, more than the music, pleased her ear.

Where her fair breasts at liberty were let,
Whose violet veins in branchèd riverets flow,
And Venus' swans, and milky doves were set
Upon those swelling mounts of driven snow;
Whereon whilst Love to sport himself doth get,
He lost his way, nor back again could go,
 But with those banks of beauty set about,
 He wand'red still, yet never could get out.

Her loose hair looked like gold (Oh word too base!
Nay, more than sin, but so to name her hair)
Declining as to kiss her fairer face;
No word is fair enough for thing so fair,
Nor never was there epithet could grace
That, by much praising, which we much impair;
    And where the pen fails, pencils cannot show it,
    Only the soul may be supposed to know it.


She laid her fingers on his manly cheek,
The Gods' pure sceptres, and the darts of Love,
That with their touch might make a tiger meek,
Or might great Atlas from his seat remove;
So white, so soft, so delicate, so sleek,
As she had worn a lily for a glove,
    As might beget life, where was never none
    And put a spirit into the hardest stone.


The fire of precious wood; the light, perfume,
Which left a sweetness on each thing it shone,
As ev'ry thing did to itself assume
The scent from them, and made the same their own;
So that the painted flowers within the room
Were sweet, as if they naturally had grown;
    The light gave colours, which upon them fell,
    And to the colours the perfume gave a smell.


When on those sundry pictures they devise[1]
And from one piece they to another run,
Commend that face, that arm, that hand, those eyes,
Show how that bird, how well that flower was done,
How this part shadowed, and how that did rise,
This top was clouded, and that trail was spun,
    The landskip, mixture and delineatings,
    And in that art a thousand curious things.

Looking upon proud Phaethon, wrapped in fire,
The gentle Queen did much bewail his fall;
But Mortimer commended his desire,
To lose one poor life or to govern all:
What though (quoth he) he madly did aspire
And his great mind made him proud Fortune's thrall?
 Yet, in despite when she her worst had done,
 He perished in the chariot of the Sun.

[1603]


## How Many Paltry, Foolish, Painted Things[1]

How many paltry, foolish, painted things,
That now in coaches trouble every street,
Shall be forgotten, whom no poet sings,
Ere they be well-wrapped in their winding sheet?
Where I to thee Eternity shall give,
When nothing else remaineth of these days,
And queens hereafter shall be glad to live
Upon the alms of thy superfluous praise;
Virgins and matrons reading these my rhymes,
Shall be so much delighted with thy story,
That they shall grieve, they lived not in these times,
To have seen thee, their Sex's only glory:
 So shalt thou fly above the vulgar throng,
 Still to survive in my immortal song.

[Idea, 1619]

## An Evil Spirit

An evil spirit, your beauty haunts me still,
Wherewith, alas, I have been long possessed,
Which ceaseth not to tempt me to each ill,
Nor gives me once but one poor minute's rest;
In me it speaks, whether I sleep or wake,
And when by means to drive it out I try,
With greater torments then it me doth take,
And tortures me in most extremity;
Before my face it lays down my despairs,
And hastes me on unto a sudden death,[1]
Now tempting me to drown myself in tears,
And then in sighing to give up my breath.
    Thus am I still provoked to every evil
    By this good wicked spirit, sweet angel-devil.

*[Idea, 1599]*

## Since There's No Help

Since there's no help, come let us kiss and part:
Nay, I have done; you get no more of me;
And I am glad, yea, glad with all my heart
That thus so cleanly I myself can free.
Shake hands forever; cancel all our vows;
And when we meet at any time again,
Be it not seen in either of our brows
That we one jot of former love retain.
Now at the last gasp of love's latest breath
When, his pulse failing, passion speechless lies,
When faith is kneeling by his bed of death
And innocence is closing up his eyes;
    Now, if thou would'st, when all have given him over,
    From Death to Life thou might'st him yet recover.

*[Idea, 1619]*

## MICHAEL DRAYTON

## The Ballad of Agincourt[1]

FAIR stood the wind for France,
When we our sails advance,
Nor now to prove our chance,
    Longer will tarry;
But putting to the main,
At Caux, the mouth of Seine,
With all his martial train,
    Landed King Harry.

And taking many a fort,
Furnished in warlike sort,
Marcheth towards Agincourt,
    In happy hour;
Skirmishing day by day,
With those that stopped his way,
Where the French general lay,
    With all his power.

Which in his height of pride,
King Henry to deride,
His ransom to provide
    To the King sending.
Which he neglects the while,
As from a nation vile,
Yet with an angry smile,
    Their fall portending.

And turning to his men
Quoth our brave Henry then:
'Though they to one be ten,
    Be not amazèd.
Yet have we well begun,
Battles so bravely won,
Have ever to the sun,
    By fame been raisèd.'

'And for myself,' quoth he,
'This me full rest shall be,
England ne'er mourn for me,
    Nor more esteem me.
Victor I will remain,
Or on this earth lie slain,
Never shall she sustain
    Loss to redeem me.'


'Poitiers and Cressy tell,
When most their pride did swell,
Under our swords they fell,
    No less our skill is,
Than when our grandsire great,
Claiming the regal seat,
By many a warlike feat,
    Lopped the French lilies.'


The Duke of York so dread
The eager vaward led;
With the main, Henry sped
    Amongst his henchmen.
Exeter had the rear,
A braver man not there,
Oh Lord, how hot they were,
    On the false Frenchmen!


They now to fight are gone,
Armour on armour shone,
Drum now to drum did groan,
    To hear, was wonder;
That with cries they make,
The very earth did shake,
Trumpet to trumpet spake,
    Thunder to thunder.

Well it thine age became,
Oh noble Erpingham,
Which didst the signal aim,
　To our hid forces;
When from a meadow by,
Like a storm suddenly,
The English archery
　Stuck the French horses.


With Spanish yew so strong,
Arrows a cloth-yard long,
That like to serpents stung,
　Piercing the weather;
None from his fellow starts,
But playing manly parts,
And like true English hearts,
　Stuck close together.


When down their bows they threw,
And forth their bilbows drew,
And on the French they flew,
　Not one was tardy;
Arms were from shoulders sent,
Scalps to the teeth were rent,
Down the French peasants went,
　Our men were hardy.


This while our noble King,
His broad sword brandishing,
Down the French host did ding,
　As to o'erwhelm it;
And many a deep wound lent,
His arms with blood besprent,
And many a cruel dent
　Bruisèd his helmet.

Gloucester, that Duke so good,
Next of the royal blood,
For famous England stood
   With his brave brother;
Clarence, in steel so bright,
Though but a maiden knight,
Yet in that furious fight,
   Scarce such another.

Warwick in blood did wade,
Oxford the foe invade,
And cruel slaughter made
   Still as they ran up;
Suffolk his axe did ply,
Beaumont and Willoughby
Bare them right doughtily,
   Ferrers and Fanhope.

Upon St Crispin's day
Fought was this noble fray,
Which fame did not delay
   To England to carry;
Oh, when shall English men
With such acts fill a pen,
Or England breed again,
   Such a King Harry?

[*Odes*, 1606]


## The Thirteenth Song
From *Poly-Olbion*

WHEN Phoebus lifts his head out of the winter's wave,
No sooner doth the earth her flowery bosom brave,
At such time as the year brings on the pleasant spring,
But hunts-up to the morn the feathered sylvans sing:

And in the lower grove, as on the rising knoll,
Upon the highest spray of every mounting pole,
Those quiristers are perched with many a speckled breast.
Then from her burnished gate the goodly glitt'ring east
Gilds every lofty top, which late the humorous night
Bespangled had with pearl to please the morning's sight:
On which the mirthful choirs with their clear open throats
Unto the joyful morn so strain their warbling notes
That hills and valleys ring, and even the echoing air
Seems all composed of sounds, about them everywhere.
The throstle, with shrill sharps; as purposely he sung
T'awake the lustless sun; or chiding, that so long
He was in coming forth that should the thickets thrill:
The woosell¹ near at hand, that hath a golden bill;
As nature had him marked of purpose, t'let us see
That from all other birds his tunes should different be:
For, with their vocal sounds, they sing to pleasant May;
Upon his dulcet pipe the merle doth only play.
When in the lower brake, the nightingale hard by,
In such lamenting strains the joyful hours doth ply,
As though the other birds she to her tunes would draw.
And, but that nature (by her all constraining law)
Each bird to her own kind this season doth invite,
They else, alone to hear that charmer of the night
(The more to use their ears) their voices sure would spare,
That moduleth her tunes so admirably rare,
As man to set in parts, at first had learned of her.

[1612-13]

# SIR EDWARD DYER
## (d. 1604)

Dyer's claim to fame, apart from one anthology piece, is his friendship with Sidney and Fulke Greville. However, his contemporaries knew him as a poet, and we must suppose that much of his work is lost. He served on diplomatic missions to the Low Countries and Denmark, and later lived quietly in the country.

## *My Mind to Me a Kingdom Is*

My mind to me a kingdom is,
  Such present joys therein I find,
That it excels all other bliss
  That world affords or grows by kind.
Though much I want which most would have,
Yet still my mind forbids to crave.

No princely pomp, no wealthy store,
  No force to win the victory,
No wily wit to salve a sore,
  No shape to feed a loving eye;
To none of these I yield as thrall,
For why my mind doth serve for all.

I see how plenty suffers oft,
  And hasty climbers soon do fall;
I see that those which are aloft
  Mishap doth threaten most of all;
They get with toil, they keep with fear:
Such cares my mind could never bear.

Content I live, this is my stay,
  I see no more than may suffice;
I press to bear no haughty sway;
  Look, what I lack my mind supplies.
Lo! thus I triumph like a king,
Content with that my mind doth bring.

Some have too much, but still do crave;
   I have little, and seek no more.
They are but poor, though much they have.
   And I am rich with little store.
They poor, I rich; they beg, I give;
They lack, I leave; they pine, I live.

I laugh not at another's loss;
   I grudge not at another's gain;
No worldly waves my mind can toss;
   My state at one doth still remain.
I fear no foe, I fawn no friend;
I loathe not life, nor dread my end.

Some weigh their pleasure by their lust,
   Their wisdom by their rage of will;
Their treasure is their only trust,
   A cloakèd craft their store of skill:
But all the pleasure that I find
Is to maintain a quiet mind.

My wealth is health and perfect ease,
   My conscience clear my choice defence;
I neither seek by bribes to please,
   Nor by deceit to breed offence.
Thus do I live; thus will I die;
Would all did so as well as I!

[Rawlinson Poet MS. 85. Another version in
William Byrd, *Psalms, Sonnets, and Songs*, 1588]

# THOMAS EDWARDS
## (*fl.* 1595)

About Edwards nothing is known except his name.

### *L'Envoy*[1]

From *Cephalus and Procris*

BETWIXT extremes
Are ready paths and fair,
One straight and narrow went
   Leads passengers in dreams,
And ever as the air
Doth buzz them with content,
   A cruel ugly fen,
   Hated of gods and men


   Calls out amain:
'Oh, whither but this way?
Or now, or never bend
   Your steps this goal to gain.'
The to'ther tells you stray,
And never will find end,
   Thus hath the gods decreed,
   To pain souls for their deeds.


   These monsters tway
Yclepèd are of all
Despair and eke Debate,
   Which are (as poets say)
Of Envy's whelps the fall,
And never come too late:
   By Procris it appears,
   Whose proof is bought so dear.

Debate afoot,
And Jealousy abroad,
For remedy, Despair
    Comes in a yellow coat,
And acts where wizards trod,
To shew the gazers fair,
    How subtly he can cloak
    The tale another spoke.

Oh, time of times,
When monster-mongers show,
As men in painted clothes,
    For food even like to pine,
And are in weal gods know[1]
Upheld with spicèd broths,
    So as the weakest seem
    What often we not deem.

Abandon it,
That breeds such discontent,
Foul Jealousy the sore,
    That vile despite would hit,
Debate, his chorus spent,
Comes in a tragic more
    Than actors on this stage
    Can plausively engage.

[1595]

# ROBERT DEVEREUX,
## EARL OF ESSEX
### (1567–1601)

Arrogant, glittering, wilful, and tragic, Elizabeth's last favourite sums up much that was truly 'Elizabethan'. Poet in his hours of relaxation, Essex was also important as a patron of poets. Sir Henry Wotton says that Essex liked to 'evaporate his thoughts in a sonnet'. His surviving work bears out this account, showing amateurishness and a certain impatience as well as brilliance.

## Change Thy Mind Since She Doth Change

CHANGE thy mind since she doth change,
    Let not fancy still abuse thee;
Thy untruth cannot seem strange,
    When her falsehood doth excuse thee.
Love is dead, and thou art free.
She doth live, but dead to thee.

Whilst she loved thee best awhile,
    See how she hath still delayed thee,
Using shows for to beguile
    Those vain hopes that have betrayed thee.
Now thou seest, although too late,
Love loves truth, which women hate.

Love no more since she is gone;
    She is gone and loves another.
Being once deceived by one,
    Leave her love, but love none other.
She was false, bid her adieu.
She was best, but yet untrue.

Love, farewell, more dear to me,
    Than my life which thou preservest.

Life, all joys are gone from thee,
   Others have what thou deservest.
Oh! my death doth spring from hence,
I must die for her offence.

Die, but yet before thou die,
   Make her know what she hath gotten.
She in whom my hopes did lie
   Now is changed, I quite forgotten.
She is changed, but changèd base,
Baser in so vild a place.

[R. Dowland, *A Musical Banquet*, 1610]

# EDWARD FAIRFAX

## (d. 1635)

Fairfax, one of the most important of the Elizabethan translators,
lived in retirement in Yorkshire. His work shows the influence of
Spenser (who had previously been influenced by Tasso). *Godfrey of
Bulloigne* is an English classic which stands seriously in need of re-
publication.

## *Armida Entertains Rinaldo*

From *Tasso's Godfrey of Bulloigne* (*Gerusalemne
Liberata*), Book Sixteen

HER breasts were naked, for the day was hot,
Her locks unbound waved in the wanton wind,
Somedeal she sweat (tired with the game you wot),
Her sweat drops bright, white, round, like pearls of Ind,
Her humid eyes a fiery smile forth shot,
That like sun-beams in silver fountains shined,
   O'er him her looks she hung, and her soft breast
   The pillow was, here he and love took rest.

His hungry eyes upon her face he fed,
And feeding them so pined himself away;
And she, declining often down her head,
His lips, his cheeks, his eyes kissed, as he lay,
Wherewith he sighed, as if his soul had fled
From his frail breast to hers, and there would stay
   With her beloved sprite: the armèd pair[1]
   These follies all beheld and this hot fare.

Down by the lovers' side there pendant was
A crystal mirror, bright, pure, smooth and neat;
He rose and to his mistress held the glass
(A noble page, graced with that service great);

She with glad looks, he with inflamed (alas!)
Beauty and love beheld, both in one seat;
 Yet them in sundry objects each espies,
 She, in the glass; he saw them in her eyes.

Her, to command; to serve, it pleased the knight;
He proud of bondage; of her empire, she;
My dear (she said) that blessest with thy sight
Even blessed angels, turn thine eyes to me,
For painted in my heart and portrayed right
Thy worth, thy beauties, and perfections be,
 Of which the form, the shape, and fashion best,
 Not in this glass is seen, but in my breast.

And if thou me disdain, yet be content
At least so to behold thy lovely hue,
That while thereon thy looks are fixed and bent,
Thy happy eyes themselves may see and view;
So rare a shape, no crystal can present,
No glass contain that heav'n of beauties true;
 Oh let the skies thy worthy mirror be,
 And in clear stars thy shape and image see!

And with that word she smiled, and ne'ertheless
Her love-toys still she used, and pleasures bold:
Her hair that done she twisted up in tress,
And looser locks in silken laces rolled,
Her curlés garland-wise she did updress,
Wherein (like rich enamel laid on gold)
 The twisted flow'rets smiled, and her white breast
 The lilies (there that spring) and roses dressed.

[1600]

# GEORGE GASCOIGNE
## (1542?–77)

The most important poet of Elizabeth's reign before the advent of Spenser, Gascoigne forms the bridge between the Wyatt/Surrey tradition and the mature Elizabethans. His work has recently attracted much attention in America, especially from Professor Yvor Winters, who praises it for its 'classicism'. Gascoigne had many careers, as courtier, soldier, and adventurer, and his poems show a keen enjoyment of his own variousness.

## The Lullaby of a Lover

SING lullaby, as women do,
Wherewith they bring their babes to rest,
And lullaby can I sing too
As womanly as can the best.
With lullaby they still the child,
And if I be not much beguiled,
Full many wanton babes have I
Which must be stilled with lullaby.

First, lullaby my youthful years,
It is now time to go to bed,
For crooked age and hoary hairs
Have won the haven within my head;
With lullaby, then, youth be still,
With lullaby, content thy will,
Since courage quails and comes behind,
Go sleep, and so beguile thy mind.

Next, lullaby my gazing eyes,
Which wonted were to glance apace.
For every glass may now suffice
To show the furrows in my face;
With lullaby, then, wink awhile,
With lullaby, your looks beguile,

GEORGE GASCOIGNE

Let no fair face nor beauty bright
Entice you eft with vain delight.

And lullaby, my wanton will,
Let reason's rule now reign thy thought,
Since all too late I find by skill
How dear I have thy fancies bought;
With lullaby, now take thine ease,
With lullaby, thy doubts appease;
For trust to this, if thou be still,
My body shall obey thy will.

Eke, lullaby my loving boy,
My little Robin, take thy rest;
Since age is cold, and nothing coy,
Keep close thy coin, for so is best;
With lullaby, be thou content,
With lullaby, thy lusts relent,
Let others pay which have mo pence,
Thou art too poor for such expense.

Thus lullaby, my youth, mine eyes,
My will, my ware, and all that was!
I can no mo delays devise,
But welcome pain, let pleasure pass;
With lullaby, now take your leave,
With lullaby, your dreams deceive,
And when you rise with waking eye,
Remember Gascoigne's lullaby.

[*A Hundreth Sundry Flowers*, 1573]

## And If I Did, What Then?

'AND if I did, what then?
Are you aggrieved therefore?
The sea hath fish for every man,
And what would you have more?'

Thus did my mistress once
Amaze my mind with doubt;
And popped a question for the nonce,
To beat my brains about.

Whereto I thus replied:
'Each fisherman can wish
That all the seas at every tide
Were his alone to fish;

And so did I, in vain;
But since it may not be,
Let such fish there as find the gain,
And leave the loss for me.

And with such luck and loss
I will content myself,
Till tides of turning time may toss
Such fishers on the shelf.

And when they stick on sands,
That every man may see,
Then will I laugh and clap my hands,
As they do now at me.'

[*The Adventures of Master F.I.*, 1573]

## The Green Knight's Farewell to Fancy[1]

FANCY (quoth he) farewell, whose badge I long did bear,
And in my hat full hairbrainedly thy flowers did I wear:
Too late I find, at last, thy fruits are nothing worth,
Thy blossoms fall and fade full fast, though bravery bring them
    forth.
By thee I hoped always in deep delights to dwell,
But since I find thy fickleness, *Fancy* (quoth he) *farewell*.


Thou mad'st me live in love, which wisdom bids me hate,
Thou bleard'st mine eyes and made me think that faith was mine
    by fate.
By thee those bitter sweets did please my taste alway,
By thee I thought that love was light and pain was but a play;
I thought that Beauty's blaze was meet to bear the bell,
And since I find myself deceived, *Fancy* (quoth he) *farewell*.


The gloss of gorgeous courts, by thee did please mine eye,
A stately sight methought it was to see the brave go by;
To see their feathers flaunt, to mark their strange device,
To lie along in ladies' laps, to lisp and make it nice;
To fawn and flatter both, I likèd sometimes well,
But since I see how vain it is, *Fancy* (quoth he) *farewell*.


When court had cast me off, I toilèd at the plough;
My fancy stood in strange conceits, to thrive I wot not how;
By mills, by making malt, by sheep and eke by swine,
By duck and drake, by pig and goose, by calves and keeping
    kine;
By feeding bullocks fat, when price at markets fell,
But since my swains eat up my gains, *Fancy* (quoth he) *farewell*.


In hunting of the deer, my fancy took delight;
All forests knew my folly still, the moonshine was my light;

In frosts I felt no cold, a sunburnt hue was best,
I sweat and was in temper still, my watching seemèd rest;
What dangers deep I passed, it folly were to tell,
And since I sigh to think thereon, *Fancy* (quoth he) *farewell.*


A fancy fed me once, to write in verse and rhyme,
To wray my grief, to crave reward, to cover still my crime;
To frame a long discourse, on stirring of a straw,
To rumble rhyme in raff and ruff, yet all not worth an haw;
To hear it said, there goeth the man that writes so well;
But since I see what poets be, *Fancy* (quoth he) *farewell.*


At music's sacred sound, my fancies eft begone,
In concords, discords, notes and clefs, in tunes of unison;
In hierarchies and strains, in rests, in rule and space,
In monochords[1] and moving modes, in burdens under bass;
In descants and in chants, I strainèd many a yell,
But since musicians be so mad, *Fancy* (quoth he) *farewell.*


To plant strange country fruits, to sow such seeds likewise,
To dig and delve for new found roots, where old might well
    suffice;
To prune the water boughs,[2] to pick the mossy trees,
Oh how it pleased my fancy once to kneel upon my knees,
To griff[3] a pippin stock, when sap begins to swell;
But since the gains scarce quit the cost, *Fancy* (quoth he) *farewell.*


Fancy (quoth he) farewell, which made me follow drums,
Where powdered bullets serves for sauce, to every dish that
    comes;
Where treason lurks in trust, where hope all hearts beguiles,
Where mischief lieth still in wait when fortune friendly smiles;
Where one day's prison proves that all such heavens are hell;
And such I feel the fruits thereof, *Fancy* (quoth he) *farewell.*

If reason rule my thoughts, and God vouchsafe me grace,
Then comfort of philosophy shall make me change my race;
And fond I shall it find, that Fancy sets to show,
For weakly stands that building still, which lacketh grace below;
But since I must accept my fortunes as they fell,
I say God send me better speed, and *Fancy now farewell.*

[*The Posies*, 1575]

# HUMFREY GIFFORD

## (*fl.* 1580)

Gifford came from a Devonshire family of some breeding, and was
an official at the Poultry Counter, a prison for debtors. Otherwise
nothing is known of him.

## *For a Gentlewoman*

WHAT luckless lot had I, alas,
   To plant my love in such a soil,
As yields no corn nor fruitful grass,
   But crops of care, and brakes of toil?


When first I chose the plot of ground
   In which mine anchor forth was cast,
I thought it stable, firm, and sound,
   But found it sand and slime at last.


Like as the fowler with his gins,
   Beguiles the birds that think no ill
By filèd speech, so divers wins
   The simple sort to work their will.


But I, whom good advice had taught
   To shun their snares and subtle charms,
Am not into such danger brought
   But that I can eschew the harms.


The skilful falconer still doth prove
   And praise the hawk which makes best wing,
So I by some that seemed to love
   Have had the proof of such a thing.

From first they did pursue their game
   With swiftest wing and eager mind,
But when in midst of flight they came
   They turned their trains against the wind.

Ye haggards strange, therefore adieu,
   Go seek some other for your mate;
Ye false your faith and prove untrue,
   I like and love the sole estate.

Like as Ulysses' wandering men,
   In red seas as they past along,
Did stop their ears with wax as then,
   Against the subtle mermaid's tongue.

So shall their crafty filèd talk
   Hereafter find no listening ear,
I will bid them go pack and walk,
   And spend their words some other where.

By proof experience tells me not
   What fickle trust in them remains,
And tract of time hath learned me how
   I should eschew their subtle trains.

Such as are bound to lovers' toys
   Make shipwreck of their freedom still;
They never taste but brittle joys,
   For one good chance a thousand ill.

Cease now your suits, and glose no more,
   I mean to lead a virgin's life,
In this of pleasure find I store,
   In doubtful suits but care and strife.

                    [*A Posy of Gilly flowers*, 1580]

# From *A Delectable Dream*

A WOMAN'S face is full of wiles,
   Her tears are like the crocadill:
With outward cheer on thee she smiles,
   When in her heart she thinks thee ill;

Her tongue still chats of this and that,
   Than aspen leaf it wags more fast,
And as she talks she knows not what,
   There issues many a truthless blast.

Thou far dost take thy mark amiss
   If thou think faith in them to find:
The weathercock more constant is,
   Which turns about with every wind.

Oh, how in pity they abound!
   Their heart is mild, like marble stone:
If in thyself no hope be found,
   Be sure of them thou gettest none.

I know some pepper-nosèd dame
   Will term me fool, and saucy jack,
That dare their credit so defame,
   And lay such slanders on their back.

What though on me they pour their spite?
   I may not use the glozer's trade,
I cannot say the crow is white,
   But needs must call a spade a spade.

[*A Posy of Gilly flowers*, 1580]

# ARTHUR GOLDING
## (1536?–1605?)

Golding was the son of one of the auditors of the Exchequer. By 1549 he was in the service of Protector Somerset. In 1563 he became receiver for the young Edward de Vere, Earl of Oxford, the son of his half-sister. Golding was a prolific translator – he 'englished' Caesar's *Commentaries* and Seneca's *De Beneficiis* as well as Ovid. Sidney was his friend, and Cecil, Hatton, Leicester, and Essex were numbered among his patrons. He showed a strong inclination to the Puritan cause.

## Medea Casts a Spell to Make Aeson Young Again[1]
### From *The Metamorphoses of Ovid*, Book Seven

BEFORE the moon should circlewise close both her horns in one
Three nights were yet as then to come. As soon as that she shone
Most full of light, and did behold the earth with fulsome face,
Medea with her hair not trussed so much as in a lace,
But flaring on her shoulders twain, and barefoot, with her gown
Ungirded, got her out of doors and wandered up and down
Alone the dead time of the night: both man, and beast, and bird
Were fast asleep: the serpents sly in trailing forward stirred
So softly that you would have thought they still asleep had
    been.
The moisting air was whist:[2] no leaf ye could have moving seen.
The stars alonely fair and bright did in the welkin shine.
To which she, lifting up her hands, did thrice herself incline,
And thrice with water of the brook her hair besprinkled she:
And gasping thrice she oped her mouth: and bowing down her
    knee
Upon the bare hard ground, she said: 'Oh trusty time of night,
Most faithful unto privities, oh golden stars whose light
Doth jointly with the moon succeed the beams that blaze by day,
And thou, three-headed Hecate, who knowest best the way
To compass this our great attempt, and art our chiefest stay:

Ye charms and witchcrafts, and thou earth which both with herb
    and weed
Of mighty working furnishest the wizards at their need:
Ye airs and winds: ye elves of hills, of brooks, of woods alone,
Of standing lakes, and of the night, approach ye everychone.
Through help of whom (the crooked banks much wondering at
    the thing)
I have compellèd streams to run clean backward to their spring.
By charms I make the calm seas rough, and make the rough seas
    plain,
And cover all the sky with clouds, and chase them hence again.
By charms I raise and lay the winds, and burst the viper's jaw,
And from the bowels of the earth both stones and trees do draw.
Whole woods and forests I remove: I make the mountains shake,
And even the earth itself to groan and fearfully to quake.
I call up dead men from their graves: and thee, oh lightsome
    moon,
I darken oft, though beaten brass abate thy peril soon:
Our sorcery dims the morning fair, and darks the sun at noon.
The flaming breath of fiery bulls ye quenchèd for my sake,
And causèd their unwieldy necks the bended yoke to take.
Amongst the earthbred brothers you a mortal war did set,
And brought asleep the dragon fell whose eyes were never shet;
By means whereof deceiving him that had the golden fleece
In charge to keep, you sent it thence by Jason into Greece.
Now have I need of herbs that can by virtue of their juice
To flowering prime of lusty youth old withered age reduce.
I am assured ye will it grant. For not in vain have shone
These twinkling stars, ne yet in vain this chariot all alone
By draught of dragons hither comes.' With that was fro the sky
A chariot softly glancèd down, and stayèd hard thereby.

[1567]

# BARNABE GOOGE

## (1540–94)

Googe, like Golding, was an early translator. He was also an early exponent of the pastoral mode. His contemporaries Gascoigne and Turberville are on the whole more skilled and interesting poets. Like so many Elizabethan writers, he was at one time a member of a lawyers' Inn – Gray's Inn.

## A Refusal

SITH Fortune favours not,
   and all things backward go,
And sith your mind hath so decreed
   to make an end of woe;
Sith now is no redress,
   but hence I must away –
Farewell – I waste no vainer words,
   I hope for better day.

[*Eclogues, Epitaphs, and Sonnets,* 1563]

# ROBERT GREENE

## (1558?–92)

Born at Norwich, and educated at St John's College, Cambridge, Greene came to London where he made a precarious living as a writer of plays, pamphlets, and romances. He became a famous Bohemian character, celebrated both for his picturesque appearance and for the low company he kept. His excesses, and his final repentance on his miserable deathbed, were copiously written up by himself and others (we learn that his death was caused by 'a fatal banquet of Rhenish wine and pickled herring'). Greene's talent is slight but strangely mixed – it combines the pastoral, the realistic, and the moralizing.

## Sephestia's Song

WEEP not, my wanton, smile upon my knee;
When thou art old there's grief enough for thee.
   Mother's wag, pretty boy,
   Father's sorrow, father's joy.
   When thy father first did see
   Such a boy by him and me,
   He was glad, I was woe:
   Fortune changèd made him so,
   When he left his pretty boy,
   Last his sorrow, first his joy.

Weep not, my wanton, smile upon my knee;
When thou art old there's grief enough for thee.
   Streaming tears that never stint,
   Like pearl drops from a flint,
   Fell by course from his eyes,
   That one another's place supplies:
   Thus he grieved in every part,
   Tears of blood fell from his heart,
   When he left his pretty boy,
   Father's sorrow, father's joy.

Weep not my wanton, smile upon my knee;
When thou art old there's grief enough for thee.
  The wanton smiled, father wept;
  Mother cried, baby leapt;
  More he crowed, more we cried;
  Nature could not sorrow hide.
  He must go, he must kiss
  Child and mother, baby bliss;
  For he left his pretty boy,
  Father's sorrow, father's joy.
Weep not, my wanton, smile upon my knee;
When thou art old there's grief enough for thee.

*[Menaphon, 1589]*

## Infida's Song

SWEET Adon, dar'st not glance thine eye –
  *N'oserez vous, mon bel ami?*
Upon thy Venus that must die?
  *Je vous en prie*, pity me:
*N'oserez vous, mon bel, mon bel,*
  *N'oserez vous, mon bel ami?*

See how sad thy Venus lies –
  *N'oserez vous, mon bel ami?*
Love in heart and tears in eyes,
  *Je vous en prie*, pity me:
*N'oserez vous, mon bel, mon bel,*
  *N'oserez vous, mon bel ami?*

Thy face as fair as Paphos brooks –
  *N'oserez vous, mon bel ami?*
Wherein fancy baits her hooks,
  *Je vous en prie*, pity me:
*N'oserez vous, mon bel, mon bel,*
  *N'oserez vous, mon bel ami?*

Thy cheeks like cherries that do grow –
   *N'oserez vous, mon bel ami?*
Amongst the western mounts of snow,
   *Je vous en prie,* pity me:
*N'oserez vous, mon bel, mon bel,*
   *N'oserez vous, mon bel ami?*


Thy lips vermilion, full of love –
   *N'oserez vous, mon bel ami?*
Thy neck as silver white as dove,
   *Je vous en prie,* pity me:
*N'oserez vous, mon bel, mon bel,*
   *N'oserez vous, mon bel ami?*


Thine eyes, like flames of holy fires –
   *N'oserez vous, mon bel ami?*
Burn all my thoughts with sweet desires,
   *Je vous en prie,* pity me:
*N'oserez vous, mon bel, mon bel,*
   *N'oserez vous, mon bel ami?*


All thy beauties sting my heart –
   *N'oserez vous, mon bel ami?*
I must die through Cupid's dart,
   *Je vous en prie,* pity me:
*N'oserez vous, mon bel, mon bel,*
   *N'oserez vous, mon bel ami?*


Wilt thou let thy Venus die?
   *N'oserez vous, mon bel ami?*
Adon were unkind, say I,
   *Je vous en prie,* pity me:
*N'oserez vous, mon bel, mon bel,*
   *N'oserez vous, mon bel ami?*

To let fair Venus die for woe –
   *N'oserez vous, mon bel ami?*
That doth love sweet Adon so –
   *Je vous en prie*, pity me:
*N'oserez vous, mon bel, mon bel,*
   *N'oserez vous, mon bel ami?*

[*Never Too Late*, 1590]


## Sonnet or Ditty

MARS in a fury 'gainst love's brightest Queen,
   Put on his helm and took him to his lance;
On Erycinus mount was Mavors seen,
   And there his ensigns did the god advance;
     And by Heaven's great gates he stoutly swore,
     Venus should die, for she had wronged him sore.

Cupid heard this and he began to cry,
   And wished his mother's absence for a while:
'Peace, fool,' quoth Venus, 'is it I must die?
   Must it be Mars?' With that, she coined a smile:
     She trimmed her tresses and did curl her hair,
     And made her face with beauty passing fair.

A fan of silver feathers in her hand,
   And in a coach of ebony she went:
She passed the place where furious Mars did stand,
   And out her looks a lovely smile she sent;
     Then from her brows leaped out so sharp a frown,
     That Mars for fear threw all his armour down.

He vowed repentance for his rash misdeed.
  Blaming his choler that had caused his woe;
Venus grew gracious, and with him agreed,
  But charged him not to threaten beauty so,
    For women's looks are such enchanting charms,
    As can subdue the greatest god in arms.

[*Tullie's Love*, 1589]

# FULKE GREVILLE, LORD BROOKE
## (1554–1628)

Greville's epitaph for himself was: 'Servant to Queen Elizabeth, councillor to King James, friend to Sir Philip Sidney.' The combination of pride and modesty which these words imply has perhaps prevented us from recognizing Greville's true stature as a poet. His friendship with Sidney, which began with their schooldays together at Shrewsbury, influenced his whole life, but his work reveals a different sort of talent – intellectual rather than romantic. Greville wrote verse not just as an amateur, but throughout his long career. A wealthy man, he was also a patron of literature. He helped Daniel, among others.

## I, With Whose Colours Myra Dressed Her Head

I, WITH whose colours Myra dressed her head,
I, that ware posies of her own hand-making,
I, that mine own name in the chimneys read[1]
By Myra finely wrought ere I was waking;
    Must I look on, in hope time coming may
    With change bring back my turn again to play?

I, that on Sunday at the church-stile found
A garland sweet, with true love-knots in flowers,
Which I to wear about mine arm was bound,
That each of us might know that all was ours;
    Must I now lead an idle life in wishes,
    And follow Cupid for his loaves and fishes?[2]

I, that did wear the ring her mother left,
I, for whose love she gloried to be blamed,
I, with whose eyes her eyes committed theft,
I, who did make her blush when I was named;
    Must I lose ring, flowers, blush, theft, and go naked,
    Watching with sighs, till dead love be awakèd?

137

I, that, when drowsy Argus fell asleep,
Like jealousy o'erwatchèd with desire,
Was ever warnèd modesty to keep,
While her breath, speaking, kindled nature's fire;
   Must I look on a-cold while others warm them?
   Do Vulcan's brothers in such fine nets arm them?

Was it for this that I might Myra see
Washing the water with her beauties white?
Yet would she never write her love to me.
Thinks wit of change, while thoughts are in delight?
   Mad girls must safely love, as they may leave;
   No man can print a kiss; lines may deceive.

[*Caelica*, 1633]


## The Nurse-Life Wheat

THE nurse-life[1] wheat within his green husk growing
Flatters our hope and tickles our desire,
Nature's true riches in sweet beauties showing,
Which set all hearts, with labour's love, on fire.
No less fair is the wheat when golden ear
Showers unto hope the joys of near enjoying:
Fair and sweet is the bud, more sweet and fair
The rose, which proves that time is not destroying.
Caelica, your youth, the morning of delight,
Enamelled o'er with beauties white and red,
All sense and thoughts did to belief invite
That Love and Glory there are brought to bed;
   And your ripe years' love-noon (he goes no higher)
   Turns all the spirits of man into desire.

[*Caelica*, 1633]

## Princes, Who Have (They Say) No Mind, But Thought

PRINCES, who have (they say) no mind, but thought,[1]
Whose virtue is their pleasure, and their end,
That kindness, which in their hearts never wrought,
They like in others, and will praise a friend.
Cupid, who, people say, is bold with blindness,
Free of excess, and enemy to measure,
Yet glories in the reverence of kindness,
In silent-trembling eloquence hath pleasure.
Princes we comprehend, and can delight,
We praise them for the good they never had;
But Cupid's ways are far more infinite,
Kisses at times, and curt'sies[2] make him glad:
   Then Myra give me leave, for Cupid's sake,
   To kiss thee oft, that I may curt'sies make.

*[Caelica, 1633]*


## Cynthia, Because Your Horns Look Diverse Ways

CYNTHIA, because your horns look diverse ways,
Now darkened to the East, now to the West;
Then at full glory once in thirty days,
Sense doth believe that change is nature's rest.[3]

Poor earth, that dare presume to judge the sky;
Cynthia is ever round, and never varies;
Shadows and distance do abuse the eye,
And in abusèd sense, truth oft miscarries:
   Yet who this language to the People speaks,
   Opinion's empire,[4] sense's idol breaks.

*[Caelica, 1633]*

## When All This All

WHEN all this *All*[1] doth pass from age to age,
And revolution[2] in a circle turn,
Then heavenly justice doth appear like rage,[3]
The caves do roar, the very seas do burn,
    Glory grows dark, the sun becomes a night,
    And makes this great world feel a greater might.


When love doth change his seat from heart to heart,
And worth about the wheel of Fortune goes,
Grace is diseased, desert seems overthwart,
Vows are forlorn, and truth does credit lose,
    Chance then gives law, desire must be wise,
    And look more ways than one, or lose her eyes.


My age of joy is past, of woe begun,
Absence my presence is, strangeness my grace,
With them that walk against me is my sun:
The wheel is turned, I hold the lowest place;
    What can be good to me, since my love is,
    To do me harm, content to do amiss?

[*Caelica*, 1633]


## The Little Hearts

THE little hearts, where light-winged passion reigns,
Move easily upward, as all frailties do;
Like straws to jet, these follow princes' veins,
And so, by pleasing, do corrupt them too.
    Whence, as their raising proves kings can create,
    So states prove sick, where toys bear staple-rate.[4]

Like *Atomi*[1] they neither rest nor stand,
Nor can erect; because they nothing be
But baby-thoughts, fed by Time-present's hand,
Slaves, and yet darlings of authority;
   Echoes of wrong, shadows of princes' might,
   Which, glow-worm-like, by shining, show 'tis night.

Curious of fame, as foul is to be fair;
Caring to seem that which they would not be;
Wherein chance helps, since praise is power's heir,
Honour the creature of authority:
   So, as borne high, in giddy orbs of grace,[2]
   These pictures[3] are, which are indeed but place.[4]

And as the bird in hand, with freedom lost,
Serves for a stale, his fellows to betray:
So do these darlings raised at princes' cost
Tempt man to throw his liberty away;
   And sacrifice Law, and Church, all real things,
   To soar, not in his own, but eagle's wings.[5]

Whereby, like Aesop's dog, men lose their meat;
To bite at glorious shadows which they see;
And let fall those strengths which make all states great
By free truths changed to servile flattery.
   Whence, while men gaze upon this blazing star,
   Mute slaves, not subjects, they to tyrants are.

[*Caelica*, 1633]

## Farewell, Sweet Boy

FAREWELL, sweet Boy, complain not of my truth;
Thy mother loved thee not with more devotion;
For to thy boy's play I gave all my youth,
Young master, I did hope for your promotion.
While some sought honours, princes' thoughts observing,
Many wooed fame, the child of pain and anguish,
Others judged inward good a chief deserving,
I in thy wanton visions joyed to languish.
I bowed not to thy image for succession,[1]
Nor bound thy bow to shoot reformèd kindness,
Thy plays of hope and fear were my confession,
The spectacles to my life was thy blindness;
    But Cupid now farewell, I will go play me
    With thoughts that please me less, and less betray me.

[*Caelica*, 1633]

## Chorus Sacerdotum
### From *Mustapha*

OH, wearisome condition of humanity,
Born under one law, to another bound;
Vainly begot, and yet forbidden vanity,
Created sick, commanded to be sound.
What meaneth nature by these diverse laws?
Passion and reason self-division cause.
It is the mark and majesty of power
To make offences that it may forgive.
Nature herself doth her own self deflower.
To hate those errors she herself doth give.
For how should man think that he may not do,
If nature did not fail and punish too?
Tyrant to others, to herself unjust,
Only commands things difficult and hard,
Forbids us all things which it knows is lust,

Makes easy pains, unpossible reward.
If nature did not take delight in blood,
She would have made more easy ways to good.
We that are bound by vows and by promotion,
With pomp of holy sacrifice and rites,
To teach belief in God and still devotion,
To preach of heaven's wonders and delights –
Yet, when each of us in his own heart looks,
He finds the God there far unlike his books.

[1609

## Chorus of the People
### The Fourth Chorus from *Alaham*

LIKE as strong winds do work upon the sea,
Stirring, and tossing waves to war each other;
So princes do with peoples' humours play,
As if confusion were the sceptre's mother.
  But Crowns! take heed: when humble things mount high,
  The winds oft calm before those billows lie.


When we are all wronged, had we all one mind,
Whom could you punish? what could you reserve?
Again, as hope and fear distract mankind,
Knew kings their strength, our freedom were to serve.
  But Fate doth to herself reserve both these,
  With each to punish other, when it please.


Grant that we be the stuff for princes' art,
By and on it, build their thrones above us;
Yet, if kings be the head, we be the heart;
And know we love no soul that doth not love us;
  Men's many passions judge the worst at length,
  And they that do so, easily know their strength.

With bruit and rumour, as with hope and fear,
You lay us low, or lift us from our earth;
You try what nature, what our states can bear;
By law you bind the liberties of birth;
 Making the people bellows unto fame,
 Which ushers heavy dooms with evil name.


Kings, govern people – over-wrack them not:
Fleece us, but do not clip us to the quick.
Think not with good, and ill, to write, and blot:
The good doth vanish, where the ill doth stick.
 Hope not with trifles to grow popular;
 Wounds that are healed forever leave a scar.


To offer people shows makes us too great;
Princes, descend not, keep yourselves above.
The sun draws not our brows up, but our sweat;[1]
Your safest rack to wind us up is love.
 To mask your vice in pomps is vainly done;
 Motes lie not hidden in beams of a sun.


The stamp of sovereignty makes current
Home brass to buy or sell, as well as gold:
Yet mark! the people's standard is the warrant
What man ought not to do, and what he should.
 Of words we are the grammar, and of deeds
 The harvest both is ours, and eke the seeds.


We are the glass of power, and do reflect
That image back, which it to us presents:
If princes flatter, straight we do neglect;
If they be fine, we see, yet seem content.
 Nor can the throne, which monarchs do live in,
 Shadow kings' faults, or sanctify their sin.

Make not the Church to us an instrument
Of bondage, to yourselves of liberty –
Obedience there confirms your government;
Our sovereigns, God's subalterns you be:
  Else while kings fashion God in human light,
  Men see, and scorn, what is not infinite.


Make not the end of justice 'Chequer-gain,
It is the liberality of kings;
Oppression and extortion ever reign
Where laws look more on sceptres than on things.
  Make crooked that line which you measure by,
  And mar the fashion straight of monarchy.


Why do you then profane your royal line,
Which we hold sacred, and dare not approach?
Their wounds and wrongs prove you are not divine,
And we learn, by example, to encroach.
  Your father's loss of eyes proclaims his end:
  By craft, which lets down princes, we ascend.


How shall the people hope? how stay their fear,
When old foundations daily are made new?
Uncertain is a heavy load to bear;
What is not constant sure was never true.
  Excess in one makes all indefinite;
  When nothing is our own, then what delight?


Kings then take heed! Men are the books of fate,
Wherein your vices deep engraven lie,
To show our God the grief of every state.
And though great bodies do not straightways die,
  Yet know, your errors have their proper doom,
  Even in our ruin to prepare your own.

[1633]

# JOSEPH HALL
## (1574–1656)

Hall ranks among the satirists on the strength of the two parts of *Virgidemiarum*, published in 1597 and 1598. These were admired by Pope, but modern taste finds them perhaps less interesting than Marston, an opponent of Hall. Hall was educated at Emmanuel College, Cambridge, took holy orders in about 1600, and was successively Bishop of Exeter and Bishop of Norwich. He was expelled during the Commonwealth, and his goods were sequestered.

## *Virgidemiarum*

### Book One, Satire Seven

GREAT is the folly of a feeble brain,
O'erruled with love, and tyrannous disdain:
For love, however in the basest breast,
It breeds high thoughts that feed the fancy best.
Yet is he blind, and leads poor fools awry,
While they hang gazing on their mistress' eye.
The lovesick poet, whose importune prayer
Repulsèd is with resolute despair,
Hopeth to conquer his disdainful dame,
With public plaints of his conceivèd flame.
Then pours he forth in patchèd sonnettings,
His love, his lust, and loathsome flatterings:
As though the staring world hanged on his sleeve,
When once he smiles, to laugh; and when he sighs, to grieve.
Careth the world, thou love, thou live, or die?
Careth the world how fair thy fair one be?
Fond wittol, that wouldst load thy witless head
With timely horns, before thy bridal bed.
Then can he term his dirty ill-faced bride
Lady and queen, and virgin deified:

Be she all sooty black, or berry brown,
She's white as morrow's milk, or flakes new blown.
And though she be some dunghill drudge at home,
Yet can he her resign some refuse room
Amidst the well-known stars: or if not there,
Sure will he saint her in his Calendar.

[1597]

# SIR JOHN HARINGTON
## (c. 1561–1612)

Queen Elizabeth's 'witty godson', Harington alternately amused
and irritated his royal mistress. She is supposed to have imposed the
task of translating the whole of the *Orlando Furioso* upon him after
he had translated a fragment which contains an attack on women.
Another of his publications, *The Metamorphosis of Ajax*, published
in 1596 without a licence, earned him a period of banishment from
Court. His reputation as a jester (and as the inventor of the water-
closet) has somewhat shrouded his merits as a poet. His Ariosto, like
Fairfax's Tasso, stands in urgent need of republication.

## Alcina Entertains Rogero

### From Ariosto's *Orlando Furioso*, Book Seven

Now as abroad the stately courts did sound,
Of trumpets, shagbot, cornets, and of flutes,
Even so within there wants no pleasing sound,
Of virginals, of viols, and of lutes,
Upon the which persons not few were found,
That did record their loves and loving suits,
    And in some song of love and wanton verse,
    Their good or ill successes did rehearse.

As for the sumptuous and luxurious fare,
I think not they that Ninus did succeed,
Nor Cleopatra fair, whose riot rare
To Antony such love and loss did breed,
Might with Alcina's any way compare,
Whose love did all the others far exceed,
    So deeply was she ravished by the sight
    Of this so valiant and so comely knight.

The supper done, and tables ta'en away,
To purposes[1] and suchlike toys they went,
Each one to other secretly to say
Some word, by which some pretty toy is meant;

This helped the lovers better to bewray
Each unto other what was their intent,
   For when the word was hither tossed and thither,
   Their last conclusion was to lie together.

These pretty kinds of amorous sports once ended,
With torches to his chamber he was brought,
On him a crew of gallant squires attended,
That every way to do him honour sought.
The chamber's furniture could not be mended,[1]
It seemed Arachne had the hangings wrought;
   A banquet new was made, the which once finished,
   The company by one and one diminished.

Now was Rogero couchèd in his bed,
Between a pair of cambric sheets perfumed,
And oft he hearkens with his wakeful head,
For her whole love his heart and soul consumed:
Each little noise hope of her coming bred,
Which finding false, against himself he fumed,
   And cursed the cause that did him so much wrong,
   To cause Alcina tarry thence so long.

Sometime from bed he softly doth arise,
And look abroad if he might her espy,
Sometime he with himself doth thus devise,
Now she is coming, now she draws thus nigh:
Sometime for very anger out he cries,
What meaneth she, she doth no faster hie?
   Sometimes he casts lest any let should be
   Between his hand and this desirèd tree.

But fair Alcina, when with odours sweet,
She was perfumed according to her skill,
The time once come she deemed it fit and meet,
When all the house were now asleep and still:

With rich embroidered slippers on her feet,
She goes to give and take of joys her fill,
   To him whom hope and fear so long assailed,
   Till sleep drew on, and hope and fear both failed.

Now when Astolfo's successor espied
Those earthly stars, her fair and heav'nly eyes,
As sulphur once inflamèd cannot hide,
Even so the metal in his veins that lies,
So flamed that in the skin it scant could bide:
But of a sudden straight he doth arise,
   Leaps out of bed, and her in arms embraced,
   Ne would he stay till she herself unlaced.

So utterly impatient of all stay,
That though her mantle was but cyprous[1] light,
And next upon her smock of lawn it lay,
Yet so the champion hasted to the fight,
The mantle with his fury fell away,
And now the smock remained alone in sight,
   Which smock as plain her beauties all discloses,
   As doth a glass the lilies fair and roses.

And look how close the ivy doth embrace
The tree or branch about the which it grows,
So close the lovers couchèd in the place,
Each drawing in the breath the other blows:
But how great joys they found that little space,
We well may guess, but none for certain knows:
   Their sport was such, so well they leer[2] their couth,[3]
   That oft they had two tongues within one mouth.

[1591]

## Of a Pointed Diamond
## Given By the Author to His Wife,
## At the Birth of His Eldest Son

DEAR, I to thee this diamond commend,
In which, a model of thyself I send;
How just unto thy joints this circlet sitteth,
So just thy face and shape my fancy fitteth.
The touch will try this ring of purest gold;
My touch tries thee as pure, though softer mould.
That metal precious is, the stone is true;
As true as, then, how much more precious you?
The gem is clear, and hath nor needs no foil;
Thy face, nay, more, thy fame is free from soil.
You'll deem this dear, because from me you have it;
I deem your faith more dear, because you gave it.
This pointed diamond cuts glass and steel;
Your love's like force in my firm heart I feel.
  But this, as all things else, time wastes with wearing;
    Where you my jewels multiply with bearing.

*[Epigrams, 1618]*

## Of an Accident of Saying Grace
## at the Lady Rogers', Who Used to Dine
## Exceeding Late. Written to His Wife

MY Mall, in your short absence from this place,
Myself here dining at your mother's board,
Your little son did thus begin his grace:
'The eyes of all things look on thee, Oh Lord;
And Thou their food dost give them in due season.'
'Peace, boy,' quoth I, 'not more of this a word!
For in this place this grace hath little reason:
Whenas we speak to God, we must speak true;
And though the meat be good in taste and season,

SIR JOHN HARINGTON

This season for a dinner is not due!
Then peace, I say, to lie to God is treason.'
'Say on, my boy,' saith she. 'Your father mocks.
Clowns, and not courtiers, use to go by clocks.'
'Courtiers by clocks,' said I, 'and clowns by cocks.'
    Now, if your mother chide with me for this,
    Then you must reconcile us with a kiss.

[*Epigrams*, 1618]


## To His Wife, For Striking Her Dog

YOUR little dog, that barked as I came by,
I strake by hap so hard I made him cry;
And straight you put your finger in your eye,
And louring sat. I asked the reason why.
'Love me, and love my dog,' thou didst reply.
'Love as both should be loved.' – 'I will,' said I,
And sealed it with a kiss. Then by and by,
Cleared were the clouds of thy fair frowning sky.
Thus small events, greater masteries may try.
    For I, by this, do at their meaning guess,
    That beat a whelp afore a lioness.

[*Epigrams*, 1618]


## The Author to His Wife

MALL, once in pleasant company by chance,
I wished that you for company would dance,
Which you refused, and said, your years require,
Now, matron-like, both manners and attire.
Well, Mall, if needs thou wilt be matron-like,
Then trust to this, I will a matron like:
Yet so to you my love may never lessen,
As you for Church, house, bed, observe this lesson.

Sit in the Church as solemn as a saint.
No deed, word, thought, your due devotion taint.
Veil (if you will) your head, your soul reveal
To him, that only wounded souls can heal.
Be in my house as busy as a bee,
Having a sting for everyone but me,
Buzzing in every corner, gathering honey.
Let nothing waste, that costs or yieldeth money.
And when thou seest my heart to mirth incline,
The tongue, wit, blood, warm with good cheer and wine,
And that by lawful fancy I am led,
To climb my nest, thy undefilèd bed
   Then of sweet sports let no occasion 'scape,
   But be as wanton, toying as an ape.

[*Epigrams*, 1618]

# THOMAS HEYWOOD

## (d. 1641)

*Oenone and Paris* has recently been recognized as a very early work of
this prolific dramatist. According to himself, by 1633 he had had a
hand in the composition of two hundred and twenty plays. He may
have begun to work for Henslowe around 1596, when he is men-
tioned in the *Diary*.

## Oenone's Plea

### From *Oenone and Paris*

THE Daulian bird[1] with thousand notes at least,
Reserves them till the crisping of the even,
A prickle is preparèd for her breast,[2]
To celebrate this night an happy steven.[3]
   The whistling blackbirds, and the pleasant thrushes,
   With mirthful Mavis flock about the bushes.

The Satyrs, and goat-footed Aegipines,[4]
Will with their rural music come and meet thee,
With boxen pipes, and country tambourines,
Faunus and old Sylvanus, they will greet thee
   Then leave not them which seem thus to admire thee,
   And leave not her, that doth so sore desire thee.

The fair Napaeae,[5] beauty of these banks,
As once they dancèd at thy wedding day,
So will they now, and yield thee thousand thanks,
Footing it finely to entreat thy stay.
   The fountain Nymphs, that haunt these pleasant springs,
   One sort will trip it, while another sings.

The nimble Fairies, taking hand in hand,
Will skip like rather lambkins in the downs,
The tender grass unbended still shall stand,

Cool Zephyrus still flaring up their gowns,
  And every shepherd's swain will tune his ode,
  And more than these, to welcome thy abode.

Wonder of Troy, Nature's exactest cunning,
Glory of shepherds, Ida's chief Decorum,
Directory of my choosing and my shunning,
More than a man, save in that *faex amorum*,
  That trothless Tindaris thy faith defaceth,
  That lust, thy love; that fault, thy fame disgraceth.

[1594]

# WILLIAM HUNNIS
## (d. 1597)

Poet and musician, and also an ardent Protestant, Hunnis was a Gentleman of the Chapel Royal under Edward VI. In Mary's reign he was involved in plots against the Queen. Elizabeth restored him to his position soon after her accession.

## *A Meditation to be Said of Women with Child*

THE time draws nigh,
   of bitter painful throes,
How long I shall
   the same endure, God knows.
Oh Lord my God,
   I humbly ask of thee,
Make haste, sweet Christ,
   and safe deliver me.
Although by sin
   deserved I have right well
Such pain as this,
   yea, more than tongue can tell:
Yet ah, my God,
   turn not away thy face,
Nor me forsake,
   in this so sharp a case.
This womb, and fruit
   that springeth in the same,
Hast thou create,
   to glory of thy Name.
Oppressed with pain,
   Oh Lord, when I shall be,
Make less the same,
   so much as pleaseth Thee:
And grant, good God,
   thy creature may proceed

Safely on live,
   with mercy at my need.
In Christ his name,
   I will my travail show;
Now Holy Ghost,
   come comfort me in woe.
Come Father dear,
   and let thy power descend;
Oh Jesu Christ,
   thy mercies great extend.
Ah God, behold
   my dolour and my smart;
Sweet Holy Ghost,
   my comforter thou art.
Take part with me,
   and hear my woeful cry:
*Exaudi me,*
   *miserere mei.*

[*Seven Sobs of a Sorrowful Soul*, 1583]

# BEN JONSON
## (1572–1637)

Jonson never attended a university, but was nevertheless probably the most learned and the most genuinely classical of all Elizabethan poets. On his death, an admirer wrote:

> His learning such, no author old nor new,
> Escaped his reading that deserved his view.

Jonson worked as a bricklayer, and served in Flanders before turning dramatist, *c.* 1597. In 1598 Francis Meres was already describing him as one of 'our best for Tragedy' (on the basis of plays which are now lost) but in fact Jonson seems to have made his name with his comedies – *Every Man in His Humour* was produced the same year. On the whole, posterity has preferred Jonson's comedies even to his surviving tragedies; *Volpone*, *The Alchemist*, and *Bartholomew Fair* are oftener read and played than *Sejanus*. Jonson had a very long literary career which continued into the reign of Charles I. In his later years he wrote many masques for the Stuart Court. Jonson had a genius both for friendship and for enmity. His best-known literary friendship was with Shakespeare, and Jonson's beautiful poem 'To the Memory of my Beloved, the Author', prefixed to the First Folio, stands as a memorial to it. Over poets younger than himself, the 'sons of Ben', Jonson had a great influence. On the other hand, his touchiness sometimes led him into awkward situations. In 1598, for example, he killed a man in a duel, and only escaped the rope by pleading benefit of clergy. He was involved in many literary battles.

## Inviting a Friend to Supper

TONIGHT, grave sir, both my poor house and I
    Do equally desire your company:
Not that we think us worthy such a guest,
    But that your worth will dignify our feast,
With those that come; whose grace may make that seem
    Something, which, else, could hope for no esteem.
It is the fair acceptance, sir, creates
    The entertainment perfect, not the cates.

Yet you shall have, to rectify your palate,
  An olive, capers, or some better salad
Ushering the mutton; with a short-legged hen
  If we can get her, full of eggs, and then
Lemons, and wine for sauce; to these, a coney
  Is not to be despaired of, for our money;
And though fowl now be scarce, yet there are clerks,
  The sky not falling, think we may have larks.
I'll tell you of more, and lie, so you will come:
  Of partridge, pheasant, woodcock, of which some
May yet be there; and godwit,[1] if we can;
  Gnat,[1] rail[1] and ruff[1] too. How soe'er, my man
Shall read a piece of Virgil, Tacitus,
  Livy, or some better book to us,
Of which we'll speak our minds amidst our meat;
  And I'll profess no verses to repeat:
To this, if aught appear which I not know of,
  That will the pastry, not my paper, show of.
Digestive cheese, and fruit, there sure will be;
  But that, which most doth take my Muse and me,
Is a pure cup of rich Canary wine,
  Which is the *Mermaid*'s now, but shall be mine;
Of which had Horace, or Anacreon tasted,
  Their lives, as do their lines, till now had lasted.
Tobacco, nectar, or the Thespian spring,
  Are all but Luther's beer, to this I sing.
Of this we will sup free, but moderately,
  And we will have no Pooly', or Parrot[2] by;
Nor shall our cups make any guilty men:
  But at our parting, we will be as when
We innocently met. No simple word,
  That shall be uttered at our mirthful board
Shall make us sad next morning: or affright
  The liberty, that we'll enjoy tonight.

[*Epigrams*, 1616]

## Epitaph on Elizabeth, L.H.

WOULDST thou hear, what man can say
  In a little? Reader stay.
Underneath this stone does lie
  As much beauty, as could die:
Which in life did harbour give
  To more virtue, than doth live,
If, at all, she had a fault,
  Leave it buried in this vault.
One name was Elizabeth,
  Th'other let it sleep with death:
Fitter, where it died, to tell,
  Than that it lived at all. Farewell.

[*Epigrams*, 1616]

## On Poet-Ape [1]

POOR Poet-Ape, that would be thought our chief,
  Whose works are e'en the frippery of wit,
From brocage[2] is become so bold a thief,
  As we, the robbed, leave rage, and pity it.
At first he made low shifts, would pick and glean,
  Buy the reversion of old plays; now grown
To' a little wealth, and credit in the scene,
  He takes up all, makes each man's wit his own.
And, told of this, he slights it. Tut, such crimes
  The sluggish gaping auditor devours;
He marks not whose 'twas first: and after-times
  May judge it to be his, as well as ours.
Fool, as if half eyes will not know a fleece
  From locks of wool, or shreds from the whole piece?

[*Epigrams*, 1616]

## To the World

### A Farewell for a Gentlewoman, Virtuous and Noble

FALSE world, goodnight: since thou hast brought
   That hour upon my morn of age,
Henceforth I quit thee from my thought,
   My part is ended on thy stage.
Do not once hope, that thou canst tempt
   A spirit so resolved to tread
Upon thy throat, and live exempt
   From all the nets that thou canst spread.
I know thy forms are studied arts,
   Thy subtle ways, be narrow straits;
Thy courtesy but sudden starts,
   And what thou call'st thy gifts are baits.
I know too, though thou strut, and paint,
   Yet art thou both shrunk up, and old,
That only fools make thee a saint,
   And all thy good is to be sold.
I know thou whole art but a shop
   Of toys, and trifles, traps, and snares,
To take the weak, or make them stop:
   Yet art thou falser than thy wares.
And, knowing this, should I yet stay,
   Like such as blow away their lives,
And never will redeem a day,
   Enamoured of their golden gyves?
Or, having scaped, shall I return,
   And thrust my neck into the noose,
From whence, so lately, did I burn,
   With all my powers, myself to loose?
What bird, or beast, is known so dull,
   That fled his cage, or broke his chain,
And tasting air, and freedom, will
   Render his head in there again?
If these, who have but sense, can shun

The engines, that have them annoyed;
Little, for me, had reason done,
  If I could not thy gins avoid.
Yes, threaten, do. Alas, I fear
  As little, as I hope from thee:
I know thou canst not show, nor bear
  More hatred, than thou hast to me.
My tender, first, and simple years
  Thou didst abuse, and then betray;
Since stird'st up jealousies and fears,
  When all the causes were away.
Then, in a soil hast planted me
  Where breathe the basest of thy fools;
Where envious arts professèd be,
  And pride, and ignorance the schools,
Where nothing is examined, weighed,
  But, as 'tis rumoured, so believed:
Where every freedom is betrayed,
  And every goodness taxed, or grieved.
But, what we'are born for, we must bear:
  Our frail condition it is such,
That, what to all may happen here,
  If 't chance to me, I must not grutch.
Else, I my state should much mistake,
  To harbour a divided thought
From all my kind: that, for my sake,
  There should a miracle be wrought.
No, I do know, that I was born
  To age, misfortune, sickness, grief:
But I will bear these, with that scorn,
  As shall not need thy false relief.
Nor for my peace will I go far,
  As wanderers do, that still do roam,
But make my strengths, such as they are,
  Here in my bosom, and at home.

[*The Forest*, 1616]

## An Elegy

Though beauty be the mark of praise,
   And yours of whom I sing be such
   As not the world can praise too much,
Yet is't your virtue now I raise.

A virtue, like alloy,[1] so gone
   Throughout your form; as though that move,
   And draw, and conquer all men's love,
This subjects you to love of one.

Wherein you triumph yet: because
   'Tis of yourself, and that you use
   The noblest freedom, not to choose
Against or faith, or honour's laws.

But who should less expect from you,
   In whom alone love lives again?
   By whom he is restored to men:
And kept, and bred, and brought up true?

His falling temples you have reared,
   The withered garlands ta'en away;
   His altars kept from the decay,
That envy wished, and nature feared.

And on them, burn so chaste a flame,
   With so much loyalty's expense
   As love, t'acquit such excellence,
Is gone himself into your name.

And you are he: the deity
   To whom all lovers are designed;
   That would their better object find:
Among which faithful troop am I.

Who as an offspring at your shrine,
    Have sung this hymn, and here intreat
    One spark of your diviner heat
To light upon a love of mine.


Which if it kindle not, but scant
    Appear, and that to shortest view,
    Yet give me leave t'adore in you
What I, in her, am grieved to want.

[*Underwoods*, 1640–1]


## An Ode to Himself

WHERE dost thou careless lie,
    Buried in ease and sloth?
Knowledge that sleeps doth die;
And this security,
    It is the common moth,
That eats on wits and arts, and oft destroys them both.


Are all th'Aonian springs
    Dried up? Lies Thespia waste?
Does Clarius'¹ harp want strings,
That not a nymph now sings!
    Or droop they as disgraced,
To see their seats and bowers by chattering pies defaced?


If hence thy silence be,
    As 'tis too just a cause;
Let this thought quicken thee,
Minds that are great and free,
    Should not on fortune pause,
'Tis crown enough to virtue still, her own applause.

What though the greedy fry
    Be taken with false baits
Of worded balladry,
And think it poesy?
    They die with their conceits,
And only piteous scorn upon their folly waits.


Then take in hand thy lyre,
    Strike in thy proper strain,
With Japhet's [1] line, aspire
Sol's chariot for new fire,
    To give the world again:
Who aided him, will thee, the issue of Jove's brain.


And since our dainty age
    Cannot endure reproof,
Make not thyself a page
To that strumpet, the stage,
    But sing high and aloof,
Safe from the wolf's black jaw, and the dull ass's hoof.

[*Underwoods*, 1640–1]


## An Elegy [2]

SINCE you must go, and I must bid farewell,
    Hear, mistress, your departing servant tell
What it is like: and do not think they can
    Be idle words, though of a parting man;
It is as if a night should shade noon-day,
    Or that the sun was here, but forced away;
And we were left under that hemisphere,
    Where we must feel it dark for half a year.

What fate is this, to change men's days and hours,
    To shift their seasons, and destroy their powers!
Alas, I ha' lost my heat, my blood, my prime,
    Winter is come a quarter ere his time,
My health will leave me; and when you depart,
    How shall I do, sweet mistress, for my heart?
You would restore it? No, that's worth a fear,
    As if it were not worthy to be there:
Oh, keep it still; for it had rather be
    Your sacrifice, than here remain with me.
And so I spare it: come what can become
    Of me, I'll softly tread unto my tomb;
Or like a ghost walk silent amongst men,
    Till I may see both it and you again.

[Underwoods, 1640–1]

## From Volpone

### Act Three, Scene Five[1]

CELIA: Some serene[2] blast me, or dire lightning strike
    This my offending face!
VOLPONE: Why droops my Celia?
    Thou hast, in place of a base husband, found
    A worthy lover: use thy fortune well,
    With secrecy and pleasure. See, behold,
    What thou art queen of; not in expectation,
    As I feed others: but possessed and crowned.
    See, here, a rope of pearl; and each, more orient
    Than that the brave Aegyptian queen caroused:
    Dissolve and drink them. See, a carbuncle,
    May put out both the eyes of our St Mark;
    A diamond, would have bought Lollia Paulina,[3]
    When she came in like star-light, hid with jewels,
    That were the spoils of provinces; take these,
    And wear, and lose them: yet remains an ear-ring
    To purchase them again, and this whole state.

A gem but worth a private patrimony,
Is nothing: we will eat such at a meal.
The heads of parrots, tongues of nightingales,
The brains of peacocks and of estriches,
Shall be our food: and, could we get the phoenix,
Though nature lost her kind, she were our dish.
CELIA: Good sir, these things might move a mind affected
With such delights; but I, whose innocence
Is all I can think wealthy, or worth th'enjoying,
And which, once lost, I have nought to lose beyond it,
Cannot be taken with these sensual baits:
If you have conscience –
VOLPONE: 'Tis the beggar's virtue;
If thou hast wisdom, hear me Celia.
Thy baths shall be the juice of July-flowers,
Spirit of roses and of violets,
The milk of unicorns, and panthers' breath
Gathered in bags, and mixed with Cretan wines.
Our drink shall be preparèd gold and amber;
Which we will take, until my roof whirl round
With the vertigo: and my dwarf shall dance,
My eunuch sing, my fool make up the antic,
Whilst we, in changèd shapes, act Ovid's tales,
Thou, like Europa, now, and I like Jove,
Then I like Mars, and thou like Erycine:
So, of the rest, till we have quite run through,
And wearied all the fables of the gods.
Then will I have thee in more modern forms,
Attirèd like some sprightly dame of France,
Brave Tuscan lady, or proud Spanish beauty;
Sometimes, unto the Persian sophy's wife;
Or the grand signior's mistress; and, for change,
To one of our most artful courtezans,
Or some quick Negro, or cold Russian;
And I will meet thee in as many shapes:
Where we may so transfuse our wandering souls
Out at our lips, and score up sums of pleasures,

[*sings*]

That the curious shall not know
How to tell them as they flow;
And the envious, when they find
What their number is, be pined.

[1607. Performed 1605]

## Songs

### From *Cynthia's Revels*

I

SLOW, slow, fresh fount, keep time with my salt tears;
   Yet slower yet, oh faintly, gentle springs;
List to the heavy part the music bears,
   Woe weeps out her division when she sings.
     Droop herbs and flowers,
     Fall grief in showers;
     Our beauties are not ours;
       Oh, I could still
(Like melting snow upon some craggy hill)
    Drop, drop, drop, drop,
Since nature's pride is, now, a withered daffodil.


2

    QUEEN, and huntress, chaste, and fair,[1]
    Now the sun is laid to sleep,
    Seated, in thy silver chair,
    State in wonted manner keep:
      Hesperus, entreats thy light,
      Goddess, excellently bright.

    Earth, let not thy envious shade
    Dare itself to interpose;
    Cynthia's shining orb was made
    Heaven to clear, when day did close:
      Bless us then with wishèd sight,
      Goddess excellently bright.

Lay thy bow of pearl apart,
And thy crystal shining quiver;
Give unto the flying hart
Space to breathe, how short soever:
    Thou that mak'st a day of night,
    Goddess excellently bright.

[1600]


## Song

### From *Epicoene, or The Silent Woman*

STILL to be neat, still to be dressed
As, you were going to a feast;
Still to be powdered, still perfumed:
Lady, it is to be presumed,
Though art's hid causes are not found,
All is not sweet, all is not sound.

Give me a look, give me a face,
That makes simplicity a grace;
Robes loosely flowing, hair as free:
Such sweet neglect more taketh me
Than all th'adulteries of art.
They strike mine eyes, but not my heart.

[1609]

# THOMAS LODGE

## (c. 1558–1625)

Lodge was the son of a Lord Mayor of London, and was educated at Merchant Taylors' School and at Trinity College, Oxford. Later, he was a member of Lincoln's Inn. In 1591 he took part in an expedition to America. In 1600 he took the degree of M.D. at Avignon, and in 1602 did likewise at Oxford. Thereafter, he settled down to a career as a London physician. Lodge, in his pastoral novel *Rosalynde* of 1590, provided Shakespeare with his source for *As You Like It*. He was also one of the initiators of the vogue for satire at the end of the reign.

## For Pity, Pretty Eyes, Surcease

FOR pity, pretty eyes, surcease
To give me war, and grant me peace!
Triumphant eyes, why bear you arms
Against a heart that thinks no harms,
A heart already quite appalled,
A heart that yields and is enthralled?

Kill rebels, proudly that resist,
Not those that in true faith persist,
And conquered, serve your deity.
Will you, alas, command me die?
Then die I yours, and death my cross;
But unto you pertains the loss.

[*Phoenix Nest*, 1593]

## The Earth, Late Choked with Showers[1]

THE earth, late choked with showers,
Is now arrayed in green;
Her bosom springs with flowers,
The air dissolves her teen.[2]
   The heavens laugh at her glory,
   Yet bide I sad and sorry.
The woods are decked with leaves
And trees are clothèd gay,
And Flora, crowned with sheaves,
With oaken boughs doth play;
   Where I am clad in black,
   In token of my wrack.

The birds upon the trees
Do sing with pleasant voices,
And chant in their degrees
Their loves and lucky choices;
   When I, whilst they are singing,
   With sighs mine arms are wringing.
The thrushes seek the shade,
And I my fatal grave;
Their flight to heaven is made,
My walk on earth I have.
   They free, I thrall; they jolly,
   I sad and pensive wholly.

[*Scilla's Metamorphosis*, 1589]

## He Wrote This With a Pointed Diamond in Her Glass[1]

THINK what I suffered, wanton, through thy wildness,
When, traitor to my faith, thy looseness led thee;
Think how my moody wrath was turned to mildness,
When I bad[2] best, yet baser grooms did bed thee.
Think that the stain of beauty then is stainèd,
When lewd desires do alienate the heart;
Think that the love which will not be containèd
At last will grow to hate in spite of art.
Think that those wanton looks will have their wrinkles,
And but by faith old age can merit nothing;
When time thy pale with purple over-sprinkles,
Faith is thy best, thy beauty is a woe-thing.
  In youth be true, and then in age resolve thee,
  Friends will be friends, till time with them dissolve thee.

[*The Life and Death of William Longbeard*, 1593]

## Jonas the Prophet Cast Out of the Whale's Belly Upon the Stage

From *A Looking Glass for London and England*,[3]
Act Four, Scene Two

JONAS: Lord of the light, thou maker of the world,
  Behold, thy hands of mercy rears me up;
  Lo, from the hideous bowels of this fish
  Thou hast returned me to the wishèd air;
  Lo, here, apparent witness of thy power,
  The proud Leviathan that scours the seas,
  And from his nostrils showers out stormy floods,
  Whose back resists the tempest of the wind,
  Whose presence makes the scaly troops to shake,
  With humble stress of his broad-opened chaps
  Hath lent me harbour in the raging floods.

Thus, though my sin hath drawn me down to death,
Thy mercy hath restorèd me to life.
Bow ye, my knees; and you, my bashful eyes,
Weep so for grief as you to water would.
In trouble, Lord, I callèd unto thee;
Out of the belly of the deepest hell
I cried, and thou didst hear my voice, Oh God!
'Tis thou hadst cast me down into the deep;
The seas and floods did compass me about;
I thought I had been cast from out thy sight;
The weeds were wrapped about my wretched head;
I went unto the bottom of the hills:
But thou, Oh Lord my God, hast brought me up.
On thee I thought whenas my soul did faint:
My prayers did press before thy mercy seat.
Then will I pay my vows unto the Lord,
For why, salvation cometh from his throne.

[1594]

# JOHN LYLY

## (1554?–1606)

Lyly went to Magdalen College, Oxford, and after leaving the university went to London in the hope of getting some kind of place at Court. The publication of his *Euphues* (1579 and 1580) brought him fame, and some employment from Burghley. In 1584 Lyly began writing plays to be acted at Court by the Children of the Chapel Royal and of St Paul's. He also took part in the 'Martin Mar-Prelate' controversy, supporting the bishops. In 1589 he became a member of Parliament, and sat several more times for various boroughs, being last elected in 1601.

## Songs

### From *Alexander and Campaspe*[1]

#### 1

CUPID and my Campaspe played
At cards for kisses; Cupid paid.
He stakes his quiver, bow and arrows,
His mother's doves and team of sparrows,
Loses them too; then down he throws
The coral of his lip, the rose
Growing on's cheek (but none knows how),
With these the crystal of his brow,
And then the dimple of his chin:
All these did my Campaspe win.
At last he set her both his eyes;
She won, and Cupid blind did rise.
Oh Love! has she done this to thee?
What shall, alas, become of me?

#### 2

WHAT bird so sings, yet so does wail?
Oh, 'tis the ravished nightingale,
Jug, jug, jug, jug, tereu, she cries,
And still her woes at midnight rise.

Brave prick-song![1] who is't now we hear?
None but the lark so shrill and clear;
How at heaven's gates she claps her wings,
The morn not waking till she sings.
Hark, hark, with what a pretty throat
The robin redbreast tunes his note;
Hark how the jolly cuckoos sing
Cuckoo, to welcome in the spring,
Cuckoo, to welcome in the spring.

[1584. These songs not printed till 1632]

# CHRISTOPHER MARLOWE

## (1564–93)

Marlowe was one of the great revolutionary poets of the Elizabethan age. Son of a shoemaker, he was educated at King's School, Canterbury, and at Corpus Christi College, Cambridge. A document hints that he went abroad on a secret mission for the Government during his time at university. On leaving Cambridge, Marlowe came to London and set up as a dramatist attached to the Lord Admiral's company. With *Tamburlaine*, probably composed *c.* 1587, Marlowe wrought a great change in the theatre of his day. The unfinished *Hero and Leander*, though only published after his death, also helped to create a new vogue for erotic mythological poems and was much imitated. Marlowe was an atheist and a homosexual, and eventually attracted the attention of the authorities. The Privy Council issued a warrant for his arrest, but, almost at the moment they did so, Marlowe was killed in a tavern brawl at Deptford.

## From *Tamburlaine*

### Part One, Act One, Scene Two

TAMBURLAINE: Disdains Zenocrate to live with me?
    Or you, my lords, to be my followers?
    Think you I weigh this treasure more than you?
    Not all the gold in India's wealthy arms
    Shall buy the meanest soldier in my train.
    Zenocrate, lovelier than the love of Jove,
    Brighter than is the silver Rhodope,
    Fairer than whitest snow on Scythian hills,
    Thy person is more worth to Tamburlaine
    Than the possession of the Persian crown
    Which gracious stars have promised at my birth.
    A hundred Tartars shall attend on thee,
    Mounted on steeds swifter than Pegasus.
    Thy garments shall be made of Medean silk,

Enchased with precious jewels of mine own:
More rich and valurous than Zenocrate's.
With milk-white harts upon an ivory sled
Thou shalt be drawn amidst the frozen pools,
And scale the icy mountains' lofty tops;
Which with thy beauty will be soon resolved.
My martial prizes with five hundred men,
Won on the fifty-headed Volga's waves,
Shall we offer to Zenocrate,
And then myself to fair Zenocrate.

[1590]

# From *The Tragical History of Doctor Faustus*
## Scene Fourteen

FAUSTUS [*to* HELEN]: Was this the face that launched a thousand
   ships
And burnt the topless towers of Ilium?
Sweet Helen, make me immortal with a kiss. [*Kisses her.*]
Her lips suck forth my soul; see where it flies!
Come, Helen, come, give me my soul again.
Here will I dwell, for Heaven is in these lips,
And all is dross that is not Helena.
I will be Paris, and for love of thee,
Instead of Troy, shall Wertenberg be sacked:
And I will combat with weak Menelaus,
And wear thy colours on my plumèd crest:
Yea, I will wound Achilles in the heel,
And then return to Helen for a kiss.
Oh, thou art fairer than the evening air
Clad in the beauty of a thousand stars;
Brighter art thou than flaming Jupiter

When he appeared to hapless Semele:
More lovely than the monarch of the sky
In wanton Arethusa's azured arms;
And none but thou shalt be my paramour!

[1604. A performance mentioned in
Henslowe's *Diary*, 1594]

## From *The Tragical History of Doctor Faustus*

### Scene Sixteen

FAUSTUS: Ah, Faustus,
Now hast thou but one bare hour to live,
And then thou must be damned perpetually!
Stand still, you ever-moving spheres of Heaven,
That time may cease, and midnight never come;
Fair Nature's eye, rise, rise again and make
Perpetual day; or let this hour be but
A year, a month, a week, a natural day,
That Faustus may repent and save his soul!
*O lente, lente, currite noctis equi!*[1]
The stars move still, time runs, the clock will strike,
The Devil will come, and Faustus must be damned.
Oh, I'll leap up to my God! Who pulls me down?
See, see, where Christ's blood streams in the firmament!
One drop would save my soul – half a drop: ah, my Christ!
Ah, rend not my heart for naming of my Christ!
Yet will I call on him: Oh spare me, Lucifer! –
Where is it now? 'tis gone; and see where God
Stretcheth out his arm, and bends his ireful brows!
Mountains and hills come, come and fall on me,
And hide me from the heavy wrath of God!
No! no!
Then will I headlong run into the earth;
Earth gape! Oh no, it will not harbour me!

You stars that reigned at my nativity,
Whose influence hath allotted Death and Hell,
Now draw up Faustus like a foggy mist
Into the entrails of yon labouring cloud,
That when you vomit forth into the air,
My limbs may issue from your smoky mouths,
So that my soul may but ascend to Heaven.
    [*The watch strikes*]
Ah, half the hour is past! 'twill all be past anon!
Oh God!
If thou wilt not have mercy on my soul,
Yet for Christ's sake, whose blood hath ransomed me,
Impose some end to my incessant pain;
Let Faustus live in Hell a thousand years –
A hundred thousand, and at last be saved!
Oh, no end is limited to damnèd souls!
Why wert thou not a creature wanting soul?
Or why is this immortal that thou hast?
Ah, Pythagoras' Metempsychosis! were that true,
This soul should fly from me, and I be changed
Unto some brutish beast! all beasts are happy,
For, when they die,
Their souls are soon dissolved in elements;
But mine must live, still to be plagued in Hell.
Curst be the parents that engendered me!
No, Faustus: curse thyself: curse Lucifer
That hath deprived thee of the joys of Heaven.
    [*The clock strikes twelve.*]
Oh, it strikes, it strikes! Now, body, turn to air,
Or Lucifer will bear thee quick to Hell.
    [*Thunder and lightning.*]
Oh, soul be changed into little water-drops,
And fall into the ocean – ne'er be found.
    [*Enter Devils.*]
My God! my God! look not so fierce on me!
Adders and serpents, let me breathe awhile!
Ugly Hell gape not! come not, Lucifer!

I'll burn my books! – Ah, Mephistophilis!
   [*Exeunt Devils with him.*] [1]
   [*Enter Chorus.*]
CHORUS: Cut is the branch that might have grown full straight,
   And burnèd is Apollo's laurel bough,
   That sometime grew within this learnèd man.
   Faustus is gone; regard his hellish fall,
   Whose fiendful fortune may exhort the wise
   Only to wonder at unlawful things,
   Whose deepness doth entice such forward wits
   To practice more than heavenly power permits.

                                              [1604]

# From *The Jew of Malta*
## Act Two

BARABAS: Hast thou no trade? then listen to my words,
   And I will teach that shall stick by thee:
   First be thou void of these affections,
   Compassion, love, vain hope, and heartless fear;
   Be moved at nothing, see thou pity none,
   But to thyself smile when the Christians moan.
ITHIMORE: Oh brave, master; I worship your nose for this!
BARABAS: As for myself, I walk abroad a nights
   And kill sick people groaning under walls;
   Sometimes I go about and poison wells;
   And now and then, to cherish Christian thieves,
   I am content to lose some of my crowns,
   That I may, walking in my gallery,
   See 'em go pinioned along by my door.
   Being young, I studied physick, and began
   To practice first upon the Italian;
   There I enriched the priests with burials,
   And always kept the sexton's arms in ure
   With digging graves and ringing dead men's knells;

And after that I was an engineer,
And in the wars 'twixt France and Germany,
Under pretence of helping Charles the Fifth,
Slew friend and enemy with my stratagems.
Then after that I was an usurer,
And with extorting, cozening, forfeiting,
And tricks belonging unto brokery,
I filled the jails with bankrupts in a year,
And with young orphans planted hospitals,
And every moon made some or other mad,
And now and then one hang himself for grief,
Pinning upon his breast a long great scroll
How I with interest tormented him.
But mark how I am blest for plaguing them,
I have as much coin as will buy the town.
But tell me, now, how hast thou spent thy time?

ITHIMORE:      Faith, master,
In setting Christian villages on fire,
Chaining of eunuchs, binding galley-slaves.
One time I was an hostler in an inn,
And in the night-time secretly would I steal
To travellers' chambers, and there cut their throats:
Once at Jerusalem, where the pilgrims kneeled,
I strowèd powder on the marble stones,
And therewithal their knees would rankle,[1] so
That I have laughed agood to see the cripples
Go limping home to Christendom on stilts.

BARABAS: Why, this is something! make account of me
As of thy fellow: we are villains both;
Both circumcizèd, we hate Christians both –
Be true and secret, thou shalt want no gold.

[1633. Frequently acted, 1592–6]

# Translation of *Ovid, Amores*

## Book One, V

IN summer's heat, and mid-time of the day,
To rest my limbs upon a bed I lay;
One window shut, the other open stood,
Which gave such light as twinkles in a wood,
Like twilight glimpse at setting of the sun,
Or night being past, and yet not day begun;
Such light to shamefaced maidens must be shown
Where they may sport, and seem to be unknown:
Then came Corinna in a long loose gown,
Her white neck hid with tresses hanging down,
Resembling fair Semiramis going to bed,
Or Lais of a thousand wooers sped.
I snatched her gown: being thin, the harm was small,
Yet strived she to be covered therewithal;
And striving thus, as one that would be cast,
Betrayed herself, and yielded at the last.
Stark naked as she stood before mine eye,
Not one wen in her body could I spy.
What arms and shoulders did I touch and see!
How apt her breasts were to be pressed by me!
How smooth a belly under her waist saw I,
How large a leg, and what a lusty thigh!
To leave the rest, all liked me passing well;
I clinged her naked body, down she fell:
Judge you the rest; being tired she bade me kiss;
Jove send me more such afternoons as this!

[*All Ovid's Elegies, c.*1599]

## *Love at First Sight*

From *Hero and Leander*, First Sestiad

ON this feast day, Oh cursed day and hour,
Went Hero through Sestos, from her tower
To Venus' temple, where unhappily,
As after chanced, they did each other spy.
So fair a church as this, had Venus none:
The walls were of discoloured¹ jasper stone,
Wherein was Proteus carved, and o'erhead
A lively vine of green sea-agate spread;
Where by one hand, light-headed Bacchus hung,
And with the other, wine from grapes outwrung.
Of crystal shining fair the pavement was;
The town of Sestos called it Venus' glass.
There might you see the gods in sundry shapes,
Committing heady riots, incest, rapes:
For know, that underneath this radiant floor
Was Danae's statue in a brazen tower,
Jove slily stealing from his sister's bed,
To dally with Idalian Ganymed;
And for his love, Europa, bellowing loud,
And tumbling with the Rainbow in a cloud:
Blood-quaffing Mars heaving the iron net
Which limping Vulcan and his Cyclops set:
Love kindling fire, to burn such towns as Troy,
Sylvanus weeping for the lovely boy
That now is turned into a cypress tree,
Under whose shade the wood-gods love to be.
And in the midst a silver altar stood;
There Hero sacrificing turtles' blood,
Vailed² to the ground, vailing her eyelids close,
And modest they opened as she rose:
Thence flew Love's arrow with the golden head,
And thus Leander was enamourèd.
Stone still he stood, and evermore he gazed,

Till with the fire that from his count'nance blazed,
Relenting Hero's gentle heart was strook:
Such force and virtue hath an amorous look.
It lies not in our power to love, or hate,
For will in us is overruled by fate.
When two are stript, long ere the course begin,
We wish that one should lose, the other win;
And one especially do we affect
Of two gold ingots, like in each respect.
The reason no man knows; let it suffice,
What we behold is censured by our eyes.
Where both deliberate, the love is slight;
Who ever loved, that loved not at first sight?

[1598]

# JOHN MARSTON
## (1575?–1634)

Marston's father was at one time a lecturer in the Middle Temple. Marston himself attended Brasenose College, Oxford. He began his career as one of the new generation of satirists in the late 1590s, and turned dramatist around 1600. His theatrical career spans the next fifteen years. Having taken orders at some unknown date, in 1616 Marston was promoted to the living of Christchurch, Hampshire, where he remained most of the rest of his life. Marston's smoky talent has proved a puzzle for critics. His satire, with its feeling of impotent yet violent revulsion against the society which surrounded him, catches the spirit of Juvenal more nearly than later 'classical' English satirists.

## In Lectores Prorsus Indignos

FIE, Satire, fie! shall each mechanic slave,
Each dunghill peasant, free perusal have
Of thy well-laboured lines? Shall each satin suit,
Each quaint fashion-monger, whose sole repute
Rests in his trim gay clothes, lie slavering,
Tainting thy lines with his lewd censuring?
Shall each odd puisne[1] of the lawyer's inn,
Each barmy-froth, that last day did begin
To read his little, or his ne'er a whit,
Or shall some greater ancient, of less wit
(That never turned but brown tobacco leaves,
Whose senses some damned occupant bereaves),
Lie gnawing on thy vacant time's expense,
Tearing thy rhymes, quite altering the sense?
Or shall perfumed Castilio censure thee?
Shall he o'erview thy sharp-fanged poesy
(Who ne'er read further than his mistress' lips),
Ne'er practised aught but some spruce capering skips,
Ne'er in his life did other language use,
But 'Sweet lady, fair mistress, kind heart, dear coz' –

Shall this phantasma, this Coloss peruse,
And blast with stinking breath thy budding muse?
Fie! wilt thou make thy wit a courtesan
For every broking handcraft's artisan?
Shall brainless cithern-heads,[1] each jobbernoll,
Pocket the very genius of thy soul?
   I, Phylo, I, I'll keep an open hall,
A common and a sumptuous festival;
Welcome all eyes, all ears, all tongues to me,
Gnaw peasants on my scraps of poesy;
Castilios, Cyprians,[2] court-boys, Spanish blocks,[3]
Ribanded ears, Granado-netherstocks,[4]
Fiddlers, scriveners, pedlars, tinkering knaves,
Base blue-coats,[5] tapsters, broadcloth-minded slaves[6] –
Welcome, i'faith, but may you ne'er depart
Till I have made your gallèd hides to smart.
Your gallèd hides? Avaunt, base muddy scum,
Think you a satire's dreadful sounding drum
Will brace itself,[7] and deign to terrify
Such abject peasant's basest roguery?
No, no, pass on, ye vain fantastic troop
Of puffy youths; know I do scorn to stoop
To rip your lives. Then hence, lewd nags, away,
Go read each post,[8] view what is played today,
Then to Priapus' gardens. You, Castilio,
I pray thee let my lines in freedom go,
Let me alone, the madams call for thee,
Longing to laugh at thy wit's poverty.
Sirra livery cloak, you lazy slipper[9]-slave,
Thou fawning drudge, what, wouldst thou satires have?
Base mind, away, thy master calls, begone.
Sweet Gnato, let my poesy alone:
Go buy some ballad of the Fairy King,
And of the beggar wench – some roguey thing
Which thou mayst chant unto the chamber-maid
To some vile tune, when that thy master's laid.
   But will you needs stay? Am I forced to bear

The blasting breath of each lewd censurer?
Must naught but clothes, and images of men,
But spriteless trunks, be judges of thy pen?
Nay then, come all: I prostitute my muse,
For all the swarms of idiots to abuse.
Read all, view all; even with my full consent,
So you will know that which I never meant;
So you will ne'er conceive, and yet dispraise,
That which you ne'er conceived, and laughter raise
Where I but strive in honest seriousness
To scourge some soul-polluting beastliness.
So you will rail, and find huge errors lurk
In every corner of my cynic work.
Proface,[1] read on, for your extrem'st dislikes
Will add a pinion to my praise's flights.
   Oh how I bristle up my plumes of pride,
Oh how I think my satires dignified,
When I once hear some quaint Castilio,
Some supple-mouthed slave, some lewd Tubrio,
Some spruce pedant, or some span-new come fry
Of inns-o'-court, striving to vilify
My dark reproofs! Then do but rail at me,
No greater honour craves my poesy.

### 1

   But, ye diviner wits, celestial souls,
   Whose free-born minds no kennel-thought controls,
   Ye sacred spirits, Maia's eldest sons[2] –

### 2

   Ye substance of the shadows of our age,
   In whom all graces link in marriage,
   To you how cheerfully my poem runs!

### 3

   True-judging eyes, quick-sighted censurers,
   Heaven's best beauties, wisdom's treasurers,
   Oh how my love embraceth your great worth!

### 4

Ye idols of my soul, ye blessed spirits,
How should I give true honour to your merits,
Which I can better think than here paint forth!

You sacred spirits, Maia's eldest sons,
To you how cheerfully my poem runs!
Oh how my love embraceth your great worth,
Which I can better think than here paint forth!
                                    Oh rare!

[*The Scourge of Villainy*, 1598]


## Inamorato Curio
### Satire Eight

WHAT should I say? Lust hath confounded all;
The bright gloss of our intellectual
Is foully soiled. The wanton wallowing
In fond delights, and amorous dallying,
Hath dusked the fairest splendour of our soul;
Nothing now left but carcass, loathsome, foul;
For sure, if that some sprite remainèd still,
Could it be subject to lewd Lais' will?
    Reason, by prudence in her function,
Had wont to tutor all our action,
Aiding, with precepts of philosophy,
Our feeblèd natures' imbecility;
But now affection, will, concupisence,
Have got o'er reason chief pre-eminence.
'Tis so; else how, how should such baseness taint
As force it be made slave to nature's paint?
Methinks the spirit's Pegase, Fantasy,
Should hoise the soul from such base slavery;
But now I see, and can right plainly show,

From whence such abject thoughts and actions grow.
  Our adverse body, being earthly, cold,
Heavy, dull, mortal, would not long enfold
A stranger inmate, that was backward still
To all his dungy, brutish, sensual will:
Now hereupon our intellectual,
Compact of fire all celestial,
Invisible, immortal, and divine,
Grew straight to scorn his landlord's muddy slime;
And therefore now is closely slunk away
(Leaving his smoky house of mortal clay),
Adorned with all his beauty's lineaments
And brightest gems of shining ornaments,
His parts divine, sacred, spiritual,
Attending on him; leaving the sensual
Base hangers-on lusking at home in slime,
Such as wont to stop Port Esquiline.[1]
Now doth the body, led with senseless will
(The which, in reason's absence, ruleth still),
Rave, talk idly, as 'twere some deity,
Adoring female painted puppetry;
Playing at put-pin,[2] doting on some glass
(Which, breathed but on, his falsèd gloss doth pass);
Toying with babies, and with fond pastime,
Some children's sport, deflowering of chaste time;
Employing all his wits in vain expense,
Abusing all his organons of sense.
  Return, return, sacred Synderesis![3]
Inspire our trunks! Let not such mud as this
Pollute us still. Awake our lethargy,
Raise us from out our brain-sick foolery!

[From *The Scourge of Villainy*, 1598]

## To Everlasting Oblivion[1]

THOU mighty gulf, insatiate cormorant,[2]
Deride me not, though I seem petulant
To fall into thy chops. Let others pray
Forever their fair poems flourish may;
But as for me, hungry Oblivion,
Devour me quick, accept my orison,
    My earnest prayers, which do impórtune thee
    With gloomy shade of thy still empery,
    To veil both me and my rude poesy.

Far worthier lines in silence of thy state
Do sleep securely, free from love or hate,
From which this, living, ne'er can be exempt,
But whilst it breathes will hate and fury tempt.
Then close his eyes with thy all-dimming hand,
Which not right glorious actions can withstand.
Peace, hateful tongues, I now in silence pace;
Unless some hound do wake me from my place,
    I with this sharp, yet well-meant poesy,
    Will sleep secure, right free from injury
    Of cankered hate or rankest villainy.

[*The Scourge of Villainy*, 1598]

## The Prologue

From *Antonio's Revenge*

THE rawish damp of clumsy winter ramps
The fluent summer's vein; and drizzling sleet
Chilleth the wan bleak cheek of the numbed earth,
Whilst snarling gusts nibble the juiceless leaves
From the nak'd shuddering branch; and pills the skin
Off from the soft and delicate aspects.
Oh now, methinks, a sullen tragic scene
Would suit the time with pleasing congruence.
May we be happy in our weak devoir,
And all part pleasèd in most wished content!
But sweat of Hercules can ne'er beget
So blest an issue. Therefore, we proclaim,
If any spirit breathes within this round,
Uncapable of weighty passion,
(As from his birth being huggèd in the arms,
And nuzzled 'twixt the breasts of happiness)
Who winks, and shuts his apprehension up
From common sense of what men were and are,
Who would not know what men be – let such
Hurry amain from our black-visaged shows:
We shall affright their eyes. But if a breast
Nailed to the earth with grief; if any heart
Pierced through with anguish pant within this ring;
If there be any blood whose heat is choked
And stifled with true sense of misery;
If aught of these strains fills his consort up –
Th'arrive most welcome. Oh that our power
Could lackey or keep wing with our desires,
That with unusèd paize of style and sense,
We might weigh massy in judicious scale.
Yet here's the prop that doth support our hopes:
When our scenes falter, or invention halts,
Your favour will give crutches to our faults.

[1602]

## From *The Dutch Courtesan*
### Act Two, Scene One

MALHEUREUX: The studious morn with paler cheek draws on
   The day's bold light. Hark! how the freeborn birds
   Carol their unaffected passions!
   Now sing they sonnets; thus they cry, we love.
   Oh breath of heaven! thus they, harmless souls,
   Give entertain to mutual affects.
   They have no bawds, no mercenary beds,
   No politic restraints, no artificial heats,
   No faint dissemblings; no custom makes them blush,
   No shame afflicts their name. Oh, you happy beasts
   In whom an inborn heat is not held sin!
   How far trascend you wretched, wretched man,
   Whom national custom, tyrranous respects
   Of slavish order, fetters, lames his power,
   Calling that sin in us, which in all things else
   Is nature's highest virtue.
     (*O miseri quorum gaudia crimen habent.*)
   Sure, nature against virtue cross doth fall,
   Or virtue's self is oft unnatural.

[1605]

# THOMAS MIDDLETON

## (1580–1627)

Middleton studied at Queen's College, Oxford, after a childhood marked by violent quarrels among his relations. Later he entered Gray's Inn. By 1601–2 he was writing plays for the Admiral's Men. Later still, he became both writer and producer of pageants for the City of London. Middleton does not seem to have achieved any great esteem as a dramatist, though his anti-Spanish play, *A Game at Chess*, produced in 1624, was one of the great box-office successes of its time. *The Changeling*, written in collaboration with Thomas Rowley, is, however, the play of Middleton's which is best known today. His earlier, non-dramatic verse has received scant consideration, but contains passages which deserve a second look.

## From *The Wisdom of Solomon Paraphrased*

### Chapter Seven

Now know I how the world was first created,
    How every motion of the air was framed,
How man was made, the devil's pride abated,
    How time's beginning, midst, and end was named;
Now know I time, time's change, time's date, time's show,
And when the seasons come, and when they go:

I know the changing courses of the years,
    And the division of all differing climes,
The situation of the stars and spheres,
    The flowing tides, and the flow-ebbing times;
I know that every year hath his four courses,
I know that every course hath several forces.

I know that nature is in everything,
    Beasts furious, winds rough, men wicked are,
Whose thoughts their scourge, whose deeds their judgements
      sting,
    Whose words and works their peril and their care;

I know that every plant hath difference,
I know that every root hath influence.

True knowledge have I got in knowing truth,
   True wisdom purchasèd in wisest wit;
A knowledge fitting age, wit fitting youth,
   Which makes me young, though old with gain of it:
True knowledge have I, and true wisdom's store,
True hap, true hope: what wish, what would I more?

[1597]

## Dedicatory Sonnet

From *The Ghost of Lucrece*[1]

TO THE RIGHT HONOURABLE,
AND MY VERY BOUNTIFUL GOOD LORD,
MY LORD COMPTON,[2]
T.M. WISHETH THE FRUIT OF ETERNAL FRUITION

THOU, that rock'st comely honour in thine arms;
Thou, patron to the child-house of my vein;
Thou, hive unto the Muses' honey-swarms,
And godfather to th'issue of my brain:
To thee, baptizer of mine infant lines
With golden water in a silver font
(Thy bounty, gold, thy fingers' silver twines[3]
Silver my paper's ink, as they were wont);
To thee, the bloody crystal of a Ghost
Wrapt in a fiery web I spin to thee;
To thee, the thawer of Diana's frost
(Tarquin the hot) in Lucrece' tragedy;
   To thee, I consecrate these ashy fires:
   She, quenched in blood, he burnt in his desires.

[1600]

## THOMAS MIDDLETON

# To Vesta

### From *The Ghost of Lucrece*

Saint Vesta! Oh thou sanctifying saint,
That lends a beam unto the clearest sun,
Which else within his fiery course would faint,
And end his race ere he had half begun,
Making the world believe his power were done,
   His oil burnt out, his lamp returned to slime,
   His fires extinguished by the breath of time;

Oh thou, the pearl that hangs on Juno's brow
Like to the moon, the massy pearl of night;
Thou jewel in the ear of Jove to show
The pride of love, the purity of light;
Thou Atlas of both worlds; umpire of right;
   Thou haven of heaven; th'assigner of each sign;
   Sanctity's saint; Divinity's divine;

Oh thou, the silver taper of the moon
Set in an alabaster candlestick
That by the bed of heaven at afternoon
Stands like a lily (which fair virgins pick
To match it with the lily of their cheek);
   Thou lily lamb; thou crystal-feathered dove
   That nestles in the palace of thy Jove;

Oh, touch my veins again, thou blood divine!
Oh, feed my spirit, thou food angelical,
And all chaste functions with my soul combine!
Colour my ghost with chastity, whose all
Feeds fat lean Death and Time in general!
   Come silver dove, heaven's alabaster nun,
   I'll hug thee more than ever I have done.

[1600]

## *A Moral*[1]

### *Lucifer Ascending, as Prologue to His Own Play*

Now is hell landed here upon the earth,
When Lucifer, in limbs of burning gold,
Ascends this dusty theatre of the world,
To join his powers; and, were it numbered well,
There are more devils of earth than are in hell.
Hence springs my damnèd joy; my tortured spleen
Melts into mirthful humour at this fate,
That heaven is hung so high, drawn up so far,
And made so fast, nailed up with many a star;
And hell the very shop-board[2] of the earth,
Where, when I cut out souls, I throw the shreds
And the white linings of a new soiled spirit,
Pawned to luxurious and adulterous merit.
Yea, that's the sin, and now it takes her turn,
For which the world shall like a strumpet burn;
And for an instance to fire false embraces,
I make the world burn now in secret places;
I haunt invisible corners as a spy,
And in adulterous circles there rise I;
There am I conjured up through hot desire,
And where hell rises, there must needs be fire.
And now that I have vaulted up so high
Above the stage-rails of this earthen globe,
I must turn actor and join companies,
To share my comic sleek-eyed villainies;
For I must weave a thousand ills in one,
To please my black and burnt affection.

[*The Black Book*, 1604]

# From *Father Hubburd's Tales*[1]

## I

### Description of the Nightingale

THIS poor musician, sitting all alone
  On a green hawthorn from the thunder blest,
Carols in varied notes her antique moan,
  Keeping a sharpened briar against her breast:
Her innocence this watchful pain doth take,
To shun the adder and the speckled snake.

These two, like her old foe the lord of Thrace,
  Regardless of her dulcet-changing song,
To serve their own lust have her life in chase;
  Virtue by vice is offered endless wrong:
Beasts are not all to blame, for now and then
We see the like attempted amongst men.

## 2

### The Golden Age

THERE was a golden age – who murdered it?
How died that age, or what became of it?
  Then poets, by divinest alchemy,
Did turn their ink to gold; kings in that time
Hung jewels at the ear of every rhyme.

But Oh, those days are wasted! and behold
The golden age that was is coined to gold:
  And why Time now is called an iron man,
Or this an iron-age, 'tis thus expressed, –
The golden age lies in an iron chest.

[1604]

# THOMAS NASHE

## (1567–1601)

Nashe survives as a poet largely on the strength of a single famous
lyric. He was primarily a writer of prose, and one of the liveliest
controversialists of his day. After being a sizar at St John's College,
Cambridge, Nashe settled in London. He soon became famous for
his attacks on contemporary writers, even those who were his
friends. He conducted a particularly bitter feud with Gabriel
Harvey, the friend of Spenser. He also took part in the 'Martin Mar-
Prelate' controversy, as an opponent of the Puritans. Most of his life
was spent in poverty – in 1597 he admitted to being 'without a
penny' in his purse. Middleton seems to describe the sordid cir-
cumstances in which he lived in *The Black Book*: 'the spindle shank
spiders . . . went stalking over his head as if they had been conning
of *Tamburlaine*.'

## Song

### From *Summer's Last Will and Testament*

ADIEU, farewell earth's bliss,
This world uncertain is;
Fond are life's lustful joys,
Death proves them all but toys,
None from his darts can fly.
I am sick, I must die.
      Lord have mercy on us![1]


Rich men, trust not in wealth,
Gold cannot buy you health;
Physic himself must fade,
All things to end are made.
The plague full swift goes by;
I am sick, I must die.
      Lord have mercy on us!

Beauty is but a flower
Which wrinkles will devour:
Brightness falls from the air,[1]
Queens have died young and fair,
Dust hath closed Helen's eye.
I am sick, I must die.
      Lord have mercy on us!

Strength stoops unto the grave,
Worms feed on Hector brave,
Swords may not fight with fate.
Earth still holds ope her gate;
Come! come! the bells do cry.
I am sick, I must die.
      Lord have mercy on us!

Wit with his wantonness
Tasteth death's bitterness;
Hell's executioner
Hath no ears for to hear
What vain art can reply.
I am sick, I must die.
      Lord have mercy on us!

Haste, therefore, each degree,
To welcome destiny.
Heaven is our heritage,
Earth but a player's stage;
Mount we unto the sky.
I am sick, I must die.
      Lord have mercy on us!

[1600]

# EDWARD DE VERE,
## EARL OF OXFORD
### (1550–1604)

Oxford was a remnant of the medieval aristocracy, and came of one of the few great families which survived the Wars of the Roses. He succeeded to the earldom young, and at the same time inherited a large fortune. Burghley was his guardian, and Oxford's first wife was Burghley's daughter. His early career consisted of a succession of escapades of which the best remembered is his quarrel with Sidney. He squandered his fortune as he grew more eccentric. The latter part of his life, after a second marriage, was spent in retirement. Though a great noble, Oxford associated freely with comparatively humble men of letters, and also with actors. His poetry, however, has a distinctive 'courtly' flavour.

## Were I a King

WERE I a king, I could command content;
　　Were I obscure, hidden should be my cares;
Or were I dead, no cares should me torment,
　　Nor hopes, nor hates, nor loves, nor griefs, nor fears.
　　　　A doubtful choice, of these three which to crave;
　　　　A kingdom, or a cottage, or a grave.

[*Chetham* MS. 8012]

## The Lively Lark Stretched Forth
## Her Wing

THE lively lark stretched forth her wing,
The messenger of morning bright,
And with her cheerful voice did sing
The day's approach, discharging night,
　　When that Aurora, blushing red,
　　Descried the guilt of Thetis' bed.

I went abroad to take the air,
And in the meads I met a knight
Clad in carnation colour fair;
I did salute this gentle wight,
   Of him I did his name enquire,
    He sighed, and said it was Desire.

Desire I did desire to stay,
And while with him I cravèd talk
The courteous knight said me no nay,
But hand in hand with me did walk;
   Then of Desire I asked again
    What thing did please, and what did pain?

He smiled, and thus he answered than:
Desire can have no greater pain
Than for to see another man
The thing desirèd to obtain;
   Nor greater joy can be than this,
    That to enjoy that others miss.

[Rawlinson Poet. MS. 85]

## If Women Could be Fair and Yet Not Fond

IF women could be fair and yet not fond,
Or that their love were firm, not fickle, still,
I would not marvel that they make men bond,
By service long to purchase their goodwill.
   But when I see how frail those creatures are,
   I muse that men forget themselves so far.

To mark the choice they make and how they change,
How oft from Phoebus they do fly to Pan,
Unsettled still, like haggards wild they range,

These gentle birds that fly from man to man;
  Who would not scorn, and shake them from the fist,
  And let them fly, fair fools, which way they list?

Yet for disport we fawn and flatter both,
To pass the time when nothing else can please;
And train them to our lure with subtle oath
Till, weary of their wiles, ourselves we ease;
  And then we say, when we their fancy try,
  To play with fools, oh, what a fool was I!

      [Rawlinson Poet. MS. 85. Set to music by William Byrd,
      *Psalms, Sonnets, and Songs,* 1588]

# GEORGE PEELE

## (1558?–97?)

Peele was a free scholar at Christ's Hospital, and later studied at
Oxford. He made a reputation as a poet while still at university. His
earliest known play, *The Arraignment of Paris*, was acted before 1584.
There is some evidence that he was an actor as well as a dramatist.
Peele had a colourful reputation, and *The Merry Conceited Jests of
George Peele*, a collection of stories which was entered in the
Stationers' Registers in 1605, suggests that his contemporaries took
an interest in his doings. Dekker represents him as a boon companion
of Greene and Marlowe, and Marlowe's influence is visible in his
work.

## A Sonnet

His golden locks time hath to silver turned;
   Oh time too swift, Oh swiftness never ceasing!
His youth 'gainst time and age hath ever spurned,
   But spurned in vain; youth waneth by increasing:
Beauty, strength, youth, are flowers but fading seen;
Duty, faith, love, are roots, and ever green.

His helmet now shall make a hive for bees,
   And, lovers' sonnets turned to holy psalms,
A man-at-arms must now serve on his knees,
   And feed on prayers, which are age his alms:
But though from court to cottage he depart,
His saint is sure of his unspotted heart.

And when he saddest sits in homely cell,
   He'll teach his swains this carol for a song:
'Blest be the hearts that wish my sovereign well,
   Cursed be the souls that think her any wrong!'
Goddess, allow this agèd man his right,
To be your beadsman now, that was your knight.

*[Polyhymnia,*[1] 1590]

## Enter Muly Mahamet with Flesh
## Upon His Sword

From *The Battle of Alcazar*,[1] Act Two, Scene Three

MULY MAHAMET: Hold thee, Calipolis, feed, and faint no more;
  This flesh I forcèd from a lioness,
  Meat of a princess, for a princess meet:
  Learn by her noble stomach to esteem
  Penury plenty in extremest dearth;
  Who, when she saw her foragement bereft,
  Pined not in melancholy or childish fear,
  But as brave minds are strongest in extremes,
  So she, redoubling her former force,
  Ranged through the woods, and rent the breeding vaults
  Of proudest savages to save herself.
  Feed, then, and faint not, fair Calipolis;
  For rather than fierce Famine shall prevail
  To gnaw thy entrails with her thorny teeth,
  The conquering lioness shall attend on thee,
  And lay huge heaps of slaughtered carcasses,
  As bulwarks in her way, to keep her back.
  I will provide thee of a princely osprey,[2]
  That as she flieth over fish in pools,
  The fish shall turn their glistering bellies up,
  And thou shalt take thy liberal choice of all:
  Jove's stately bird with wide-commanding wings
  Shall hover still about thy princely head,
  And beat down fowl by shoals into thy lap:
  Feed then, and faint not, fair Calipolis!

[1594]

# From *The Old Wives' Tale*

### 1. *Song*

WHEN as the rye reach to the chin,
And chopcherry, chopcherry ripe within,
Strawberries swimming in the cream,
And schoolboys playing in the stream;
Then Oh, then Oh, then Oh, my true-love said,
Till that time come again
She could not live a maid.

### 2

BE not afraid of every stranger;
Start not aside for every danger;
Things that seem are not the same;
Blow a blast at every flame;
For when one flame of fire goes out,
Then come your wishes well about:
If any ask who told you this good,
Say, the white bear of England's wood.

### 3

SPREAD, table, spread,
Meat, drink and bread,
Ever may I have
What I ever crave,
When I am spread,
Meat for my black cock,
And meat for my red.[1]

### 4. *The Heads speak in the well*

A: GENTLY dip, but not too deep,
For fear you make the golden beard to weep.
Fair maiden, white and red,
Comb me smooth, and stroke my head,[1]
And thou shalt have some cockle-bread.[2]

B: Gently dip, but not too deep,
For fear thou make the golden beard to weep.

Fair maid, white and red,
Comb me smooth, and stroke my head,
And every hair a sheaf shall be,
And every sheaf a golden tree.

[1595]

## From *David and Bethsabe*[1]

### *Scene One – Bethsabe's Song*

HOT sun, cool fire, tempered with sweet air,
Black shade, fair nurse, shadow my white hair:
Shine, sun; burn, fire; breathe, air, and ease me;
Black shade, fair nurse, shroud me, and please me:
Shadow, my sweet nurse, keep me from burning,
Make not my glad cause cause of my mourning.
      Let not my beauty's fire
      Inflame unstaid desire,
      Nor pierce any bright eye
      That wandereth lightly.

### *Scene Thirteen – The battle; and Absalon hangs by the hair*

ABSALON: What angry angel, sitting in these shades,
Hath laid his cruel hands upon my hair,
And holds my body thus 'twixt heaven and earth?
Hath Absalon no soldier near his hand
That may untwine me this unpleasant curl,
Or wound this tree that ravisheth his lord?
Oh God, behold the glory of thy hand,
And choicest fruit of nature's workmanship,
Hang, like a rotten branch, upon this tree,
Fit for the axe and ready for the fire!
Since thou withold'st all ordinary help
To loose my body from this bond of death,
Oh, let my beauty fill these senseless plants
With sense and power to loose me from this plague,
And work some wonder to prevent his death
Whose life thou mad'st a special miracle!

[1599]

# WILLIAM PERCY

## (1575-1648)

Third son of the third Earl of Northumberland, Percy was educated at Gloucester Hall (later Worcester College), Oxford. He was a close friend of Barnabe Barnes, and it was to him that Barnes dedicated *Parthenophe and Parthenophil*. Percy repaid the compliment by praising Barnes in the concluding poem of his *Sonnets to Coelia* (1594). After a period of turbulence – he was once in the Tower on a charge of homicide – Percy withdrew from the world. He died at Oxford, where, says Wood, he had 'lived a melancholy and retired life many years'.

## *It Shall be Said I Died For Coelia!*

IT shall be said I died for Coelia!
Then quick, thou grisly man of Erebus,
Transport me hence unto Proserpina,
To be adjudged as 'wilful amorous':
To be hung up within the liquid air,
For all the sighs which I in vain have wasted:
To be through Lethe's waters cleansèd fair,
For those dark clouds which have my looks o'ercasted:
To be condemned to everlasting fire,
Because at Cupid's fire I wilful brent me;
And to be clad, for deadly dumps, in mire.
Among so many plagues which shall torment me
   One solace I shall find, when I am over:
   It will be known I died a constant lover!

*[Coelia, 1594]*

# SIR WALTER RALEGH
## (1552?–1618)

Ralegh arrived at Court in 1582 and rose rapidly in the Queen's favour, at the same time incurring the hatred of many of his contemporaries, who were offended by his arrogance. The rise of Essex, and his clandestine marriage with Elizabeth Throckmorton, deprived him of his paramount position, but he remained an important person in Elizabeth's orbit. In 1589, after a retirement to Ireland, he introduced Spenser at Court. The year 1595 saw his expedition to Guiana, 1596 his participation in the successful attack on Cadiz, and with Essex he shared the blame for the failure of the 'Islands Voyage' in 1597. James's accession was a disaster for Ralegh, who had always been anti-Spanish, and who was bitterly disliked by the new king. He was soon arrested, tried, and condemned to death. After being reprieved, he spent twelve years in the Tower, writing his *History of the World*. In 1616 he was released for a doomed final voyage to Guiana, which led to his re-arrest and execution on his return. Ralegh associated with the best poets of the day, and was even suspected of atheism because of his connexion with Marlowe.


## The Passionate Man's Pilgrimage[1]
### Supposed to be Written by One at the Point of Death

GIVE me my scallop shell of quiet,
My staff of faith to walk upon,
My scrip of joy, immortal diet,
My bottle of salvation:
My gown of glory, hope's true gage,
And thus I'll take my pilgrimage.

Blood must be my body's balmer,
No other balm shall there be given,
Whilst my soul, like a white palmer,
Travels to the land of heaven,
Over the silver mountains,
Where spring the nectar fountains:

And there I'll kiss
The bowl of bliss,
And drink my eternal fill
On every milken hill.
My soul will be a-dry before,
But after, it will ne'er thirst more.

And by the happy blissful way
More peaceful pilgrims I shall see,
That have shook off their gowns of clay,
And go apparelled fresh like me.
I'll bring them first
To slake their thirst,
And then to taste those nectar suckets
At the clear wells
Where sweetness dwells,
Drawn up by saints in crystal buckets.

And when our bottles and all we
Are filled with immortality:
Then the holy paths we'll travel
Strewed with rubies thick as gravel,
Ceilings of diamonds, sapphire floors,
High walls of coral and pearl bowers.

From thence to heaven's bribeless hall
Where no corrupted voices brawl,
No conscience molten into gold,
No forged accusers bought and sold,
No cause deferred, no vain spent journey,
For there Christ is the King's Attorney:
Who pleads for all without degrees,
And he hath Angels, but no fees.[1]

When the grand twelve million jury,
Of our sins with sinful fury,
'Gainst our souls black verdicts give,
Christ pleads his death, and then we live,

Be thou my speaker, taintless pleader,
Unblotted lawyer, true proceeder,
Thou movest salvation even for alms:
Not with a bribèd lawyer's palms.

And this is my eternal plea,
To him that made Heaven, Earth and Sea,
Seeing my flesh must die so soon,
And want a head to dine next noon,
Just at the stroke when my veins start and spread,
Set on my soul an everlasting head.
Then am I ready like a palmer fit,
To tread those blest paths which before I writ.

[Daiphantus, 1604]

## The Lie

Go soul, the body's guest,
    upon a thankless arrant,
Fear not to touch the best,
    the truth shall be thy warrant:
Go, since I needs must die,
    and give the world the lie.

Say to the Court it glows,
    and shines like rotten wood,
Say to the Church it shows
    what's good, and doth no good.
If Church and Court reply,
    then give them both the lie.

Tell potentates they live
    acting by others' action,
Not loved unless they give,
    not strong but in affection.
If potentates reply,
    give potentates the lie.

Tell men of high condition,
   that manage the estate,
Their purpose is ambition,
   their practice only hate:
And if they once reply,
   then give them all the lie.


Tell them that brave it most,
   they beg for more by spending,
Who in their greatest cost
   like nothing but commending.
And if they make reply,
   then give them all the lie.


Tell zeal it wants devotion,
   tell love it is but lust,
Tell time it meets but motion,
   tell flesh it is but dust.
And wish them not reply,
   for thou must give the lie.


Tell age it daily wasteth,
   tell honour how it alters.
Tell beauty how it blasteth,
   tell favour how it falters,
And as they shall reply,
   give every one the lie.


Tell wit how much it wrangles
   in tickle points of niceness,
Tell wisdom she entangles
   herself in overwiseness.
And when they do reply,
   straight give them both the lie.

Tell physick of her boldness,
   tell skill it is prevention:
Tell charity of coldness,
   tell law it is contention,
And as they do reply,
   so give them still the lie.

Tell fortune of her blindness,
   tell nature of decay,
Tell friendship of unkindness,
   tell justice of delay.
And if they will reply,
   then give them all the lie.

Tell arts they have no soundness,
   but vary by esteeming,
Tell schools they want profoundness
   and stand so much on seeming.
If arts and schools reply,
   give arts and schools the lie.

Tell faith it's fled the city,
   tell how the country erreth,
Tell manhood shakes off pity,
   tell virtue least preferreth,
And if they do reply,
   spare not to give the lie.

So when thou hast, as I
   commanded thee, done blabbing,
Because to give the lie,
   deserves no less than stabbing,
Stab at thee he that will,
   no stab thy soul can kill.

[*A Poetical Rhapsody*, second ed., 1608]

## To the Translator of Lucan

HAD Lucan hid the truth to please the time,
He had been too unworthy of thy pen:
Who never sought, nor ever cared to climb
By flattery, or seeking worthless men.
For this thou hast been bruised: but yet those scars
Do beautify no less, than those wounds do
Received in just, and in religious wars;
Though thou hast bled by both, and bear'st them too.
Change not, to change thy fortune 'tis too late.
Who with a manly faith resolves to die,
May promise to himself a lasting state,
Though not so great, yet free from infamy.
    Such was thy Lucan, whom so to translate
    Nature thy Muse (like Lucan's) did create.

               [Prefixed to Sir Arthur Gorges'[1] translation of
               Lucan's *Pharsalia*, 1614]

## Nature That Washed Her Hands In Milk

NATURE that washed her hands in milk
    And had forgot to dry them,
Instead of earth took snow and silk
    At Love's request to try them,
If she a mistress could compose
To please Love's fancy out of those.

Her eyes he would should be of light,
    A violet breath and lips of jelly,
Her hair not black, nor over-bright,
    And of the softest down her belly,
As for her inside he'd have it
Only of wantonness and wit.

At Love's entreaty, such a one
   Nature made, but with her beauty
She hath framed a heart of stone,
   So as Love by ill destiny
Must die for her whom Nature gave him,
Because her darling would not save him.

But Time which Nature doth despise,
   And rudely gives her love the lie,
Makes Hope a fool, and Sorrow wise,
   His hands doth neither wash, nor dry,
But being made of steel and rust,
Turns snow, and silk, and milk to dust.

The light, the belly, lips and breath,
   He dims, discolours, and destroys,
With those he feeds, but fills not death,
   Which sometimes were the food of joys;
Yea, Time doth dull each lively wit,
And drys all wantonness with it.

Oh cruel Time, which takes in trust
   Our youth, our joys, and all we have,
And pays us but with age and dust,
   Who in the dark and silent grave
When we have wandered all our ways
Shuts up the story of our days.

[Harleian MS. 6917]

## As You Came From the Holy Land[1]

As you came from the holy land
   Of Walsingham
Met you not with my true love
   By the way as you came?

How shall I know your true love
    That have met many one [1]
As I went to the holy land
    That have come, that have gone?


She is neither white nor brown
    But as the heavens fair,
There is none hath a form so divine
    In the earth or the air.


Such an one did I meet, good Sir,
    Such an angelic face,
Who like a queen, like a nymph, did appear
    By her gait, by her grace.


She hath left me here all alone,
    All alone as unknown,
Who sometimes did me lead with herself,
    And me loved as her own.


What's the cause that she leaves you alone
    And a new way doth take;
Who loved you once as her own
    And her joy did you make?


I have loved her all my youth,
    But now old, as you see,
Love likes not the falling fruit
    From the withered tree.


Know that love is a careless child
    And forgets promise past,
He is blind, he is deaf when he list
    And in faith never fast.

His desire is a dureless content
    And a trustless joy,
He is won with a world of despair
    And lost with a toy.

Of women-kind such indeed is the love,
    Or the word love abused,
Under which many childish desires
    And conceits are excused.

But true love is a durable fire
    In the mind ever burning;
Never sick, never old, never dead,
    From itself never turning.

[Rawlinson Poet. MS. 85. First printed Deloney,
*The Garland of Goodwill*, 1678]

## On the Life of Man

WHAT is our life? a play of passion,
Our mirth the music of division,
Our mothers' wombs the tiring houses be,
Where we are dressed for this short comedy,
Heaven the judicious sharp spectator is,
That sits and marks who still doth act amiss,
Our graves that hide us from the searching sun,
Are like drawn curtains when the play is done,
Thus march we playing to our latest rest,
Only we die in earnest, that's no jest.

[Orlando Gibbons, *Madrigals and Motets*, 1612]

## To His Son[1]

THREE things there be that prosper up apace,
And flourish, whilst they grow asunder far,
But on a day, they meet all in one place,
And when they meet, they one another mar;
And they be these – the wood, the weed, the wag.
The wood is that, which makes the gallows-tree,
The weed is that, which strings the hangman's bag,
The wag, my pretty knave, betokeneth thee.
Mark well, dear boy, whilst these assemble not,
Green springs the tree, hemp grows, the wag is wild;
But when they meet, it makes the timber rot,
It frets the halter, and it chokes the child.
    Then bless thee, and beware, and let us pray,
    We part not with thee at this meeting day.

[B.M. MS. Add. 23, 229]

## Translation of *Ausonius*
### Epigram 118

I AM that Dido which thou here dost see,
Cunningly framed in beauteous imagery.
Like this I was, but had not such a soul
As Maro feigned, incestuous and foul.
Aeneas never with his Trojan host
Beheld my face, or landed on this coast.
But flying proud Iarbas villainy,
Not moved by furious love or jealousy,
I did with weapon chaste, to save my fame,
Make way for death untimely, ere it came.
This was my end; but first I built a town,
Revenged my husband's death, lived with renown.

Why didst thou stir up Virgil, envious Muse,
Falsely my name and honour to abuse?
Readers, believe Historians, not those
Which to the world Jove's thefts and vice expose.
Poets are liars, and for verses' sake
Will make the gods of human crimes partake.

[*The History of the World*, 1614]

# WILLIAM SHAKESPEARE

## (1564–1616)

The few facts which are known about Shakespeare give a picture of bourgeois success. His father held office as an alderman and as a Bailiff in the corporation of Stratford. Shakespeare married in 1582, and in 1583 his first child – a daughter – was born, followed by twins in February 1585. The first dated knowledge which we have of Shakespeare in London is the publication of *Venus and Adonis* in 1593, followed by the *Rape of Lucrece* the next year. By this time, however, he must have been established both as a dramatist and as an actor. In 1599 he became one of the shareholders in the Globe Theatre. In 1601 he bought New Place, one of the finest houses in Stratford. In 1608 he was one of the original shareholders in the new Private Theatre at the Blackfriars. He seems to have retired from writing plays around 1612. The picture given by these established facts must be set against that provided by the *Sonnets*. This sequence, perhaps not intended for publication, suggests a divided character with a streak of sexual ambiguity. Biographers differ so radically about Shakespeare that it is difficult to reach any firm conclusions about him.


## From *Love's Labour's Lost*

### Act Three, Scene One

BIRON: Oh! And I, forsooth, in love!
    I that have been love's whip;
    A very beadle to a humorous sigh;
    A critic, nay, a night-watch constable;
    A domineering pedant o'er the boy;
    Than whom no mortal so magnificent!
    This wimpled, whining, purblind, wayward boy;
    This Signior Junior, giant-dwarf, Dan Cupid;
    Regent of love-rhymes, lord of folded arms,
    Th' anointed sovereign of sighs and groans,
    Liege of all loiterers and malcontents,
    Dread prince of plackets, king of codpieces,

Sole imperator and great general
Of trotting paritors:[1] – Oh my little heart! –
And I to be a corporal of his field,
And wear his colours like a tumbler's hoop!
What I! I love! I sue! I seek a wife!
A woman, that is like a German clock,
Still a-repairing, ever out of frame,
And never going aright, being a watch,
But being watched that it may still go right!
Nay, to be perjured, which is worst of all;
And, among three, to love the worst of all;
A whitely wanton with a velvet brow,
With two pitch-balls stuck in her face for eyes:
Ay, and, by heaven, one that will do the deed,
Though Argus were her eunuch and her guard.
And I to sigh for her! to watch for her!
To pray for her! Go to: it is a plague
That Cupid will impose for my neglect
Of his almighty dreadful little might.
Well, I will love, write, sigh, pray, sue and groan:
Some men must love my lady, and some Joan.

[1598]

# From *Richard III*
## Act One, Scene Four

[*London. The Tower. Enter Clarence and Keeper.*]
KEEPER: Why looks your Grace so heavily to-day?
CLARENCE: Oh, I have passed a miserable night,
So full of fearful dreams, of ugly sights,
That, as I am a Christian faithful man,
I would not spend another such a night,
Though 'twere to buy a world of happy days,
So full of dismal terror was the time!

KEEPER: What was your dream, my lord? I pray you tell me.
CLARENCE: Methoughts that I had broken from the Tower,
   And was embarked to cross to Burgundy;
   And, in my company, my brother Gloucester,
   Who from my cabin tempted me to walk
   Upon the hatches. There we looked toward England,
   And cited up a thousand heavy times,
   During the wars of York and Lancaster,
   That had befall'n us. As we paced along
   Upon the giddy footing of the hatches,
   Methought that Gloucester stumbled; and, in falling,
   Struck me, that thought to stay him, overboard,
   Into the tumbling billows of the main.
   Oh Lord! methought, what pain it was to drown!
   What dreadful noise of water in mine ears!
   What sights of ugly death within mine eyes!
   Methoughts I saw a thousand fearful wracks;
   A thousand men that fishes gnawed upon;
   Wedges of gold, great anchors, heaps of pearl,
   Inestimable stones, unvalued jewels,
   All scattered in the bottom of the sea.
   Some lay in dead men's skulls; and in the holes
   Where eyes did once inhabit, there were crept,
   As 'twere in scorn of eyes, reflecting gems,
   That wooed the slimy bottom of the deep,
   And mocked the dead bones that lay scattered by.
KEEPER: Had you such leisure in the time of death
   To gaze upon these secrets of the deep?
CLARENCE: Methought I had; and often did I strive
   To yield the ghost: but still the envious flood
   Stopped in my soul, and would not let it forth
   To find the empty, vast and wand'ring air;
   But smothered it within my panting bulk,
   Who almost burst to belch it in the sea.
KEEPER: Awaked you not in this sore agony?
CLARENCE: No, no, my dream was lengthened after life:
   Oh, then began the tempest to my soul.

I passed, methought, the melancholy flood,
With that sour ferryman which poets write of,
Unto the kingdom of perpetual night.
The first that there did greet my stranger-soul,
Was my great father-in-law, renownèd Warwick;
Who spake aloud, 'What scourge for perjury
Can this dark monarchy afford false Clarence?'
And so he vanished. Then came wand'ring by
A shadow like an angel, with bright hair[1]
Dabbled in blood; and he shrieked out aloud,
'Clarence is come, false, fleeting, perjured Clarence,
That stabbed me in the field by Tewkesbury.
Seize on him, Furies, take him unto torment!'
With that, methought, a legion of foul fiends
Environed me, and howlèd in mine ears
Such hideous cries, that with the very noise
I trembling waked, and for a season after
Could not believe but that I was in hell,
Such terrible impression made my dream.

[1597]


## From *The Merchant of Venice*

### Act Five, Scene One

LORENZO: How sweet the moonlight sleeps upon this bank!
    Here will we sit, and let the sounds of music
    Creep in our ears. Soft stillness and the night
    Become the touches of sweet harmony.
    Sit, Jessica. Look how the floor of heaven
    Is thick inlaid with patens of bright gold.
    There's not the smallest orb which thou behold'st
    But in his motion like an angel sings,
    Still quiring to the young-eyed cherubins:

Such harmony is in immortal souls;
But whilst this muddy vesture of decay
Doth grossly close it in, we cannot hear it.

[1600. Entered in the *Stationers' Register*, 1598]


## From *Measure For Measure*
### Act Three, Scene One

ISABELLA: What says my brother?
CLAUDIO:                    Death is a fearful thing.
ISABELLA: And shamèd life a hateful.
CLAUDIO: Ay, but to die, and go we know not where;
  To lie in cold obstruction[1] and to rot;
  This sensible warm motion to become
  A kneaded clod; and the delighted spirit
  To bathe in fiery floods, or to reside
  In thrilling region of thick-ribbèd ice;
  To be imprisoned in the viewless winds,
  And blown with restless violence round about
  The pendent world; or to be worse than worst
  Of those that lawless and incertain thought
  Imagine howling! 'Tis too horrible!
  The weariest and most loathèd worldly life
  That age, ache, penury, and imprisonment
  Can lay on nature is a paradise
  To what we fear of death.

[1623. Played at Court, 26 December 1604]

## *Lear and Cordelia as Prisoners*

### From *King Lear,* Act Five, Scene Three

CORDELIA: We are not the first
  Who with best meaning have incurred the worst.
  For thee, oppressèd King, I am cast down;
  Myself could else outfrown false Fortune's frown.
  Shall we not see these daughters and these sisters?[1]
LEAR: No, no, no, no! Come, let's away to prison.
  We two alone will sing like birds i' th' cage.
  When thou dost ask me blessing, I'll kneel down
  And ask of thee forgiveness: so we'll live,
  And pray, and sing, and tell old tales, and laugh
  At gilded butterflies, and hear poor rogues
  Talk of court news; and we'll talk with them too,
  Who loses and who wins, who's in, who's out;
  And take upon's the mystery of things,
  As if we were God's spies: and we'll wear out,
  In a walled prison, packs and sects of great ones
  That ebb and flow by th' moon.
EDMUND: Take them away.
LEAR: Upon such sacrifices, my Cordelia,
  The gods themselves throw incense. Have I caught thee?
  He that parts us shall bring a brand from heaven,
  And fire us hence like foxes. Wipe thine eyes.
  The good years shall devour them, flesh and fell,
  Ere they shall make us weep: we'll see 'em starved first.
  Come.

[1608]

## *Enobarbus' Description of Cleopatra*

From *Antony and Cleopatra*, Act Two, Scene Two

ENOBARBUS: The barge she sat in, like a burnished throne,
Burned on the water. The poop was beaten gold;
Purple the sails, and so perfumèd that
The winds were lovesick with them; the oars were silver,
Which to the tune of flutes kept stroke and made
The water which they beat to follow faster,
As amorous of their strokes. For her own person,
It beggared all description. She did lie
In her pavilion, cloth-of-gold of tissue,
O'erpicturing that Venus where we see
The fancy outwork nature. On each side her
Stood pretty dimpled boys, like smiling Cupids,
With divers-coloured fans, whose wind did seem
To glow the delicate cheeks which they did cool,
And what they undid did.

AGRIPPA: Oh, rare for Antony!

ENOBARBUS: Her gentlewomen, like the Nereides,
So many mermaids, tended her i' th' eyes,
And made their bends adornings.[1] At the helm
A seeming mermaid steers. The silken tackle
Swell with the touches of those flower-soft hands
That yarely[2] frame the office. From the barge
A strange invisible perfume hits the sense
Of the adjacent wharfs. The city cast
Her people out upon her; and Antony,
Enthroned i' th' market-place, did sit alone,
Whistling to th' air; which, but for vacancy,
Had gone to gaze on Cleopatra too,
And made a gap in nature.

AGRIPPA: Rare Egyptian!

ENOBARBUS: Upon her landing, Antony sent to her,
Invited her to supper. She replied,
It should be better he became her guest,
Which she entreated. Our courteous Antony,

Whom ne'er the word of 'No' woman heard speak,
Being barbered ten times o'er, goes to the feast,
And, for his ordinary, pays his heart
For what his eyes eat only.
AGRIPPA: Royal wench!
    She made great Caesar lay his sword to bed.
    He ploughed her, and she cropped.[1]
ENOBARBUS: I saw her once
    Hop forty paces through the public street;
    And having lost her breath, she spoke, and panted,
    That she did make defect perfection,
    And, breathless, power breathe forth.
MAECENAS: Now Antony must leave her utterly.
ENOBARBUS: Never! He will not.
    Age cannot wither her nor custom stale
    Her infinite variety. Other women cloy
    The appetites they feed, but she makes hungry
    Where most she satisfies: for vilest things
    Become themselves in her, that the holy priests
    Bless her when she is riggish.[2]

[1623. Entered in the *Stationers' Register*, 1608]


## Song

### From *Love's Labour's Lost*

#### Spring

WHEN daisies pied and violets blue
    And lady-smocks all silver white
And cuckoo-buds of yellow hue
    Do paint the meadows with delight,
The cuckoo then, on every tree,
Mocks married men; for thus sings he,
        Cuckoo;
    Cuckoo, cuckoo: Oh word of fear,
    Unpleasing to a married ear!

When shepherds pipe on oaten straws,
   And merry larks are ploughmen's clocks,
When turtles tread, and rooks, and daws,
   And maidens bleach their summer smocks,
The cuckoo then, on every tree,
Mocks married men; for thus sings he,
      Cuckoo;
Cuckoo, cuckoo: Oh word of fear,
Unpleasing to a married ear!

     *Winter*
When icicles hang by the wall,
   And Dick the shepherd blows his nail,
And Tom bears logs into the hall,
   And milk comes frozen home in pail,
When blood is nipped and ways be foul,
Then nightly sings the staring owl,
     Tu-whit, to-who,
A merry note,
While greasy Joan doth keel[1] the pot.

When all aloud the wind doth blow,
   And coughing drowns the parson's saw
And birds sit brooding in the snow,
   And Marian's nose looks red and raw,
When roasted crabs hiss in the bowl,
Then nightly sings the staring owl,
     Tu-whit, tu-who,
A merry note,
While greasy Joan doth keel the pot.

                      [1598]

## Feste's Songs

From *Twelfth Night*

### 1

OH mistress mine, where are you roaming?
Oh, stay and hear, your true love's coming,
  That can sing both high and low.
Trip no further, pretty sweeting;
Journeys end in lovers meeting,
  Every wise man's son doth know.

What is love? 'Tis not hereafter:
Present mirth hath present laughter;
  What's to come is still unsure.
In delay there lies no plenty;
Then come kiss me, sweet-and-twenty:
  Youth's a stuff will not endure.

### 2

COME away, come away, death,
  And in sad cypress let me be laid.
Fly away, fly away, breath;
  I am slain by a fair cruel maid.
My shroud of white, stuck all with yew,
    Oh, prepare it!
My part of death, no one so true
    Did share it.

Not a flower, not a flower sweet,
  On my black coffin let there be strown;
Not a friend, not a friend greet
  My poor corpse, where my bones shall be thrown:
A thousand thousand sighs to save,
    Lay me, Oh, where
Sad true lover never find my grave,
    To weep there!

3

WHEN that I was and a little tiny boy,
   With hey, ho, the wind and the rain,
A foolish thing was but a toy,
   For the rain it raineth every day.

But when I came to man's estate,
   With hey, ho, the wind and the rain,
'Gainst knaves and thieves men shut their gate,
   For the rain it raineth every day.

But when I came, alas! to wive,
   With hey, ho, the wind and the rain,
By swaggering could I never thrive,
   For the rain it raineth every day.

But when I came unto my beds,
   With hey, ho, the wind and the rain,
With toss-pots still had drunken heads,
   For the rain it raineth every day.

A great while ago the world begun,
   With hey, ho, the wind and the rain,
But that's all one, our play is done,
   And we'll strive to please you every day.

   [1623. A performance in the Middle Temple recorded
   at Candlemas, 1601–2]

## *Dirge for Fidele*
### From *Cymbeline*

FEAR no more the heat o' the sun,
　　Nor the furious winter's rages;
Thou thy worldly task hast done,
　　Home art gone, and ta'en thy wages.
Golden lads and girls all must,
As chimney-sweepers, come to dust.

Fear no more the frown o' the great,
　　Thou art past the tyrant's stroke;
Care no more to clothe and eat,
　　To thee the reed is as the oak.
The sceptre, learning, physic, must
All follow this, and come to dust.

Fear no more the lightning-flash,
　　Nor the all-dreaded thunder-stone;
Fear not slander, censure rash;
　　Thou hast finished joy and moan.
All lovers young, all lovers must
Consign to thee, and come to dust.

No exorciser harm thee!
Nor no witchcraft charm thee!
Ghost unlaid forbear thee!
Nothing ill come near thee!
Quiet consummation have,
And renownèd be thy grave!

[1623]

## *Autolycus' Song*

From *The Winter's Tale*

WHEN daffodils begin to peer,
   With heigh! the doxy, over the dale,
Why, then comes the sweet o' the year;
   For the red blood reigns in the winter's pale.

The white sheet bleaching on the hedge,
   With heigh! the sweet birds, Oh how they sing!
Doth set my pugging[1] tooth on edge,
   For a quart of ale is a dish for a king.

The lark, that tirra-lirra chants,
   With heigh! with heigh! the thrush and the jay,
Are summer songs for me and my aunts,
   While we lie tumbling in the hay.

[1623]


## *Shall I Compare Thee To a Summer's Day*

SHALL I compare thee to a summer's day?
Thou art more lovely and more temperate:
Rough winds do shake the darling buds of May,
And summer's lease hath all too short a date:
Sometime too hot the eye of heaven shines,
And often is his gold complexion dimmed;
And every fair from fair sometime declines,
By chance, or nature's changing course untrimmed:
But thy eternal summer shall not fade,
Nor lose possession of that fair thou ow'st,
Nor shall death brag thou wander'st in his shade,
When in eternal lines to time thou grow'st;
   So long as men can breathe, or eyes can see,
   So long lives this, and this gives life to thee.

[*Sonnets*, 1609]

## Full Many a Glorious Morning Have I Seen

FULL many a glorious morning have I seen
Flatter the mountain-tops with sovereign eye,
Kissing with golden face the meadows green,
Gilding pale streams with heavenly alchemy;
Anon permit the basest clouds to ride
With ugly rack on his celestial face,
And from the forlorn world his visage hide,
Stealing unseen to west with this disgrace.
Even so my sun one early morn did shine
With all-triumphant splendour on my brow;
But, out! alack! he was but one hour mine,
The region cloud hath masked him from me now.
   Yet him for this my love no whit disdaineth;
    Suns of the world may stain when heaven's sun staineth.

[*Sonnets*, 1609]


## Not Marble, Nor the Gilded Monuments

NOT marble, nor the gilded monuments
Of princes, shall outlive this powerful rime;
But you shall shine more bright in these contents
Than unswept stone, besmeared with sluttish time.
When wasteful war shall statues overturn,
And broils root out the work of masonry,
Nor Mars his sword nor war's quick fire shall burn
The living record of your memory.
'Gainst death and all-oblivious enmity
Shall you pace forth; your praise shall still find room,
Even in the eyes of all posterity
That wear this world out to the ending doom.
   So, till the judgement that yourself arise,
    You live in this, and dwell in lovers' eyes.

[*Sonnets*, 1609

## Or I Shall Live Your Epitaph To Make

Or I shall live your epitaph to make,
Or you survive when I in earth am rotten,
From hence your memory death cannot take,
Although in me each part will be forgotten.
Your name from hence immortal life shall have,
Though I, once gone, to all the world must die:
The earth can yield me but a common grave,
When you entombèd in men's eyes shall lie.
Your monument shall be my gentle verse,
Which eyes not yet created shall o'er-read;
And tongues to be your being shall rehearse,
When all the breathers of this world are dead;
 You still shall live – such virtue hath my pen –
 Where breath most breathes – even in the mouths of men.

             *[Sonnets, 1609]*

## That Time of Year Thou Mayst In Me Behold

That time of year thou mayst in me behold
When yellow leaves, or none, or few, do hang
Upon those boughs which shake against the cold,
Bare ruined choirs, where late the sweet birds sang.
In me thou see'st the twilight of such day
As after sunset fadeth in the west,
Which by and by black night doth take away,
Death's second self, that seals up all in rest.
In me thou see'st the glowing of such fire,
That on the ashes of his youth doth lie,
As the death-bed whereon it must expire
Consumed with that which it was nourished by.
 This thou perceiv'st, which makes thy love more strong,
 To love that well which thou must leave ere long.

             *[Sonnets, 1609]*

## Was It the Proud Full Sail Of His
## Great Verse[1]

WAS it the proud full sail of his great verse,
Bound for the prize of all too precious you,
That did my ripe thoughts in my brain inhearse,
Making their tomb the womb wherein they grew?
Was it his spirit, by spirits taught to write
Above a mortal pitch, that struck me dead?
No, neither he, nor his compeers by night
Giving him aid, my verse astonishèd.
He, nor that affable familiar ghost
Which nightly gulls him with intelligence,
As victors of my silence cannot boast;
I was not sick of any fear from thence:
    But when your countenance filled up his line,
    Then lacked I matter; that enfeebled mine.

[*Sonnets*, 1609]

## Farewell! Thou Art Too Dear For
## My Possessing

FAREWELL! thou art too dear for my possessing,
And like enough thou know'st thy estimate:
The charter of thy worth gives thee releasing;
My bonds in thee are all determinate.
For how do I hold thee but by thy granting?
And for that riches where is my deserving?
The cause of this fair gift in me is wanting,
And so my patent back again is swerving.

Thyself thou gav'st, thy own worth then not knowing,
Or me, to whom thou gav'st it, else mistaking;
So thy great gift, upon misprision growing,
Comes home again, on better judgement making.
  Thus have I had thee, as a dream doth flatter,
  In sleep a king, but, waking, no such matter.

[*Sonnets*, 1609]


## Let Me Not To The Marriage Of
## True Minds

LET me not to the marriage of true minds
Admit impediments. Love is not love
Which alters when it alteration finds,
Or bends with the remover to remove.
Oh, no! it is an ever-fixèd mark,
That looks on tempests and is never shaken;
It is the star to every wand'ring bark,
Whose worth's unknown, although his height be taken.
Love's not Time's fool, though rosy lips and cheeks
Within his bending sickle's compass come;
Love alters not with his brief hours and weeks,
But bears it out even to the edge of doom.
  If this be error, and upon me provèd,
  I never writ, nor no man ever lovèd.

[*Sonnets*, 1609]

WILLIAM SHAKESPEARE

## Th' Expense of Spirit In a Waste of Shame

Th' expense of spirit in a waste of shame
Is lust in action; and till action, lust
Is perjured, murd'rous, bloody, full of blame,
Savage, extreme, rude, cruel, not to trust:
Enjoyed no sooner but despisèd straight;
Past reason hunted, and no sooner had,
Past reason hated, as a swallowed bait
On purpose laid to make the taker mad:
Mad in pursuit and in possession so;
Had, having, and, in quest to have, extreme;
A bliss is proof, and, proved, a very woe;
Before, a joy proposed; behind, a dream.
  All this the world well knows; yet none knows well
  To shun the heaven that leads men to this hell.

[*Sonnets,* 1609]

# SIR PHILIP SIDNEY
## (1554–86)

Sidney was the *preux chevalier* of the Elizabethan age, and the elegies written for him show what glamour he possessed in the eyes of his contemporaries. After going to Shrewsbury School, he studied at both Oxford and Cambridge, but did not take a degree. In 1572 he accompanied an English ambassador on a mission to France. In 1577 he himself went as ambassador to the Emperor and the Elector Palatine. He began the *Arcadia* during a banishment from Court in 1580. In 1583 he married and was knighted. In 1585 he was sent as Governor to Flushing. In 1586 he was mortally wounded in a skirmish at Zutphen. *Astrophel and Stella* (addressed to Penelope Rich, to whom he had once been engaged) was published without the consent of Sidney's family in 1591, and immediately triggered off a remarkable outburst of sonnet-cycles. In 1598 a fully authorized edition of Sidney's works appeared, prepared for the press by his sister, the Countess of Pembroke. Sidney was the centre of an important circle of poets, including Greville (his friend from school-days), Dyer, and Spenser. This group was sometimes referred to as the Areopagus.

## *Fly, Fly, My Friends*

FLY, fly, my friends; I have my death-wound, fly;
See there that boy, that murth'ring boy, I say,
Who, like a thief, hid in dark bush doth lie
Till bloody bullet get him wrongful prey.
So tyrant he no fitter place could spy,
Nor so fair level¹ in so secret stay,
As that sweet black which veils the heav'nly eye;
There himself with his shot he close doth lay.
Poor passenger, pass now thereby I did,
And stayed, pleased with the prospect of the place,
While that black hue from me the bad guest hid;
But straight I saw motions of lightning grace,
   And then descried the glist'ring of his dart;
   But ere I could fly thence, it pierced my heart.

[*Astrophel and Stella*, 1591]

## Having This Day My Horse, My Hand, My Lance [1]

HAVING this day my horse, my hand, my lance
Guided so well that I obtained the prize,
Both by the judgement of the English eyes
And of some sent from that sweet enemy, France;
Horsemen my skill in horsemanship advance,
Town-folks my strength; a daintier judge applies
His praise to sleight which from good use doth rise;
Some lucky wits impute it but to chance;
Others, because of both sides I do take
My blood from them who did excel in this,
Think nature me a man of arms did make.
How far they shot awry! The true cause is,
   Stella looked on, and from her heav'nly face
   Sent forth the beams which made so fair my race.

*[Astrophel and Stella, 1591]*

## Who Is It That This Dark Night . . . ?

'WHO is it that this dark night
   Underneath my window plaineth?'
It is one who from thy sight
   Being, ah! exiled, disdaineth
Every other vulgar light.

'Why, alas! and are you he?
   Be not yet those fancies changèd?'
Dear, when you find change in me,
   Though from me you be estrangèd,
Let my change to ruin be.

'Well, in absence this will die;
    Leave to see and leave to wonder.'
Absence sure will help, if I
    Can learn how myself to sunder
From what in my heart doth lie.


'But time will these thoughts remove;
    Time doth work what no man knoweth.'
Time doth as the subject prove;
    With time still the affection groweth
In the faithful turtle dove.


'What if you new beauties see,
    Will not they stir new affection?'
I will think they pictures be,
    Image like of saint's perfection,
Poorly counterfeiting thee.


'But your reason's purest light
    Bids you leave such minds to nourish.'
Dear, do reason no such spite;
    Never doth thy beauty flourish
More than in my reason's sight.


'But the wrongs love bears will make
    Love at length leave undertaking.'
No, the more fools it do shake,
    In a ground of so firm making
Deeper still they drive the stake.


'Peace, I think that some give ear;
    Come no more lest I get anger.'
Bliss, I will my bliss forbear,
    Fearing, sweet, you to endanger;
But my soul shall harbour there.

'Well, begone, begone, I say,
    Lest that Argus' eyes perceive you.'
Oh, unjust Fortunè's sway,
    Which can make me thus to leave you,
And from louts to run away.

[*Astrophel and Stella*, 1591]


## Leave Me, Oh Love[1]

LEAVE me, Oh Love which reacheth but to dust;
And thou, my mind, aspire to higher things;
Grow rich in that which never taketh rust;
Whatever fades but fading pleasure brings.
Draw in thy beams, and humble all thy might
To that sweet yoke where lasting freedoms be;
Which breaks the clouds and opens forth the light,
That doth both shine and give us sight to see.
Oh take fast hold; let that light be thy guide
In this small course which birth draws out to death,
And think how evil becometh him to slide,
Who seeketh heaven, and comes of heavenly breath.
    Then farewell, world; thy uttermost I see;
    Eternal Love, maintain thy life in me.

[*Certain Sonnets*, 1598]


## Oh Sweet Woods

OH sweet woods, the delight of solitariness![2]
Oh, how much I do like your solitariness!
Where man's mind hath a freed consideration,
Of goodness to receive lovely direction;
Where senses do behold th'order of heavenly host,
And wise thoughts do behold what the Creator is.
Contemplation here holdeth his only seat,
Bounded with no limits, borne with a wing of hope,

Climbs even unto the stars; Nature is under it.
Nought disturbs thy quiet, all to thy service yields;
Each sight draws on a thought (thought, mother of science);
Sweet birds kindly do grant harmony unto thee;
Fair trees' shade is enough fortification,
Nor danger to thyself if be not in thyself.

Oh sweet woods, the delight of solitariness!
Oh, how much I do like your solitariness!
Here nor treason is hid, veilèd in innocence;
Nor envy's snaky eye finds any harbour here;
Nor flatterers' venomous insinuations,
Nor cunning humourists' puddled opinions,
Nor courteous ruin of proffered usury,
Nor time prattled away, cradle of ignorance,
Nor causeless duty, nor cumber of arrogance,
Nor trifling title of vanity dazzleth us,
Nor golden manacles stand for a paradise.
Here wrong's name is unheard, slander a monster is.
Keep thy spright from abuse; here no abuse doth haunt.
What man grafts in a tree dissimulation?

Oh sweet woods, the delight of solitariness!
Oh, how well I do like your solitariness!
Yet, dear soil, if a soul closed in a mansion
As sweet as violets, fair as lily is,
Straight as cedar, a voice stains the canary bird's,
Whose shade safely doth hold, danger avoideth her;
Such wisdom that in her lives speculation;
Such goodness that in her simplicity triumphs;
Where envy's snaky eye winketh or else dieth;
Slander wants a pretext, flattery gone beyond;
Oh! if such a one have bent to a lonely life,
Her steps glad we receive, glad we receive her eyes,
And think not she doth hurt our solitariness,
For such company decks such solitariness.

[*The Countess of Pembroke's Arcadia*, 1593]

## Sestina

FAREWELL, Oh sun, Arcadia's clearest light;
Farewell, Oh pearl, the poor man's plenteous treasure;
Farewell, Oh golden staff, the weak man's might;
Farewell, Oh joy, the joyful's only pleasure;
Wisdom, farewell, the skilless man's direction;
Farewell, with thee farewell, all our affection.

For what place now is left for our affection,
Now that of purest lamp is quenched the light
Which to our dark'ned minds was best direction?
Now that the mine is lost of all our treasure;
Now death hath swallowed up our worldly pleasure,
We orphans made, void of all public might!

Orphans, indeed, deprived of father's might,
For he our father was in all affection,
In our well-doing placing all his pleasure,
Still studying how to us to be a light;
As well he was in peace a safest treasure,
In war his wit and word was our direction.

Whence, whence, alas, shall we seek our direction,
When that we fear our hateful neighbour's might,
Who long have gaped to get Arcadians' treasure?
Shall we now find a guide of such affection,
Who for our sakes will think all travail light,
And make his pain to keep us safe his pleasure?

No, no; forever gone is all our pleasure,
For ever wandering from all good direction,
For ever blinded of our clearest light,
For ever lamèd of our surèd might,
For ever banished from well placed affection,
For ever robbed of all our royal treasure.

Let tears for him therefore be all our treasure,
And in our wailful naming him our pleasure;
Let hating of our selves be our affection,
And unto death bend still our thought's direction;
Let us against our selves employ our might,
And putting out our eyes seek we our light.

Farewell, our light; farewell, our spoilèd treasure;
Farewell, our might; farewell, our daunted pleasure;
Farewell, direction; farewell, all affection.

[*The Countess of Pembroke's Arcadia*, 1593]

# Ring Out Your Bells, Let Mourning Shows be Spread

RING out your bells, let mourning shows be spread;
For Love is dead.
   All Love is dead, infected
With plague of deep disdain;
   Worth, as nought worth, rejected,
And Faith fair scorn doth gain.
   From so ungrateful fancy,
   From such a female franzy,
     From them that use men thus,
     Good Lord, deliver us!

Weep, neighbours, weep! do you not hear it said
That Love is dead?
   His death-bed, peacock's folly;
His winding-sheet is shame;
   His will, false-seeming holy;
His sole executor, blame
   From so ungrateful fancy,
   From such a female franzy,
     From them that use men thus,
     Good Lord, deliver us!

Let dirge be sung and trentals rightly read,
For Love is dead.
   Sir Wrong his tomb ordaineth
My mistress Marble-heart,
   Which epitaph containeth,
'Her eyes were once his dart.'
   From so ungrateful fancy,
   From such a female franzy,
    From them that use men thus,
    Good Lord, deliver us!

Alas! I lie, rage hath this error bred;
Love is not dead.
   Love is not dead, but sleepeth
In her unmatchèd mind,
   Where she his counsel keepeth,
Till due desert she find.
   Therefore from so vile fancy,
   To call such wit a franzy,
    Who Love can temper thus,
    Good Lord, deliver us!

[*Certain Sonnets*, 1598]

# ROBERT SOUTHWELL

## (c. 1561–95)

A Jesuit, Southwell was educated abroad, at Douai and at Paris, and served for a time as prefect of studies in the English College at Rome. In 1584 he was ordained priest, and in 1586 he returned to England. In 1589 he became chaplain to the Countess of Arundel. In 1592 he was arrested, and spent the rest of his life in prison, sometimes being tortured. Finally he was executed by hanging. His poems were published soon after his death and enjoyed considerable popularity.

## The Burning Babe

As I in hoary winter's night stood shivering in the snow,
Surprised I was with sudden heat which made my heart to glow;
And lifting up a fearful eye to view what fire was near,
A pretty babe all burning bright did in the air appear;
Who, scorchèd with excessive heat, such floods of tears did shed
As though his floods should quench his flames which with his tears
    were fed.
'Alas,' quoth he, 'but newly born in fiery heats I fry,
Yet none approach to warm their hearts or feel my fire but I!
My faultless breast the furnace is, the fuel wounding thorns,
Love is the fire, and sighs the smoke, the ashes shame and scorns,
The fuel Justice layeth on, and Mercy blows the coals,
The metal in this furnace wrought are men's defilèd souls,
For which, as now on fire I am to work them to their good,
So will I melt into a bath to wash them in my blood.'
With this he vanished out of sight and swiftly shrunk away,
And straight I callèd unto mind that it was Christmas day.

[*St Peter's Complaint*, 1595]

## Upon the Image of Death

BEFORE my face the picture hangs,
That daily should put me in mind
Of those cold qualms and bitter pangs,
That shortly I am like to find:
   But yet, alas, full little I
   Do think hereon that I must die.

I often look upon a face
Most ugly, grisly, bare, and thin;
I often view the hollow place,
Where eyes and nose had sometimes been;
   I see the bones across that lie,
   Yet little think that I must die.

I read the label underneath,
That telleth me whereto I must;
I see the sentence eke that saith
'Remember, man, that thou art dust!'
   But yet, alas, but seldom I
   Do think indeed that I must die.

Continually at my bed's head
A hearse[1] doth hang, which doth me tell,
That I ere morning may be dead,
Though now I feel myself full well:
   But yet, alas, for all this, I
   Have little mind that I must die.

The gown which I do use to wear,
The knife wherewith I cut my meat,
And eke that old and ancient chair
Which is my only usual seat;
   All these do tell me I must die,
   And yet my life amend not I.

My ancestors are turned to clay,
And many of my mates are gone;
My youngers daily drop away,
And can I think to 'scape alone?
   No, no, I know that I must die,
   And yet my life amend not I.

Not Solomon, for all his wit,
Nor Samson, though he were so strong,
No king nor person ever yet
Could 'scape, but death laid him along:
   Wherefore I know that I must die,
   And yet my life amend not I.

Though all the East did quake to hear
Of Alexander's dreadful name,
And all the West did likewise fear
To hear of Julius Caesar's fame,
   Yet both by death in dust now lie.
   Who then can 'scape, but he must die?

I none can 'scape death's dreadful dart,
If rich and poor his beck obey,
If strong, if wise, if all do smart,
Then I to 'scape shall have no way.
   Oh! grant me grace, Oh God, that I
   My life may mend sith I must die.

[*Maeoniae*, 1595]

# From *St Peter's Complaint*

SLEEP, Death's ally, oblivion of tears,
   Silence of passions, balm of angry sore,
Suspense of loves, security of fears,
   Wrath's lenitive, heart's ease, storm's calmest shore;
Senses and souls reprievèd from all cumbers,
Benumbing sense of ill with quiet slumbers.

Not such my sleep, but whisperer of dreams,
   Creating strange chimaeras, faining frights;
Of day-discourses giving fancy themes,
   To make dumb-shows with worlds of antic sights;
Casting true griefs in fancy's forging mould,
Brokenly telling tales rightly foretold.

[1595]

# EDMUND SPENSER
## (1552–99)

Educated as a 'poor scholar' at Merchant Taylors', and later as a sizar at Pembroke Hall (later Pembroke College), Cambridge. At Cambridge he formed a friendship with Gabriel Harvey. Spenser left the University in 1576, and in 1579 entered the household of the Earl of Leicester. This brought him the friendship of Sidney, Leicester's nephew. *The Shepheardes Calender* was completed, and *The Faerie Queene* begun under Leicester's roof. *The Shepheardes Calender* had a great impact on Elizabethan poetry, and its publication brought Spenser an immediate reputation as a poet. By 1580 Spenser had become estranged from Leicester, and accepted the post of secretary to Lord Grey of Wilton (an opponent of Leicester's), who was going to Ireland as Lord Deputy. Spenser spent most of the rest of his life in Ireland, which he continued to regard as a land of exile. However, in 1589 he accompanied Ralegh (whose friendship he had gained either during his time with Leicester or in Ireland itself) back to England and the Court. Ralegh procured for him an audience with the Queen, but in the end Spenser failed to establish himself and find preferment, and was forced to return to Ireland. In 1594 he married. In 1595 he once more visited England to see the second part of *The Faerie Queene* through the press. In 1597 he returned to Ireland, and in September 1598 was nominated High Sheriff of Cork. Almost immediately catastrophe fell, with Tyrone's invasion of Munster. Spenser's house was burnt about his ears, and he fled to England an impoverished and dying man. Three weeks after his arrival, he died at Westminster. Essex, who had previously offered him help, paid for the funeral. In death he was treated as England's chief poet, and his fellow poets paid tributes at his grave.

## Like As a Huntsman After Weary Chase

LIKE as a huntsman after weary chase,
Seeing the game from him escaped away,
Sits down to rest him in some shady place,
With panting hounds beguilèd of their prey:
So after long pursuit and vain assay,

When I all weary had the chase forsook,
The gentle deer returned the self-same way,
Thinking to quench her thirst at the next brook.
There she beholding me with milder look,
Sought not to fly, but fearless still did bide:
Till I in hand her yet half trembling took,
And with her own goodwill her firmly tied.
   Strange thing me seemed to see a beast so wild,
    So goodly won with her own will beguiled.

[*Amoretti*, 1595]


## One Day I Wrote Her Name Upon the Strand[1]

ONE day I wrote her name upon the strand,
But came the waves and washèd it away:
Again I wrote it with a second hand,
But came the tide, and made my pains his prey.
Vain man, said she, that dost in vain assay,
A mortal thing so to immortalise,
But I myself shall like to this decay,
And eke my name be wipèd out likewise.
Not so (quod I), let baser things devise
To die in dust, but you shall live by fame:
My verse your virtues rare shall eternise,
And in the heavens write your glorious name.
   Where whenas death shall all the world subdue,
    Our love shall live, and later life renew.

[*Amoretti*, 1595]

## Let Not One Spark of Filthy
## Lustful Fire

LET not one spark of filthy lustful fire
Break out, that may her sacred peace molest:
Ne one light glance of sensual desire
Attempt to work her gentle mind's unrest.
But pure affections bred in spotless breast,
And modest thoughts breathed from well-tempered sprites
Go visit her in her chaste bower of rest,
Accompanied with angelick delights.
There fill yourself with those most joyous sights,
The which myself could never yet attain:
But speak no word to her of these sad plights,
Which her too constant stiffness doth constrain.
   Only behold her rare perfection,
   And bless your fortune's fair election.

[*Amoretti*, 1595]

## Prothalamion [1]

CALM was the day, and through the trembling air
Sweet breathing Zephyrus did softly play,
A gentle spirit, that lightly did delay
Hot Titan's beams, which then did glister fair;
When I whose sullen care,
Through discontent of my long fruitless stay
In prince's court, and expectation vain
Of idle hopes, which still do fly away
Like empty shadows, did afflict my brain,
Walked forth to ease my pain
Along the shore of silver streaming Thames,
Whose rutty bank, the which his river hems,
Was painted all with variable flowers,
And all the meads adorned with dainty gems,

Fit to deck the maidens' bowers,
And crown their paramours,
Against the bridal day, which is not long:
  Sweet Thames, run softly, till I end my song.

There, in a meadow, by the river's side,
A flock of nymphs I chancèd to espy,
All lovely daughters of the flood thereby,
With goodly greenish locks all loose untied,
As each had been a bride;
And each one had a little wicker basket,
Made of fine twigs entrailèd curiously,
In which they gathered flowers to fill their flasket,
And with fine fingers cropped full feateously[1]
The tender stalks on high.
Of every sort, which in that meadow grew,
They gathered some, the violet pallid blue,
The little daisy that at evening closes,
The virgin lily, and the primrose true,
With store of vermeil roses,
To deck their bridegrooms' posies,
Against the bridal day, which was not long:
  Sweet Thames, run softly, till I end my song.

With that, I saw two swans of goodly hue
Come softly swimming down along the Lee;
Two fairer birds I yet did never see.
The snow, which doth the top of Pindus strew,
Did never whiter shew,
Nor Jove himself, when he a swan would be
For love of Leda whiter did appear:
Yet Leda was they say as white as he,
Yet not so white as these, nor nothing near.
So purely white they were,
That even the gentle stream, the which them bare,
Seemed foul to them, and bade his billows spare
To wet their silken feathers, lest they might

Soil their fair plumes with water not so fair,
And mar their beauties bright,
That shone as heaven's light,
Against their bridal day, which was not long:
  Sweet Thames, run softly, till I end my song.

Eftsoons the nymphs, which now had flowers their fill,
Ran all in haste, to see that silver brood,
As they came floating on the crystal flood.
Whom when they saw, they stood amazèd still,
Their wondering eyes to fill.
Them seemed they never saw a sight so fair,
Of fowls so lovely, that they sure did deem
Them heavenly born, or to be that same pair
Which through the sky draws Venus' silver team;
For sure they did not seem
To be begot of any earthly seed,
But rather angels or of angels' breed:
Yet were they bred of summer's heat they say,
In sweetest season, when each flower and weed
The earth did fresh array,
So fresh they seemed as day,
Even as their bridal day, which was not long:
  Sweet Thames, run softly, till I end my song.

Then forth they all out of their baskets drew
Great store of flowers, the honour of the field,
That to the sense did fragrant odours yield,
All which upon those goodly birds they threw,
And all the waves did strew,
That like old Peneus' waters they did seem,
When down along by pleasant Tempe's shore,
Scattered with flowers, through Thessaly they stream,
That they appear through lilies' plenteous store,
Like a bride's chamber floor.
Two of these nymphs, meanwhile, two garlands bound,
Of freshest flowers which in that mead they found,

The which presenting all in trim array,
Their snowy foreheads therewithal they crowned,
Whilst one did sing this lay,
Prepared against this day,
Against their bridal day, which was not long:
   Sweet Thames, run softly, till I end my song.


'Ye gentle birds, the world's fair ornament,
And heaven's glory, whom this happy hour
Doth lead unto your lovers' blissful bower,
Joy may you have and gentle heart's content
Of your love's complement:
And let fair Venus, that is queen of love,
With her heart-quelling son upon you smile,
Whose smile, they say, hath virtue to remove
All love's dislike, and friendship's faulty guile
For ever to assoil.
Let endless peace your steadfast hearts accord,
And blessed plenty wait upon your board,
And let your bed with pleasures chaste abound,
That fruitful issue may to you afford,
Which may your foes confound,
And make your joys redound,
Upon your bridal day, which is not long:
   Sweet Thames, run softly, till I end my song.'


So ended she; and all the rest around
To her redoubled that her undersong,
Which said, their bridal day should not be long.
And gentle echo from the neighbour ground
Their accents did resound.
So forth those joyous birds did pass along,
Adown the Lee, that to them murmured low,
As he would speak, but that he lacked a tongue,
Yet did by signs his glad affection show,
Making his stream run slow.
And all the fowl which in his flood did dwell

'Gan flock about these twain, that did excel
The rest so far as Cynthia doth shend
The lesser stars. So they, enrangèd well,
Did on those two attend,
And their best service lend,
Against their wedding day, which was not long:
   Sweet Thames, run softly, till I end my song.

At length they all to merry London came,
To merry London, my most kindly nurse,
That to me gave this life's first native source;
Though from another place I take my name,
An house of ancient fame.
There when they came, whereas these bricky towers,
The which on Thames' broad aged back do ride,
Where now the studious lawyers have their bowers
There whilom wont the Templar Knights to bide,
Till they decayed through pride:
Next whereunto there stands a stately place,
Where oft I gainèd gifts and goodly grace
Of that great lord, which therein wont to dwell,
Whose want too well now feels my friendless case.
But ah! here fits not well
Old woes but joys to tell
Against the bridal day, which is not long:
     Sweet Thames, run softly, till I end my song.

Yet therein now doth lodge a noble peer,
Great England's glory and the world's wide wonder,
Whose dreadful name late through all Spain did thunder,
And Hercules' two pillars standing near
Did make to quake and fear.
Fair branch of honour, flower of chivalry,
That fillest England with thy triumph's fame,
Joy have thou of thy noble victory,
And endless happiness of thine own name
That promiseth the same:

That through thy prowess and victorious arms,
Thy country may be freed from foreign harms;
And great Elisa's glorious name may ring
Through all the world, filled with thy wide alarms,
Which some brave Muse may sing
To ages following,
Upon the bridal day, which is not long:
   Sweet Thames, run softly, till I end my song.

From those high towers this noble lord issuing,
Like radiant Hesper when his golden hair
In th' Ocean billows he hath bathèd fair,
Descended to the river's open viewing,
With a great train ensuing.
Above the rest were goodly to be seen
Two gentle knights of lovely face and feature
Beseeming well the bower of any queen,
With gifts of wit and ornaments of nature,
Fit for so goodly stature;
That like the twins of Jove they seemed in sight,
Which deck the baldric of the heavens bright.
These two forth pacing to the river's side,
Received those two fair birds, their love's delight,
Which at th' appointed tide
Each one did make his bride,
Against their bridal day, which is not long:
   Sweet Thames, run softly, till I end my song.

[*Prothalamion, or, A Spousal Verse*, 1596]

EDMUND SPENSER

# From *An Hymn of Heavenly Love*

BEFORE this world's great frame, in which all things
Are now contained, found any being place
Ere flitting Time could wag his eyas[1] wings
About that mighty bound, which doth embrace
The rolling spheres, and parts their hours by space,
That high eternal power, which now doth move
In all these things, moved in itself by love.

It loved itself, because itself was fair
(For fair is loved); and of itself begot
Like to itself his eldest son and heir,
Eternal, pure, and void of sinful blot,
The firstling of his joy, in whom no jot
Of love's dislike, or pride was to be found,
Whom he therefore with equal honour crowned.

With him then reigned, before all time prescribed,
In endless glory and immortal might,
Together with that third from them derived,
Most wise, most holy, most almighty Sprite,
Whose kingdom's throne no thought of earthly wight
Can comprehend, much less my trembling verse
With equal words can hope it to rehearse.

Yet Oh most blessed Spirit, pure lamp of light,
Eternal spring of grace and wisdom true,
Vouchsafe to shed into my barren sprite
Some little drop of thy celestial dew,
That may my rhymes with sweet infuse embrew,[2]
And give me words equal unto my thought,
To tell the marvels by thy mercy wrought.

[*Four Hymns*, 1596]

EDMUND SPENSER

## The Garden of Adonis

From *The Faerie Queene*, Book Three, Canto Six

RIGHT in the middest of that paradise
There stood a stately mount, on whose round top
A gloomy grove of myrtle trees did rise,
Whose shady boughs sharp steel did never lop,
Nor wicked beasts their tender buds did crop,
But like a garland compassèd the height,
And from their fruitful sides sweet gum did drop,
That all the ground with precious dew bedight,
Threw forth most dainty odours, and most sweet delight.

And in the thickest covert of that shade,
There was a pleasant arbor, not by art,
But of the trees' own inclination made,
Which knitting their rank branches part to part,
With wanton ivy-twine entrailed athwart,
And eglantine, and caprifole among,
Fashioned above within their inmost part,
That neither Phoebus' beams could through them throng,
Nor Aeolus sharp blast could work them any wrong.

And all about grew every sort of flower,
To which sad lovers were transformed of yore;
Fresh Hyacinthus, Phoebus' paramour,
And dearest love,
Foolish Narcisse, that likes the watery shore,
Sad Amaranthus, made a flower but late,
Sad Amaranthus, in whose purple gore
Me seems I see Amintas' wretched fate,
To whom sweet poets' verse hath given endless date.

There wont fair Venus often to enjoy
Her dear Adonis' joyous company
And reap sweet pleasure of the wanton boy;

There yet, some say, in secret he does lie,
Lappèd in flowers and precious spicery,
By her hid from the world, and from the skill
Of Stygian Gods, which do her love envy;
But she herself, whenever that she will,
Possesseth him, and of his sweetness takes her fill.

And sooth it seems they say: for he may not
For ever die, and ever buried be
In baleful night, where all things are forgot;
All be he subject to mortality,
Yet is eterne in mutability,
And by succession made perpetual,
Transformèd oft, and changèd diversely:
For him the Father of all forms they call;
Therefore needs mote[1] he live, that living gives to all.

There now he liveth in eternal bliss,
Joying his goddess, and of her enjoyed:
Ne feareth he henceforth that foe of his,
Which with his cruel tusk him deadly cloyed:
For that wild boar, the which him once annoyed,
She firmly hath emprisonèd for aye,
That her sweet love his malice mote avoid,
In a strong rocky cave, which is they say,
Hewen underneath that mount, that none him loosen may.

There now he lives in everlasting joy,
With many of the Gods in company,
Which thither haunt, and with the wingèd boy
Sporting himself in safe felicity:
Who when he hath with spoils and cruelty
Ransacked the world, and in the woeful hearts
Of many wretches set his triumphs high,
Thither resorts, and laying his sad darts
Aside, with fair Adonis plays his wanton parts.

[1590]

### EDMUND SPENSER

## An Epitaph Upon the
## Right Honourable Sir Philip Sidney, Knight:
## Lord Governor of Flushing[1]

To praise thy life, or wail thy worthy death,
And want thy wit, thy wit high, pure, divine,
Is far beyond the power of mortal line,
Nor anyone hath worth that draweth breath.

Yet rich in zeal, though poor in learning's lore,
And friendly care obscured in secret breast,
And love that envy in thy life suppressed,
Thy dear life done, and death, hath doubled more.

And I, that in thy time and living state,
Did only praise thy virtues in my thought,
As one that seeld the rising sun hath sought,
With words and tears now wail thy timeless fate.

Drawn was thy race, aright from princely line,
Nor less than such (by gifts that nature gave,
The common mother that all creatures have),
Doth virtue show and princely lineage shine.

A king gave thee thy name,[2] a kingly mind
That God thee gave, who found it now too dear
For this base world, and hath resumed it near,
To sit in skies, and sort with powers divine.

Kent thy birth days, and Oxford held thy youth,
The heavens made haste, and stayed not years, nor time,
The fruits of age grew ripe in thy first prime,
Thy will, thy words: thy words the seals of truth.

Great gifts and wisdom rare imployed thee thence,
To treat from kings, with those more great than kings,
Such hope men had to lay the highest things
On thy wise youth, to be transported hence.

Whence to sharp wars sweet honour did thee call,
Thy country's love, religion, and thy friends:
Of worthy men, the marks, the lives and ends,
And her defence, for whom we labour all.

There didst thou vanquish shame and tedious age,
Grief, sorrow, sickness, and base fortune's might:
Thy rising day saw never woeful night,
But passed with praise from off this worldly stage.

Back to the camp by thee that day was brought
First thine own death, and after thy long fame;
Tears to the soldiers, the proud Castilians shame;
Virtue expressed, and honour truly taught.

What hath he lost, that such great grace hath won,
Young years, for endless years, and hope unsure
Of fortune's gifts, for wealth that still shall dure,
Oh, happy race with so great praises run!

England doth hold thy limbs that bred the same,
Flanders thy valour where it last was tried,
The camp thy sorrow where thy body died,
Thy friends, thy want; the world, thy virtue's fame.

Nations thy wit, our minds lay up thy love,
Letters thy learning, thy loss, years long to come,
In worthy hearts sorrow hath made thy tomb,
Thy soul and sprite enrich the heavens above.

Thy liberal heart embalmed in grateful tears,
Young sighs, sweet sighs, sage sighs, bewail thy fall,
Envy her sting, and spite hath left her gall,
Malice herself a mourning garment wears.

That day their Hannibal died, our Scipio fell,
Scipio, Cicero, and Petrarch of our time,
Whose virtues wounded by my worthless rhyme,
Let angels speak, and heaven thy praises tell.

[*Colin Clouts Come Home Again*, 1595]


## *Iambicum Trimetrum* [1]

UNHAPPY Verse, the witness of my unhappy state,
   Make thyself flutt'ring wings of thy fast flying
   Thought, and fly forth unto my Love, wheresoever she be;
Whether lying restless in heavy bed, or else
   Sitting so cheerless at the cheerful board, or else
   Playing alone careless on her heavenly virginals.
If in bed, tell her that my eyes can take no rest;
   If at board, tell her that my mouth can eat no meat;
   If at her virginals, tell her I can hear no mirth.
Askèd, why? say: Waking love suffereth no sleep;
   Say that raging love doth appal the weak stomach;
   Say that lamenting marreth the musical.
Tell her that her pleasures were wont to lull me asleep;
   Tell her that her beauty was wont to feed mine eyes;
   Tell her that her sweet tongue was wont to make me mirth.
Now do I nightly waste, wanting my kindly rest;
   Now do I daily starve, wanting my lively food;
   Now do I always die, wanting thy timely mirth.
And if I waste, who will bewail my heavy chance?
   And if I starve, who will record my cursèd end?
   And if I die, who will say, 'This was Immerito'? [2]

[From a letter to Gabriel Harvey, 16 October 1579]

# RICHARD STANYHURST

(1547–1618)

Stanyhurst was educated at University College, Oxford, and after 1579 left England never to return. He went to the Low Countries, where he became a Catholic convert. His translation – or rather adaptation – of the first four books of the *Aeneid* into English was published in Leyden in 1582. Stanyhurst was praised by Gabriel Harvey, an ardent partisan of classical metres in English, and was attacked by Harvey's opponent, Nashe. Later Stanyhurst turned historian and hagiographer, writing a history of Ireland, and a life of St Patrick, both of them in Latin. He is also said to have 'professed alchemy' at this period. In 1590 he went to Spain, and acted as adviser to the Spanish government on English affairs. In 1602, after the death of his second wife, he became a priest, and was appointed chaplain to the governors of the Netherlands, the Archduke Albert and his wife Isabella.

## The Royal Hunt and Storm

From *The First Four Books of Virgil*, Book Four

THE whilst the dawning Aurora fro the Ocean hast'ned,[1]
And the May-fresh yoonckers to the gates do make their assembly
With nets and catch toils, and huntspears plentiful ironed,
With the hounds quickscenting, with pricking galloper horseman,
Long for the princess the Moors' gentility waited,
As yet in her prinking not pranked with trinkery trinkets;
As they stood attending the whilst her trapped jennet[2] haughty,
Decked with rich scarlet, with gold-stood[3] furniture hanging,
Pranceth on all startling, and on bit jingled[4] he champeth.
At length forth she fleeth with swarming company circled,
In cloak Sidonical with rich dye brightly besprinkled.
Her locks are broyded[5] with gold, her quiver is hanging
Backward; with gold tache[6] the vesture purple is holden.
The band of Trojans likewise, with wanton Iulus
Do march on forward; but, of all, the Lucifer-heav'nly-
In-beauty Aeneas himself to the company ranketh.

263

Like when as hard-frozen Lycia and Zanth floods be relinquished
By Phoebe, to Delos, his native country seat, hast'ning.
He 'points a dancing; forth with the rustical hoblobs
Of Cretes, of Dryopes, and painted clowns Agathyrsi
Do fetch their gambols hopping near consecrate altars,
He trips on Zanthus mountain, with delicate hair-locks
Trailing, with green shrubs and pure gold neatly becrampound.[1]
His shafts on shoulder rattle; the like haughty resemblance
Carried Aeneas with glitt'ring comeliness heav'nly.

When they to the mountains and to lairs uncouth approachèd,
Then, lo, behold ye, breaking,[2] the goats do trip from the rock-
tops
Near to the plain; the herd deer doth stray from mountain
unharboured,
The chase is ensuèd with passage dusty bepowdered.
But the lad Ascanius, with prancing courser high mounted,
Doth manage in valley, now them, now these over-ambling;
He scorns these rascal tame games, but a sounder[3] of hogsters,[4]
Or the browny lion to stalk fro the mountain he wisheth.

The whilst in the sky-seat great bouncing rumbelo thund'ring
Rattleth; down-pouring to sleet thick hail-knob is added;
The Tyrian fellowship with youthful Trojan assembly
And Venus' haughty nephew do run to sundry-set houses.
Huge floods loudly freaming[5] from mountains lofty betrolling,[6]
Dido and the Trojan captain do jumble in one den.
Then the earth crau's[7] the bans; there too, wat'ry Juno, the
chaplain,
Seams up the bedmatch; the fire and air testify wedlock,
And nymphs in mountains' high tip do squeak, hullelo, yearning;
That day cross and dismal was cause of mischief all after,
And bane of her killing; her fame for slight she regarded,
No more doth she labour to mask her fancy with hoodwink,
With the name of wedlock her carnal lechery cloaking,
Straight through towns Lybical this fame with an infamy rangeth.

[1582]

## *A Prayer to the Trinity* [1]

TRINITY blessèd, deity co-equal,
Unity sacred, God one eke in essence,
Yield to thy servant, pitifully calling,
               Merciful hearing.
Virtuous living did I long relinquish,
Thy will and precepts miserably scorning.
Grant to me, sinful, patient repenting,
               Healthful amendment.
Blessèd I judge him that in heart is healèd;
Cursèd I know him that in health is harmèd:
Thy physic therefore to me, wretch unhappy,
               Send, my redeemer!
Glory to God, the father, and his only
Son the protector of us earthly sinners,
The sacred spirit, labourers refreshing,
               Still be renownèd!

[*The First Four Books of Virgil*, 1582]

# CHIDIOCK TICHBORNE

## (1558?–86)

Both Tichborne and his father were ardent Catholics. In 1583 Tichborne was interrogated about 'popish relics' imported after he had gone abroad without permission. In 1586 he became involved in the Babington Plot, was arrested, and hanged on 20 September. The poem 'My prime of youth' is supposed to have been written the night before his execution.

## Elegy For Himself

### Written in the Tower before His Execution, 1586

My prime of youth is but a frost of cares;
   My feast of joy is but a dish of pain;
My crop of corn is but a field of tares;
   And all my good is but vain hope of gain:
The day is past, and yet I saw no sun;
And now I live, and now my life is done.

My tale was heard, and yet it was not told;
   My fruit is fall'n, and yet my leaves are green;
My youth is spent, and yet I am not old;
   I saw the world, and yet I was not seen:
My thread is cut, and yet it is not spun;
And now I live, and now my life is done.

I sought my death, and found it in my womb;
   I looked for life, and saw it was a shade;
I trod the earth, and knew it was my tomb;
   And now I die, and now I was but made;
My glass is full, and now my glass is run;
And now I live, and now my life is done.

[*Verses of Praise and Joy*, 1586]

# CYRIL TOURNEUR
## (1575?–1625)

Tourneur probably came of a family which possessed some interest with the Cecils. He seems to have served for many years in the Low Countries – at any rate, he was given a pension by the United Provinces. He died in Ireland of sickness contracted on the expedition to Cadiz of 1625–6. His literary reputation is usually held to rest on two plays – *The Revenger's Tragedy*, and *The Atheist's Tragedy*. There is now, however, a tendency to attribute *The Revenger's Tragedy* to Middleton.

## From *The Transformed Metamorphosis*

AWAKE, oh Heaven, for (lo) the heavens conspire;
    The silver feathered moon, and both the Bears,
Are posted down for Phlegetontike[1] fire:
    Lo, now they are upon the azure spheres,
    (Thy soul is vexed with sense confounding fears)
Now are they mounted into Carol's wain,
With all the stars like to an armèd train.

Ay, even those stars, which for their sacred minds
    (They once terrestrial) were stellified,[2]
With all the force of Aeol's sail – swelled winds
    And fearful thunder, vailer of earth's pride –
    Upon the lofty firmament do ride:
All with infernal concord do agree
To shake the strength of heaven's axletree.

[1600]

## From *A Funeral Poem Upon the Death . . .*
## *of Sir Francis Vere*[1]

FOR when
He did bestow preferment on a man
The gift descended from no second hand
That might divide a general command;

267

But from himself, as a propriety
Reserved unto his own authority
And often, unrequested, singled forth
Some private men, whom for desert and worth
He did advance to some employment fit,
Before they sought it or expected it.
Hence did his troops not only understand
Their hopes to rise depended on his hand
But that he carried an observing eye
That would inform him how deservingly
They bore themselves, which did as well produce
Endeavour to do well, as curb abuse,
And made example emulation breed
Which, leading unto generous ends doth feed
The active disposition of the spirit
With a desire to go beyond in merit.
In which pursuit his action still was wont
To lead the way to honour. And i' the front
Of danger where he did his deeds advance
In all his gestures and his countenance
He did so pleasing a consent express
Of noble courage and free cheerfulness
That his assurance had the power to raise
The most dejected spirit into praise
And imitation of his worth. And thus
By means heroic and judicious
He did incline his army's gen'rous part
With love unto the practice of desert.
And in that moving orb of active war
His high command was the transcendent star
Whose influence, for production of men's worths,
Did govern at their military births
And made them fit for arms. Witness the merits
Ev'n of the chiefest ranks of war-like spirits
Who for our Prince's service do survive
Which from his virtues did their worths derive.

[1609]

268

# GEORGE TURBERVILLE

## (1540?–1610?)

Turberville was educated at Winchester. In 1561 he was elected perpetual fellow of New College, Oxford. Later, he joined one of the Inns of Court. In 1567 he published *Epitaphs, Epigrams, Songs and Sonnets*, on which his fame as a poet chiefly rests. In 1568 he accompanied Thomas Randolph, Elizabeth's ambassador to Ivan the Terrible, on his mission to Russia. Turberville wrote a book of poems about this visit, which is lost (some poems survive, reprinted in a later book). He also published a compilation of hawking, a book of *Tragical Tales* (mostly taken from Boccaccio), and translations from the Latin. Turberville was influenced by Googe, but surpasses him. His work received praise from Harington, but by 1590 was considered hopelessly old-fashioned, as is plain from references made both by Nashe and by Gabriel Harvey.

## To His Love

That sent him a ring wherein was graved
'Let reason rule'

SHALL reason rule where reason hath no right
Nor never had? Shall Cupid lose his lands?
His claim? his crown? his kingdom? name of might?
And yield himself to be in reason's bands?
No, friend, thy ring doth will me thus in vain.
Reason and love have ever yet been twain.
They are by kind of such contrary mould
As one mislikes the other's lewd device;
What reason wills, Cupido never would;
Love never yet thought reason to be wise.
To Cupid I my homage erst have done,
Let reason rule the hearts that she hath won.

[*Epitaphs, Epigrams, Songs, and Sonnets*, 1567

## Of Venus in Armour

In complete Pallas saw
   the Lady Venus stand:
Who said, let Paris now be judge,
   encounter we with hand.

Replied the goddess: what?
   scorn'st thou in armour me,
That naked erst in Ida Mount
   so foiled and conquered thee?

[*Epitaphs, Epigrams, Songs, and Sonnets*, 1567]


## The Lover Whose Mistress Feared a Mouse, Declareth That He Would Become a Cat, If He Might Have His Desire

If I might alter kind,
   what think you I would be?
Nor fish, nor fowl, nor flea, nor frog,
   nor squirrel on the tree.
The fish the hook, the fowl
   the limèd twig doth catch;
The flea the finger, and the frog
   the buzzard doth dispatch.
The squirrel thinking naught,
   that featly cracks the nut,
The greedy goshawk wanting prey
   in dread of death doth put.
But scorning all these kinds,
   I would become a cat,
To combat with the creeping mouse
   and scratch the screeking rat.

I would be present aye,
   and at my lady's call,
To guard her from the fearful mouse
   in parlour and in hall.
In kitchen for his life
   he should not show his head;
The pear in poke should lie untouched
   when she were gone to bed.
The mouse should stand in fear,
   so should the squeaking rat:
All this would I do if I were
   converted to a cat.

*[Epitaphs, Epigrams, Songs, and Sonnets. 1567]*

# RICHARD VERSTEGAN
## (*fl.* 1565–1620)

Richard Verstegan, alias Rowlands, was educated at Christ Church, Oxford, but as a Catholic was debarred from taking a degree. He went to live in Antwerp, where he dropped his English name, and adopted that of his Dutch grandfather. He set up a printing press, and acted as agent for the transmission of Catholic literature to England. About 1587 he was living in Paris, where the English ambassador succeeded in getting him imprisoned for a book about Elizabeth's treatment of the Catholics. In 1595 he went to Spain, where he had an interview with Philip II. Later he returned to Antwerp, where he was still living in 1620.

## Our Blessed Lady's Lullaby [1]

UPON my lap my sovereign sits
  And sucks upon my breast,
Meanwhile his love sustains my life,
  And gives my body rest.
    Sing lullaby, my little boy,
    Sing lullaby, my only joy.


When thou hast taken thy repast,
  Repose, my babe, on me;
So may thy mother and thy nurse
  Thy cradle also be.
    Sing lullaby, my little boy,
    Sing lullaby, my only joy.


I grieve that duty doth not work
  All what my wishing would,
Because I would not be to thee
  But in the best I should.
    Sing lullaby, my little boy,
    Sing lullaby, my only joy.

## RICHARD VERSTEGAN

Yet as I am, and as I may,
   I must and will be thine,
Though all too little for thyself,
   Vouchsafing to be mine.
     Sing lullaby, my little boy,
     Sing lullaby, my only joy.

[*Odes in Imitation of the Seven Penitential Psalms*, 1601]

# THOMAS WATSON
## (1557?–92)

Watson appears to have gone to Oxford, but to have left without a degree. He also seems to have been a member of one of the Inns of Court. He began his literary career as a writer of Latin verse. In 1581 he went to Paris, where he attracted the attention of Sir Francis Walsingham, a notable patron. Watson became prominent in the London literary society of his time, and was a friend of both Lyly and Peele. He is represented in most of the poetical miscellanies of the period. Most of his sonnets were published before those of Sidney, and there is evidence that his work was studied by Shakespeare.

## This Latter Night Amidst My Troubled Rest

THIS latter night amidst my troubled rest
A dismal dream my fearful heart appalled,
Whereof the sum was this: Love made a feast
To which all neighbour saints and gods were called;
    The cheer was more than mortal men can think,
    And mirth grew on, by taking in their drink.

Then Jove amidst his cups, for service done,
'Gan thus to jest with Ganymede his boy:
'I fain would find for thee, my pretty son,
A fairer wife than Paris brought to Troy.' –
    'Why sir,' quoth he, 'if Phoebus stand my friend,
    Who knows the world, this gear will soon have end.'

Then Jove replied that Phoebus should not choose,
But do his best to find the fairest face;
And she, once found, should neither will nor choose
But yield herself, and change her dwelling place:
    Alas, how much then was my heart affright,
    Which bade me wake and watch my fair delight.

[*Hekatompathia*, 1582]

## Come, Gentle Death!

COME, gentle Death! *Who calls? One that's oppressed.*
*What is thy will? That thou* abridge my woe
By cutting off my life. *Cease thy request,*
*I cannot kill thee yet.* Alas! why so?
  *Thou want'st thy heart.* Who stole the same away?
  *Love, whom thou serv'st. Intreat him, if thou may.*

Come, come, come, Love! *Who calleth me so oft?*
Thy vassal true, whom thou shouldst know by right.
*What makes thy cry so faint?* My voice is soft
And almost spent by wailing day and night.
  *Why then, what's thy request?* That thou restore
  To me my heart, and steal the same no more.

And thou, Oh Death! when I possess my heart,
Dispatch me then at once. *Why so?*
By promise thou art bound to end my smart.
*Why, if thy heart return, then what's thy woe?*
  That, brought from cold, it never will desire
  To rest with me, which am more hot than fire.

[Hekatompathia, 1582]

## Though Somewhat Late

THOUGH somewhat late, at last I found the way
To leave the doubtful labyrinth of love,
Wherein, alas, each minute seemed a day:
Himself was minotaur; whose force to prove
  I was enforced, till Reason taught my mind
  To slay the beast, and leave him there behind.

But being scapèd thus from out his maze,
And past the dang'rous den so full of doubt,
False Theseus-like, my credit shall I craze,
Forsaking her, whose hand did help me out?
   With Ariadne Reason shall not say,
   *I saved his life, and yet he runs away.*

No, no, before I leave the golden rule,
Or laws of her, that stood so much my friend,
Or once again will play the loving fool,
The sky shall fall, and all shall have an end:
   I wish as much to you that lovers be,
   Whose pains will pass, if you beware by me.

                                   [*Hekatompathia*, 1582]

# NOTES

p. 26. 1. Skip.

p. 27. 1. A sort of tag, played by three couples.

p. 28. 1. A volcanic island in the Cape Verde group.

p. 38. 1. Raging mad. The play on the two senses of 'wood' continues throughout the poem.

p. 43. 1. Simple.

p. 44. 1. Crop-tailed.

p. 45. 1. It has been suggested that this poem is addressed to the poet, Richard Lynche. In *The Passionate Pilgrim* it is attributed to Shakespeare.
2. A vessel into which dirty dishes and scraps of food were put.

p. 49. 1. Centaurs, or else half-bulls? 2. Keep his distance.

p. 50. 1. Marshy.

p. 51. 1. Pious. 2. That is, they were Puritans constrained to observe outward forms.

p. 52. 1. The highest note in the gamut.

p. 56. 1. Philosophical term, meaning 'essential being', or 'essence'.

p. 59. 1. 'To lead apes in Hell' was a proverbial phrase for sexual frustration.

p. 62. 1. In his *Observations in the Art of English Poesy*, Campion says of this metre that it is 'passing graceful in our English tongue, and will excellently fit the subject of a Madrigal, or any other lofty or tragical matter'.

p. 63. 1. Campion offers this as a specimen of English trochaic verse.

p. 64. 1. This provides the 'due praise of your mother tongue above all others' promised by Chapman in the preface to his *Seven Books of the Iliads*, 1598.

p. 66. 1. Laurentius Valla, who translated Homer into Latin, 1474.
2. Eobanus Hessus, German sixteenth-century poet who also translated the *Iliad* into Latin. 3. La Badessa Messinese, who translated the first five books of the *Iliad* into Italian, 1564. 4. Hugues Salel, who translated the first five books of the *Iliad* into French, 1555.

p. 67. 1. The 'fourteener' which Chapman uses in his translation of the *Iliad*.

p. 68. 1. Caught (a term used in hawking). 2. Wild goose.

p. 70. 1. This passage may be compared with Pound's Canto I, which uses the same material.

p. 73. 1. Bussy has been lured into an ambush by Montsurry, husband of his mistress, Tamyra. Monsieur (brother to Henry III of France), and the Duke of Guise are concerned in the plot. Umbra is the ghost of a Friar who has earlier played some part. 2. Nineteen lines omitted.

p. 75. 1. This sonnet expounds orthodox Catholic doctrine concerning the Trinity.

p. 77. 1. Stonehenge, always a subject of great interest to the Elizabethans.

p. 79. 1. The theme of this sonnet is exceedingly common in Elizabethan poetry. Compare Drayton's '*How many paltry, foolish, painted things*' in this volume. 2. *Cleopatra* is very different from Shakespeare's treatment of the theme, being a 'literary' tragedy on the strict Senecan model.

p. 86. 1. Davies's image of the universe is still based upon the theories of the Greek astronomers, as summed up in Ptolemy. He does, however, make a reference to the rival theory of Copernicus. Like the Greek, Davies assumes that Earth is the centre of the universe, around which all other bodies move – the sun, the moon, the planets, and the fixed stars in an outermost orbit of their own. The 'great long year' was the period which it took this imagined outermost orbit to complete one rotation. Following Ptolemy, Davies envisages the sun as moving in an eccentric orbit, to account for the apparent changes in its distance from the earth about which it was supposed to revolve. The references to Venus, which 'with divers cunning passages doth err', reflect the great difficulty which early astronomers found in accounting for the motion of the two planets nearest to the sun, Venus and Mercury. Earth itself, in Davies's account as in Ptolemy's, is thought of as consisting of the Four Elements – Fire, Air, Water, and Earth, of which Fire is outermost.

p. 92. 1. This parodies the extravagances of contemporary sonneteers. 2. Laces for fastening clothes. 3. Over-shoes.

p. 93. 1. A potgun was a shot-gun with a big bore. Here used figuratively to mean 'pip-squeaks'.

p. 99. 1. This has been considered to be the source for a similar passage in *King Lear*.

p. 100. 1. Written on the 'Islands Voyage' in 1597. 2. One of several references in the verse of the period to the famous miniaturist (1547–1619). 3. An early editor, Grosart, suggests that this strange phrase is probably derived from the Latin word *firmamentum*, one of the spheres of the element of air.

p. 101. 1. A reference to the terrible conditions in Elizabethan prisons. Prisoners were dependent on friends and outside charity for sustenance (only after Elizabeth's reign was a small living allowance made to them). Favours of all kinds had to be bought from the gaolers; for example, prisoners could be loaded with heavy irons unless they paid for lighter ones.

p. 102. 1. The Bermudas enjoyed a very bad reputation with Elizabethan mariners. The reference antedates the famous one in *The Tempest*. 2. A reference to *Genesis* (1, 3) in the Latin of the Vulgate. Here the Creator says '*Fiat Lux*'. The reference would spring the more naturally to Donne's mind because he was brought up as a Catholic.

p. 103. 1. This poem was rewritten from the earlier *Mortimeriados*, published in 1596. The main source is Holinshed, but the passage quoted here stems from Stow. 2. Canopy.

# NOTES

p. 104. 1. This stanza is important evidence for Elizabethan attitudes to the visual arts.

p. 105. 1. This and the following two sonnets are from *Idea*. The sequence grew by a process of accretion, which accounts for the differences in date.

p. 106. 1. Evil spirits were supposed to urge men to suicide.

p. 107. 1. The source is again Holinshed.

p. 111. 1. Ouzel.

p. 114. 1. The first six stanzas of seventeen.

p. 115. 1. The sense is that the times are awry, that those who seem to be starving are in fact prosperous. The imagery of both this and the preceding stanza is very interesting, as it is obviously drawn from what the author saw in the theatre. It relies more (I think) on the old moralities than on contemporary drama, and may even suggest that the poem was written somewhat earlier than 1595, when it was published.

p. 118. 1. Rinaldo's companions, come to rescue him from the enchantress.

p. 123. 1. 'The Green Knight' seems to have been Gascoigne's own sobriquet.

p. 124. 1. Harmonies. 2. Feeble shoots, overhung by the main boughs. 3. Graft.

p. 129. 1. This passage is one of the sources of Prospero's speech abjuring magic (*Tempest*, v, i, 33), which contains a number of verbal echoes of it. Apparently, Shakespeare also consulted the original Latin. 2. Quiet.

p. 137. 1. Written in the soot. 2. That is, depend on miracles.

p. 138. 1. Life-fostering.

p. 139. 1. That is, princes who are reputed to be without fixed principles, and to have instead only passing thoughts. 2. Obeisances. 3. Permanent law. 4. That is, public report as opposed to true knowledge.

p. 140. 1. The Universe. 2. A cycle, or epoch. 3. Mad confusion. 4. Staple-towns appointed by the monarch had bodies of merchants who were allowed to fix the prices of important commodities for export.

p. 141. 1. Motes or atoms. 2. That is, within the circle of royal favour. 3. That is, they are mere copies of what is real. 4. That is, they have rank, but are without real substance. 5. In the fable, the wren soars by riding on the back of the eagle.

p. 142. 1. In the hope of begetting heirs.

p. 144. 1. That is, we do not despise it, instead we labour by its light.

p. 148. 1. A game of questions and answers.

p. 149. 1. Bettered.

p. 150. 1. Probably cypress lawn, a light transparent material. 2. Learn. 3. Friendship.

p. 154. 1. According to legend, Philomena became a nightingale at Daulia in Phocis. 2. Cf. Middleton's description of the nightingale in this volume. 3. Sound. 4. The Aegipines or Aegipanes were shaped like a man above the waist, like a goat below. 5. Tutelary divinities of hills and woods.

p. 159. 1. All birds, although a ruff is also a kind of coarse fish. 2. I am unable to discover who Pooly was, but Parrot might just possibly be Henry Parrot, who in 1613 published *Laquei Ridiculosi*, containing an epigram which attacks Jonson.

p. 160. 1. The subject of this epigram is unknown. Some early editors tentatively suggest Shakespeare, but this is unlikely considering Jonson's relationship with him. 2. Illegal trafficking.

p. 163. 1. An admixture. Usually used in the opposite sense to this, to mean something tainting or sullying.

p. 164. 1. Apollo. The epithet is derived from the god's temple at Clarus.

p. 165. 1. Not the Biblical Japhet, but Japetus, father of Prometheus. 2. This is one of four poems in *Underwoods* which have sometimes been attributed to Donne. One of the group appeared as *The Expostulation* in the edition of Donne's poems printed in 1633.

p. 166. 1. The situation here is that Celia has just been handed over to Volpone by her impotent, fortune-hunting husband. 2. A noxious vapour or dew. 3. A woman of proverbially great wealth, whom the Emperor Caligula married in A.D. 38, and divorced the following year.

p. 168. 1. The song is intended as a compliment to Queen Elizabeth.

p. 171. 1. Translated from a French original by Phillipe Desportes. 2. Trouble.

p. 172. 1. A poem which should be compared with Wyatt's earlier and more famous 'They flee from me'. 2. Prayed, entreated. 3. This curious play was written by Lodge and Greene in collaboration. Though the bulk of the play is probably by Greene, this speech is generally given to Lodge.

p. 174. 1. Because these songs do not appear in the early quarto, it has been suggested that they were added later by Dekker or some other.

p. 175. 1. Literally 'descant', but also a punning reference to the legend that the nightingale presses a thorn to her breast while singing.

p. 178. 1. A slightly altered quotation from Ovid's *Amores*.

p. 180. 1. In the second edition (1616) a short scene is interpolated before the chorus enters.

p. 181. 1. Fester.

p. 183. 1. Parti-coloured. 2. Made obeisance.

p. 185. 1. Newly entered student at the Inns of Court.

p. 186. 1. The head of the fingerboard of these musical instruments was often carved in the shape of a grotesque human head. Citherns were provided for the amusement of customers in barber-shops. 2. Prostitutes. 3. Hats of a shape fashionable in Spain. 4. Granada was a centre of silk-weaving. 5. Servants wore blue livery. 6. Either 'draper's assistants' (measurers of broadcloth), or 'respectable citizens' (wearers of broadcloth). 7. A brace is the slide used for regulating the tension of a drum-skin. 8. Playbills were put up on a pillar near the theatre. 9. Slippery.

p. 187. 1. Formula of welcome to a meal, from Old French '*bon prou vous fasse*'. 2. The eloquent.

p. 189. 1. The jakes. 2. A child's game. 3. Remorse.

p. 190. 1. By tradition the inscription on Marston's tomb in the Temple Church, London, read 'Oblivioni sacrum', 'Consecrated to oblivion'. 2. Cf. *Richard II*, II, i, 38: 'Light vanity, insatiate cormorant.'

p. 194. 1. This poem is technically a 'complaint', or tragic monologue by a departed spirit. Cf. Daniel's *Complaint of Rosamund*, 1602. 2. William, Second Baron Compton of Compton Wynyates, Warwickshire, born *c.* 1568, succeeded to the title 1589. Later Earl of Northampton. 3. Twins.

p. 196. 1. The opening lines of the verse prologue to a pamphlet in prose concerned with the Elizabethan underworld. The work is not quite certainly by Middleton. 2. Elizabethan tailors had a hole under their shop-boards where odd pieces of cloth were thrown. This was known as the 'tailors' hell'.

p. 197. 1. The first extract is from the verse prologue in the form of a dialogue between the Ant and the Nightingale. The second extract is an independent poem inserted in the prose text.

p. 198. 1. A phrase from the Litany of the Saints, which was customarily recited through the streets of London in time of plague.

p. 199. 1. For a cogent argument that this famous line should read 'Beauty falls from the hair', see J. V. Cunningham, *Tradition and Poetic Structure* (Alan Swallow, Denver, 1960).

p. 203. 1. *Polyhymnia* commemorates the retirement of Sir Henry Lee from his office as Queen's Champion on the grounds of old age. He formally resigned the post to the Earl of Cumberland on 17 November 1590. 'A Sonnet' was sung before the Queen on that occasion, and has sometimes been attributed to Lee himself. It is set to music in Dowland's *First Book of Airs*, 1597.

p. 204. 1. *The Battle of Alcazar* is first mentioned by Henslowe in his *Diary* (8 February 1591–2). Although published anonymously, it is usually given to Peele. Pistol parodies: 'Feed then and faint not, fair Calipolis' In *Henry IV*, Part Two. 2. Cf. the similar description of this bird in Drayton's *Poly-Olbion*, Song XXV.

p. 205. 1. All of these are images with strong sexual as well as magical overtones. Cf. the modern calypso:
'She say to me – Kitch, come home to bed,
I got a small comb, fi comb you head.'
2. Cockle-bread is a magical cake, used as a love charm, and made with menstrual blood.

p. 206. 1. The only extant Elizabethan play with a purely scriptural subject.

p. 208. 1. Ralegh was condemned to death on 17 November 1603 and reprieved on 6 December. It has been suggested that the poem belongs to this period.

p. 209. 1. An angel was a gold coin. The pun is a common one in Elizabethan literature.

p. 213. 1. Gorges was Ralegh's first cousin.

p. 214. 1. There were several ballads on the theme of Walsingham. The tradition must have begun before 1538, when the priory there was destroyed.

p. 215. 1. In *Hamlet*, Ophelia sings:
'How shall I know your true love
From another one?'

p. 217. 1. Probably Ralegh's elder son, Walter, born 1593.

p. 220. 1. Legal officers employed in cases of adultery.

p. 222. 1. Edward Prince of Wales, taken prisoner at the Battle of Tewkesbury, and murdered there. Cf. *Henry VI*, v, 5.

p. 223. 1. Stagnation.

p. 224. 1. Goneril and Regan.

p. 225. 1. Editors quarrel about the meaning of this. It seems to mean that Cleopatra's maidens worked under the eyes of their mistress, and adorned the scene with their graceful obeisances. There seems to be a suppressed pun: adornings/adorings. 2. Nimbly.

p. 226. 1. Cleopatra had a son, Caesarion, by Julius Caesar. 2. Wanton.

p. 227. 1. Cool a hot liquid, especially by stirring or skimming.

p. 231. 1. Thieving.

p. 234. 1. The 'Rival Poet' sonnet. Chapman and Marlowe have both been suggested as the subject.

p. 237. 1. Aim.

p. 238. 1. This sonnet may refer to the court festivities held between 15 April and 1 August 1581, when a French embassy was trying to woo Elizabeth on behalf of the Duke of Anjou.

p. 240. 1. Though not included in the original edition, this is the true conclusion of *Astrophel and Stella*. 2. The metre is asclepiads.

p. 246. 1. A black canopy, designed to be hung over a coffin.

p. 250. 1. 'Her name' was Elizabeth Boyle, and she was the lady whom Spenser married.

p. 251. 1. Written to celebrate the double marriage of the Earl of Worcester's daughters, Lady Elizabeth Somerset and Lady Katherine Somerset.

p. 252. 1. Dexterously.

p. 257. 1. A young hawk. 2. Imbue.

p. 259. 1. May.

p. 260. 1. This poem is sometimes attributed to Ralegh. 2. Philip of Spain.

p. 262. 1. Sent to Gabriel Harvey in return for a copy of verses which Harvey had sent to Spenser. Spenser says: 'I dare warrant, they be precisely perfect for the feet (as you can easily judge) and vary not one inch from the Rule.' 2. Spenser signed the prefatory poem 'To His Book' in the *Shepheardes Calender* with the pseudonym Immerito.

p. 263. 1. The metre is English quantitative hexameters. 2. Small Spanish horse. 3. Gold-studded trappings. 4. Jingling. 5. Braided. 6. Fastening or buckle.

# NOTES

p. 264. 1. Set (of a jewel) – i.e. Phoebus' head is like a jewel in its setting of leaves and gold. 2. Scattering. 3. Herd of wild swine. 4. A hoggaster is a boar in its third year. 5. Roaring. 6. Moving round. 7. Cries or crows.

p. 265. 1. A poem of extremely similar style, and in the same metre, is among the A. W. poems in *A Poetical Rhapsody.*

p. 267. 1. Hellish. A word Tourneur uses often. 2. Made into stars. A mild example of the coinages in which the poem abounds.

p. 268. 1. Sir Francis Vere born 1558, died 1608. Entered the army, and served with distinction in the Low Countries. In 1596 was appointed Lord-Marshal of the army sent against Cadiz. Elizabeth made him Governor of Briel and Governor of Portsmouth. Distinguished himself at the battle of Nieuport, in 1600, and at the siege of Ostend, in 1601.

p. 273. 1. I follow Norman Ault, *Elizabethan Lyrics*, in printing only the first four stanzas, of twenty-four.

# INDEX OF FIRST LINES